ESCAPE IN TIME

By RJ Nyx

2025

Butterworth Books is a different breed of publishing house. It's a home for Indies, for independent authors who take great pride in their work and produce top quality books for readers who deserve the best. Professional editing, professional cover design, professional proof reading, professional book production—you get the idea. As Individual as the Indie authors we're proud to work with, we're Butterworths and we're *different*.

Authors currently publishing with us:

E.V. Bancroft
Valden Bush
Addison M Conley
Jo Fletcher
Helena Harte
Lee Haven
Karen Klyne
Sydney Lear
AJ Mason
Ally McGuire
James Merrick
Robyn Nyx (RJ Nyx)
JP Preston
Simon Smalley
Brey Willows

For more information visit www.butterworthbooks.co.uk

CATALOGING INFORMATION
ISBN: 978-1-915009-84-5
CREDITS
Editor: Victoria Villaseñor
Cover Design: Nicci Robinson
Production Design: Global Wordsmiths

Acknowledgements/Author's Note

I've always loved the idea of time travel, of the ability to fix things that should never have happened or twists of fate we wished weren't true. That's where the idea for this series originated, and where better to start than World War Two?

Human nature fascinates me. Our ability to endure, our compassion, and our empathy. Equally, I'm intrigued by the darker side of our nature. The part of us that can so easily descend into hatred and persecution. Both sides of that interest were perfectly evident in the Second World War, so a mission back to that time seemed like a perfect place to kick off this series (which, like Star Wars, was never intended to only be a trilogy).

Cue lots of research and reading (If this topic interests you, I highly recommend *This Is A Woman* by Sarah Helm. Though it's an incredibly tough read, it serves as a poignant documentation of the savagery of this particular war). When I came to write the scenes in Ravensbrück, I knew that research had to take me to the actual concentration camp, the only women-only camp that existed. A few days later, my wife and I were on a plane to Berlin and then in a car travelling north to the camp. We were there for many hours, and we spent them all in total silence. The brutality of the camp is still very much tangible despite it being mostly demolished, though the beauty of the surrounding area remains, including the lush lodges of the camp's officers. Much of the camp's scenes in this book are taken directly from personal accounts and historic records. None of it is there for the sake of gratuitous violence. I believe we can only learn how to behave in our present and future by looking to the past. Remembering what we have done as humans is imperative to that journey, though I'd advise you to please take care of yourself as you read those scenes (chapters 23-27).

But this book is also about redemption and the light that invades that darkness to bring hope. Germany emerged from the shadow of Hitler and the Third Reich to become a leading light in Europe.

The human race has learned from the atrocities of the past, and though some continue to perpetrate violence against each other, there are many more who combat that aggression through their gentle and kind compassion to others.

My first iteration of this idea was raw, when I was only beginning to learn my craft (back in 2017). It's been rewarding to be able to revisit it, correct the many craft issues, and create a better book because of it. The beauty of indie publishing is that level of control over your own words. Yee-ha to indies!

All that said, I hope you'll enjoy the time-travelling shenanigans of Landry and Foster, and their bromance.

And now to the thank-yous. To my wife, for her constant support. To Maggie, for her keen eye when she's proofing. And to my amazing team of ARC readers, a special thank you for taking your precious time to read my stories. And finally, of course, to you lovely readers, for whom all of us authors endeavour to entertain, amuse, and challenge with our books. May you always keep turning the pages.

Dedication

For Brey,
If I could travel back in time,
I'd go back to the moment I met you,
so I could relive every second of our lives
together all over again. And then I'd keep doing it.

CHAPTER ONE

2015: Cartagena, Colombia

Landry Donovan kicked open the Jeep door and took a deep breath of free air. Four months in this god-forsaken place had been too long, and her California king-size bed in San Francisco called to her. It was time for some hard-earned vacation and a little retreat into normal life, away from saving the future by rescuing people in the past.

She jogged across the desert road and quickly scaled the tree where she'd hidden the people retrieval unit (PRU) high in an abandoned bird nest. After she dropped to the ground, slightly off balance, she was suddenly slammed against the gnarled tree trunk. The impact forced the air from her lungs, and her face smashed against the hard bark, producing a gruesome crack as her nose connected with it. The PRU fell from her hand and skittered across the sand in its armored casing. *Shit.* Damage that, and she and her team would never return home.

Before she could turn to face her assailant, she was tossed to the ground. Another crack tore through her body as her hand jammed awkwardly between some rocks. A kick to her gut lifted her from the ground and slammed her into the tree again. Pain ripped through her body with another three kicks to her ribs. When she was yanked up by a handful of her hair, she finally caught a glimpse of the asshole knocking the shit out of her before he smashed his fist into her face. *Fucking Miguel.* Hours earlier, she hadn't put a bullet in this guy's brain because his daughter had begged her not to.

The next two kicks splintered a couple of ribs, and she swore she heard the hiss of a lung as the bones pierced it. These time-travel missions were inherently dangerous, but being beaten to death by this drugged-up fucknut was an absolutely avoidable scenario. Her mom would *not* be impressed.

Miguel slumped to the ground beside her. The intense fog of agony that cocooned her entire body subsided slightly when she saw the serrated tip of a hunting knife protruding through his right eye socket, his eyeball balanced precariously on its tip. She reached up and flicked it off before she saw a boot beside her head as the knife was removed.

"What the fuck, Landry?"

Landry squinted through her rapidly swelling eyes at her buddy, Foster, then she spat out crimson blood onto the golden sand. "I had him on the ropes."

"That's not what it looked like from where we were standing." Foster nodded to her fellow operative, Joyce, who hovered beside her. She sliced open Landry's shirt with her knife and leaned closer to listen to her chest. "You've got a punctured lung. We're gonna have to fix that now, or you won't make the jump." She dropped her backpack to the ground and pulled out a health kit.

"That's a big fucking syringe," Landry said between labored breaths.

Foster grinned. "This might sting a little."

Landry's laugh turned into an uncomfortable cough that rattled her chest. "Do it."

Foster thrust the syringe through Landry's chest wall, then pulled it away to leave the hollow needle sticking out between her ribs.

The released pressure hissed out, and the subsequent weird little clicks reverberated against her skin. Her lung refilled with air, and Landry grabbed Foster's forearm as her breathing returned to normal. "Thanks, buddy."

"Anytime." Foster listened to Landry's chest again before

tugging the needle out and wrapping the entry wound.

Joyce handed the PRU to Foster, and she gave it to Landry. "Let's get the fuck out of Dodge."

Foster and Joyce helped Landry to her feet. She pressed her finger to the print recognition plate, then she held the PRU at arm's length to trace a giant circle in the air, its line crackling into luminescent blue light as it came into being. The inside of the wormhole blurred and shredded, and Landry held her breath while pointing the PRU at its center. She released a quiet sigh when she saw the cosmic string waiting on the other side, as it always did, constantly edging into the new future they were creating with each day spent in the past. She hit buttons X and 3 on the PRU, and three thick neon light threads emerged from the single string to hover mid-air. "Damn, that's a pretty sight."

Foster wrapped one of them around Landry's wrist and folded her fingers over its end. "Hold tight, bud."

Joyce and Foster took the remaining two time threads, and Landry pressed the retrieve key. Before she entered the time circle, she glanced back at Miguel's dead body and clenched her jaw. What had she been thinking? The decision to let him live had almost killed her. As she was pulled into the time path, the pain in her ribs and face didn't concern Landry—her mom could easily fix that damage—but her mind? That was a different thing entirely.

CHAPTER TWO

December 19, 2075: Pulsus Island

LANDRY RELAXED INTO HER soft leather couch and sighed deeply. *Fucking Miguel.* Why hadn't he just stayed home and taken the win? He didn't have to die; now his eight-year-old daughter was an orphan. She glanced across at her desk and briefly considered googling the kid to see how she'd turned out but dismissed the thought almost as quickly as it had come into her head. She might work for a self-proclaimed philanthropic organization, but that didn't mean she could afford to care. The med unit stay when she'd arrived back was a reminder of what letting emotions into play could cost. Her bones and lungs had mended without issue, and she'd been right; her mom was *not* impressed. So be it. Another mission was complete, and that was what really mattered.

She placed the lit cigar onto the ashtray. The smoke rose and curled toward the extractor fan, and she watched, almost hypnotized by its graceful motion. She wouldn't actually smoke it, no more than she'd drink the bourbon she'd just poured. Watching the cracks distort the ice cubes as the two temperatures battled, before cold inevitably succumbed to the warmth of the liquor, was more satisfying than consuming the alcohol could ever be. This was all about tradition and routine, two things she needed to ground herself after returning from a mission. The third was a short break away from this community bubble, where she'd immerse herself in *real life* and make the effort to enjoy time in the present before she headed off into the future or the past once more.

Landry flicked the switch on the laser machine on the side table.

The slide in the cartridge never changed. No one would've been in her apartment since she'd left for the mission, but she pulled out the glass slide anyway. Holding it up to the light, she inspected the drawing and smiled. The tattoo used to be all she had to remember her mother by, her last piece of art before she was attacked and murdered, leaving Landry alone at seventeen.

Until Pulsus came knocking and turned her reality upside down fifteen years later.

Preparation time for missions varied greatly and removing her tattoo was the last thing she did before the jump. She couldn't have any unusual marks or features during missions, nothing to draw attention or arouse suspicion. But as soon as she returned, she had to have it etched back onto her skin before she could rest. She had to pull herself back into the present with this very special thing from her past.

Landry slipped the slide back into the cartridge and positioned her right wrist into the clamp beneath the laser pen. "Begin."

The laser danced across her skin, recreating the delicate lines and inking the twisted, gnarled branches of the two willow trees, and she barely noticed the light discomfort the process incurred. Thirty minutes later, the outline was complete, and she recognized herself again. She turned her forearm this way and that, appreciating the intricacy of the design, the wisp of a branch, the veins of a leaf, all of which hinted at her mom's brilliance.

Landry stretched out her fingers and willed her arm to remain still as the machine worked in hues of red around the top tree and shades of blue in the upside down tree. She'd restored the old machine herself since newer models no longer used color now that it was considered too dangerous. Landry didn't care for the new guidelines: no one would drain the color from her life.

By the time her tattoo was finally complete, Landry was desperate for her giant bed. After over a decade spent in tiny military cots, moving from one war-torn place to another, the luxury of a thick mattress and comforter had been a necessity to reacclimatize to a civilian life. She wanted to dream of all the possibilities of her tomorrow and revel in its delightful uncertainty. She had two weeks of downtime to look forward to, to live in the moment as if her whole life *wasn't* about saving everyone else's future, and she could enjoy catching up with the small number of people who knew nothing about what she'd been doing or where she'd been. Foster and Joyce would stay on the island, just like everyone else from Pulsus did, saying it was too problematic to navigate the "natives," as they'd taken to calling the rest of the world's population.

But Landry couldn't wait to spend her vacation among regular people; it was invaluable to her sanity. She spent so much of her time saving other people's lives that it left her little time to enjoy her own, so she planned to make the most of the next two weeks. And it'd be the first time she'd get to celebrate Christmas off-island. Maybe the little family in the lower part of her building would invite her into their home. Maybe she'd find a hot woman to celebrate the New Year with too, even if only for the night, like usual. Whatever she ended up doing, it'd be a complete release from the cage that was this island and this work.

She jumped up from the sofa and headed to her bedroom, energized with possibilities and buzzing with the freedom of it all... Time to escape into the real world.

CHAPTER THREE

Foster jerked upright, her heart pounding and her hands aching. She looked down to see them balled tightly in the sheets. And there was blood, everywhere. She squeezed her eyes tightly shut and drew in a long, deep breath before blowing it slowly out of her mouth. When she opened her eyes again, her sheets were white—they were soaked through with sweat, as was her T-shirt, but they were no longer saturated in blood.

Foster held a pillow to her face until her brain overrode her heart, and she dropped it back to the floor, gasping for breath. She squeezed her eyes tightly shut and pressed her hands over her ears to block out the crunching sounds, Landry's wounded grunts, all of her agony. God, Foster had never been so desperate to kill someone as when she drove her hunting knife, full force, through Miguel's head. She'd told Landry to kill him; he was collateral damage. But Landry was an extractor. She was all about saving lives, not taking them. If she'd seen the torture Miguel had carried out in the seven years Foster had spent with him on this mission, maybe Landry wouldn't have been so forgiving.

Foster didn't have forgiveness in her anymore. The bottles of Widow Jane washed it away, though it did little to cleanse her mind of the vivid memories of her own participation in the torture of innocents. It was *so* easy for the patch-up team to fix Landry's body—Pulsus had developed the breakthrough in restoring the physical ravages of time-travel missions years ago—but they could do fuck all to erase the malignant movies that played in Foster's mind. *Which is why I want you.* She emptied the glass of bourbon on her bedside table, and it raced down her throat, burning a path of fire as she swallowed. She'd need every drop of the two new bottles waiting on the table to haul her brain into a fitful sleep. Though the majority of Pulsus employees barely consumed alcohol anymore, it was Foster's savior, and the only way she could reconcile living the merry-go-round of her existence since becoming an operative.

She stumbled into the living room, poured herself another full glass, and dropped into her armchair, with the bottle in her lap. "Playlist three." Music the world had once known as death metal assaulted her ears. "One hundred and ten decibels."

"Volume not recommended," the warm tones of her AI assistant warned her. "Listening to music at this level will cause hearing loss after twenty-eight minutes."

"Override." No one had made her turn her music down since she was a kid, and the new legal recriminations for making noise over eighty decibels didn't apply to anyone on the island anyway. Without this, the crying voices in her head from missions long gone would do more damage than any temporary hearing loss. She glanced down at the crude gashes she'd gouged into the wood of her coffee table; twelve of them, one for each mission, on the left side, and ninety more, one for every single year she'd lived in the past. The mirror hanging on her wall tricked her into thinking she might only be thirty-six, but her mind knew better. That same mind struggled to navigate the emotional backlash of the heinous things she'd done in those ninety years in the pursuit of a "greater good."

If only she could share her pain with someone...with Landry. Foster closed her eyes and pictured the moment they'd met three years ago, when they'd both been recruited to Pulsus. It hadn't taken Foster long to grasp that Landry was an extraordinary human being with off-the-scale intelligence, unlimited resilience, and exceptional strength. Tactical, intuitive, charming, and with hazel eyes that blazed like a forest fire, Landry Donovan was every good thing a human could be.

But to be an extractor, she was also many bad things: isolated, detached, void of emotion, and remorseless. Still, Foster couldn't stop herself from wanting every bit of Landry with every fiber of her being. And when Landry disappeared to the mainland after missions, she left Foster alone with her desire until she returned for pre-mission training.

Foster grabbed her bottle and stood before wandering to her bedroom. She inhaled deeply, but the scent she was after no longer lingered. She dropped face down onto her bed and sank her face into the pillow; she hadn't changed the sheets for months, since the last time Landry's hard body had left a soft impression on her mattress, but the traces of her had long dissipated. Foster rolled over and took a swig of bourbon, then she closed her eyes again and tried to visualize Landry above her, tried to draw the picture of them making love.

She scoffed. Landry didn't make love; she didn't know how. The occasional times they'd hooked up, the sex was violent and frantic, a simple expenditure of excess energy, like Landry was exercising, not connecting emotionally. The last time she was in this bed, Foster had tried to slow things down, but Landry had shut off instantly and left, claiming she needed an early night before training the following day.

Foster pushed up from the bed and drifted back into the living room. She sat at her desk and flipped through the brief for their Cartagena mission. Drug-taking. Sexual assault. Torture. None of that was detailed in these papers. *Infiltrate the gang by any means necessary.* The Pulsus board had no idea what they were sending their operatives to do, and they didn't want to know either. They didn't care. After the PU team had fixed their bodies and rewound time, after the psych squad had performed a perfunctory evaluation of their minds, operatives like her were simply left alone with their memories, with their actions, and with their decisions.

Even the founder, Jenkin, with her immense intelligence couldn't possibly fathom the cumulative effects of a life lived five times over, of years spent committing foul acts against the very people the organization was supposed to be saving.

"All in a good cause," Landry kept telling her, but the longest she'd had to live in the past was months, not years, and she joined them when the truly distasteful part of the mission was over. Sure, she'd done awful things too, but they were always directed at the bad guys, the people they'd been sent to stop. If Landry killed someone, it was invariably someone who deserved it.

Foster had been hand-picked by Jenkin because her military record showed her as someone with an unswerving and unquestioning ability to follow orders. She slammed the manila folder closed and tossed another glass of bourbon down her throat. After ninety years of following those orders, Foster was beginning to question how much longer she'd be able to do it.

CHAPTER FOUR

WHEN LANDRY'S PHONE VIBRATED at eight a.m. sharp, she didn't have to check the screen to see who was calling. Her mom was more reliable than any alarm, but Landry was already up, showered, and packed, ready and eager to hit the mainland again. "Hi, Mom."

Her mom smiled widely. "Pumpkin, are you going to the city today?"

What was it that Einstein said about the definition of insanity? Doing the same thing over and over and expecting a different response. Her mom had the same issue with this question she asked after every mission. "I am." Having her mom around after being alone for eighteen years still didn't feel quite natural. But at the same time, after her first mission, Landry *hadn't* actually been alone. Fuck these competing memories; once the brain developed them, they didn't let them go. "We'll get together when I get back. We'll have time."

"That's not real time, Landry," her mom said.

Landry chuckled. "Is there such a thing as real time? I was an orphan for eighteen years and then I *wasn't*. Was that all real time when any of it can be taken away on the next mission?"

Her mom frowned. "You always get this way after a mission. Sometimes I wonder if you regret saving me."

"Whoa, no, don't say that." Landry shook her head and pressed her fingers to her mom's face on the screen. "It's just a mindfuck, that's all. You know that we all have competing memories of lives lived and *not* lived. Sometimes, the old orphan ones win out. I'm just trying to live a normal life when I can, Mom. You get that, don't you?"

Her mom nodded, but she didn't look any happier. "You're always too busy in pre-mission training. Can't you delay your trip and spend one day with me?" Her mom stuck out her bottom lip and pouted, almost comically.

Landry's memory of her mom's sense of humor was somehow intangible unless she was reminded of it. "How about a compromise? You come over for breakfast, and I'll catch a later train. I don't want to miss the game."

"Does watching the games make you wish you'd gone into pro basketball instead of the military?"

Landry sighed. "Isn't it too early for psycho-babble questions?"

"I'm just asking."

Landry searched her mind for conversations she'd had with her mom in the eighteen years she'd missed *actually* living and only had memories of. Yeah, deep conversations were their thing. "Sometimes," she said, her vulnerability skimming close to the surface. *This* was why she took off to the city as soon as she could. "But mostly, I just love being courtside, imagining a different life along the path unchosen. It doesn't mean that's what I want, Mom. If I hadn't gone in the military, I wouldn't have had the special skill set required for this job, and I never would've been able to go back to rescue you."

Her mom blew out a breath then smiled. "And I'd never be able to try to guilt you into spending time with me."

Landry flicked her hand at the screen, not wanting to get any deeper into a conversation like this. "Are you coming for waffles or not?"

Her mom narrowed her eyes. "Do you have bacon?"

"No, but you probably do, right?"

"I'll bring some. And I want to make sure your lungs are fully healed." Her mom swallowed and glanced away from the phone. "I've never seen you like that before."

Landry was still getting to know her mom through experience rather than recollected memory, but the concern lacing her voice was ill-concealed. "Questioning your own workmanship? I spent the recommended hours in the curatio tank, just like your assistant told me. Your machines are flawless, Mom. They've never failed us before."

"You're my daughter, pumpkin. It's my job to worry about you. And it's my *other* job to make sure my tech works perfectly."

Landry smiled. The military had been her family for a long time, and the real thing was taking some getting used to. "Don't forget the bacon," she said and hung up.

Fifteen minutes later, her mom arrived, medical kit in one hand and a package of bacon in the other. Landry snagged the meat and headed for the kitchen, but her mom grabbed her hand and proceeded to give her a full physical examination in the living room.

"You know, I'd much prefer one of the hot female patchers to examine me. Hell, I'd even take a guy over this. It's like I'm twelve again, and you're looking for lice in my hair in front of all my friends."

Her mom rolled her eyes. "And I'm sure my female patchers would *love* to be the ones getting you naked and examining every inch of you, but since I invented the tech, I get to make the rules." She gestured to the empty room. "At least no one's here to witness this."

Landry groaned and begrudgingly endured the uncomfortable humiliation, though she was grateful that they were alone.

When her mom had finished, Landry pulled her tank top back on. She'd expected to be a little sore. Neither she nor any of her team had ever had such serious injuries before, so she didn't know if her mom's machines *were* going to be fully effective. "See? I told you I was okay. Your fancy machines haven't failed me yet." Going on her vacation in top shape was a pleasant relief.

Her mom tenderly traced the branches of Landry's tattoo. "As above, so below," she said, reading out the words inked on Landry's arm. "I love that you put this back on before you go into the city again."

Landry smiled and placed her hand over her mom's. "It was

the only thing I had to remind me of you for a long time. Now that you're here again, I guess I don't need it, but I like the stability it gives me when I get home." It wasn't like her to be so maudlin. Her experience with near death had affected her more than she cared to admit. "Anyway, you fixed me up, and I'm good to go." She pushed away the negative vibes and headed to the kitchen to make breakfast.

Her mom followed her and sat on a bar stool in front of the marble counter. "What happened, pumpkin? What went wrong?"

"Things can always go wrong, Mom; I'd just been lucky until yesterday...until sixty years ago." Landry laughed, but her self-reproach for essentially facilitating the attack was like acid burning away at her mind. She'd had the chance to eliminate Miguel, and she'd been swayed by the hysterical pleas of a child. Before her first mission with Pulsus, which had *revoked* her orphan status, she would've executed him without a second thought. Having a mom again had made her soft. She took a box of strawberries from the fridge and placed them in front of her mom, along with a knife and chopping board.

Her mom arched her eyebrow. "Luck has nothing to do with your mission success, whereas your training and preparation does. Something must've gone wrong for you to end up like that." She shuddered and shook her head. "You're not telling me everything, are you? A mother knows when her baby's lying."

Landry's jaw twitched, and she busied herself gathering the ingredients for the waffle batter. How could her mom know her so well when she'd only really *known* Landry for three years? The science meant nothing to her; the memories in her head didn't feel real, didn't feel like she'd lived them. "Maybe the prep wasn't enough this time. You can't predict human behavior one hundred percent of the time."

"Maybe not a hundred percent, but close. Random and unexpected behavior is far more rare than people like to think it is."

Landry huffed as she cracked eggs into the bowl and threw

in the rest of the ingredients. "I disagree. We're capable of infinite spontaneous actions." She was sure her decision to let Miguel live had been just that. Against protocol. Against her better judgment. But the teary eyes of an innocent child moved her to act unpredictably.

Her mom smiled, but her eyes remained cold. "That's the kind of thing your father would say. He could be romantic sometimes too."

Landry scoffed and began to whisk the mixture. "I don't think anyone has ever called me that." Certainly none of the sexual partners she enjoyed on the mainland. She had no time for roses and rainbows, not in her line of work, and that suited her just fine. The mention of her dad, however, needled the heart she usually denied. "I would've liked to have seen Dad's romantic side, but Jenkin wouldn't like the competition now, would she? That's the real reason she won't authorize a mission to save him."

Her mom sighed and began to chop the strawberries. "You know that's not true. Your brother—"

"*Half*-brother." She tightened her grip on the whisk, nearly bending it in two.

Her mom tilted her head slightly. "Your *half*-brother wouldn't have been born if we stopped your father from dying on active duty. Michael wouldn't have saved Cassandra Taylor from falling to her death. And then Ms. Taylor wouldn't have de-escalated the threat of nuclear war in 2068. The world wouldn't benefit from your father staying alive."

Landry flared her nostrils and opened her mouth to protest, but her mom took Landry's hands, and she stopped whisking the waffle batter.

"I know you would have benefitted, pumpkin, but we can't change the past for the sake of our own future. That's not what all this is for."

Landry closed her eyes briefly and pulled away. "I know. But I miss him." And she was definitely sure of her memories of him, even if she only had thirteen years of them.

"I know you do, pumpkin."

Landry glanced up and saw no sign of grief in her mom's eyes. She'd remarried, had Michael, gotten divorced, and was now playing at being a lesbian with Jenkin. How long had it taken before she pushed Landry's father out of her heart?

"Speaking of Michael, he's invited us all to join his family for Christmas," her mom said, hope clear in her voice. "It would be lovely if you could come. It wouldn't mess with your normal life vacation time, because he's on the mainland too. I bet it'd only take you thirty minutes to get there."

Landry turned away and clenched her fists as she pretended to search for something in a lower cupboard. "I'll think about it," she said.

"Please, Landry. I want to spend a real Christmas with you; we've missed out on so many."

Landry blinked at the soft plea in her mom's voice. She *had* missed out on them even though she had the memories to contradict that reality. The Landry who'd benefitted from her going back to save her mom from being murdered had enjoyed nearly twenty more years of holidays with her–their–mom. And those memories were warm and comforting. Actually being able to *live* one of those Christmases would be good for her, wouldn't it? As if balking at the notion, a stabbing pain shot through her heart. But her dad wouldn't be there, so it still wouldn't feel right. And Michael was just a reminder that her mom had moved on. But Landry hadn't; she just couldn't seem to. Would her heart ever stop aching for her loss?

CHAPTER FIVE

FOSTER WOKE TO THE sounds of playlist three on repeat, and her throbbing temples reminded her that she alone had emptied both bottles of bourbon that lay discarded on the floor like abandoned hopes. She sat up and rolled her neck, and it cracked against the movement. She would've preferred to have made it to bed before she passed out, but small mercies: her sleep hadn't been entirely littered with nightmares.

"Playlist five. Minus ten decibels." Once the soft sounds of Sade began to soothe her aching head, she headed to the kitchen for her regular hangover cure. She pulled a bottle of protein and spinach elixir from the fridge and filled her bourbon glass with the green gunk. The gross-tasting liquid was now as essential to her existence as the whisky was. Dampen, drown, pass-out. Wake, fumble, drink potions to undo some of the damage. If she'd stayed in the Army, her reality wouldn't be a living hell.

But then she wouldn't have met Landry either. Foster picked up the phone and hesitated. Landry would already be on the train; she'd said she was looking forward to some stupid ball game, but more likely, it was the city girls she couldn't wait to get hip-deep in. Still, just hearing her machine message would give Foster some small comfort, so she called anyway.

"Hey, Foster. What's up?"

"You shouldn't be home." She snapped her fingers to mute the music. An actual conversation would be better for her head than the gunk she was drinking.

"Tell me about it," Landry said. "Mom came over for breakfast and was fussing all over me."

"I'd give up a year's salary to have your mom do that for me."

"Fuck off, perv. That's my mom you're talking about."

Foster grimaced. "Don't be gross. I didn't mean that. I meant it's nice that your mom cares enough about you to want to do that. My mom never did."

"Oh, sure," Landry said. "Sorry."

"Are you all good?"

"I'm a lot better than I would've been if you hadn't stepped in."

Foster chuckled at Landry's discomfort with showing gratitude. "That's one way of describing the way I saved your ass."

"What do you want?" Landry asked. "A medal for doing your job, hotshot?"

Foster chewed on her inside lip. "A thank you would suffice. And you're supposed to be the hotshot extractor, not me."

"I'm not an island," Landry said, slightly softer. "I wouldn't want anyone else by my side."

Foster shook her head. If only Landry meant that in all areas of her life. "Do you have time for coffee?"

Landry cleared her throat after a short silence. "I'm already running late. I've got tickets for the Warriors' first game since Coach Durant got canned."

"I don't get the fascination of watching ten women run from one end of the court to the other and back again for forty-eight minutes," she said, ignoring the awkward edge that had settled after her question.

"You're not serious? Aside from the fact that those ten women are usually pretty fucking sexy, there's the beauty of the game too."

"Fuck that shit. Bounce, bounce, shoot. If you want to talk about a beautiful game, let's talk soccer." *Let's just talk about anything. And don't leave the island.*

"Soccer's okay, but a basketball game is more intimate, more intense. You can't hide on a basketball court because the game is in constant flux. But if your team is bearing down on the goal in soccer, the back line can sit down and have a hot dog."

Foster grinned, knowing that Landry would be emphasizing her point with her hands, even though nobody could see her. *Chop my hands off, and I'd be mute*, she liked to say. *Chopping your hands off would be a travesty to lesbians everywhere* was Foster's stock response.

"You're just sore 'cos you never made the soccer team."

Landry huffed. "I never tried out for the—"

"Because you're too slow."

"Miguel came out of nowhere. I'd left him back at the house, begging for his life. How could I know he'd come after me?"

Foster frowned at Landry's sudden switch, which made it clear that while her body had been fixed, she hadn't gotten over the mental side of the attack. "I wasn't talking about that, Landry. And you couldn't know he'd be stupid enough to follow you. You didn't say anything, did you?" Blips like that were never raised in debriefs. It was an unspoken soldier's oath. "Because I didn't. The shit that goes on in our missions stays in that time, Landry. We both know that."

Landry didn't respond, and part of Foster wished they were in the same room so she could comfort her somehow. She scoffed at herself for the tender thought. Neither of them was good at showing their emotions; that's what made them such good soldiers.

"What if my mom hadn't invented regenerative tech? I'd be dead."

Foster laughed, trying to ignore the bile that hit the back of her throat as vicious images of Landry's broken body assaulted her mind. Landry dead? *No.* "So would I—or I'd be a decrepit one hundred and twenty-six-year-old."

"Seriously, Dee..."

"Look, buddy, we don't deal in what ifs. She did invent it, and that's because you jumped back and saved her. Now she gets to save you and the rest of us," Foster said. "You made a judgment call, and it backfired. It happens, even to you, the *great Landry Donovan*. But I bet you won't make the same mistake again."

Bubbles of possibility floated up from the vulnerability behind Landry's words. Maybe she was having the same doubts that were plaguing Foster about their work. Had nearly dying made her think harder about how she was living?

"You're right. I'm being ridiculous. I just need a break."

Foster blew out a breath. "I guess I'll see you in two weeks."

"Count on it. Have a great vacation."

Landry hung up before Foster could respond, and she tossed the phone across the kitchen counter.

"What does a great vacation look like, Landry? A long line of hot women desperate for you to take them to bed?" She drained the glass of the room-temperature liquid and hurled the tumbler at the wall. It bounced off and landed at her feet, still in one piece because some clever fuck had invented non-breakable glass. Not all inventions improved things; nothing satisfied anger like the sight and sound of smashing glass.

Foster had to face the fact that Landry wasn't emotionally available. God, she hated therapist jargon, but that lack of connection made her so good at her job. Or at least it had, until Cartagena. And Foster had been the same too, mostly thanks to her family history. So why couldn't she have just stayed that way? If only she could go back in time and keep herself from falling for someone so desperately unobtainable.

She opened the cupboard that held her stock of Widow Jane and pulled out another bottle. She couldn't stop her emotions, but this would help to numb them, and that would have to suffice. For now.

CHAPTER SIX

THE HIGH-SPEED, SUB-OCEAN TRAIN Pulsus had spent billions creating to maintain the link between the mainland and the island was now a glorified freight train, and Landry was its only regular passenger. But sitting alone in a carriage meant for twenty people was a pleasant way to decompress and make the mental transition from time-traveling soldier to wannabe civilian.

When the train came to a slow halt, Landry disembarked and made her way along to the cargo bays where the service staff were loading supplies from the dedicated supplier. They were practically self-sufficient, and their tech devices and systems were the stuff Apple and Google could only dream of, but no one made candy like M&Ms and Twizzlers. Those, and other luxury items, were still shipped over from the mainland.

"Two weeks of women-wrangling, cowboy?"

Landry jutted her chin at Garrett, who was busy throwing boxes of Pop Tarts into the boxcar. "Something like that, hoss."

Garrett grinned widely. "It's been a long few months without your stories. I'll make sure to be in the passenger carriage on your way home."

She shook her head; the island wasn't home. "You're way too invested in my sex life, Garrett. What does your man think of that?"

Garrett winked. "He thinks it's been a long few months too. He's missed stories of your city antics. Everyone has."

"What do you mean by *everyone*?" Landry pulled her bag onto her shoulder, just about done with the conversation and ready to leave. This was why she had to get away from the island; everyone knew everyone else's business, but she hadn't realized her private life was the hot topic at the water cooler.

"Chill, Donovan. Now that we're so isolated from the rest of the world, extractors are our version of movie stars, and you're top of the pile. You know that, *and* you love it."

"I wouldn't say that." She supposed there were worse things than being adored by a community of scientists and soldiers. "But I'll do my best not to let anyone down."

"That's the spirit, cowboy. Enjoy the big game."

"Sure thing," she said, though she didn't remember telling Garrett about her plans. She turned away and climbed the stairs to the discreet doorway leading to the surface, even more eager to get away from all things Pulsus.

Her first glimpse of San Francisco after a mission was like a breath of the cleanest, freshest mountain air. This was home in a way nowhere else had been since the death of her father. And though the landscape and its people had changed irrevocably since the earthquake that had leveled the whole city and the surrounding area in 2060, it still reminded her of a simpler time, one before she learned to kill people for the government, before she began hopping through space and time to save the world. This was the place her father had brought her to see the decommissioned naval ship, the USS Independence, and where he'd cemented the idea of her following in his footsteps by serving her country. He had a lot of faith in her, but she doubted that even he could've predicted her years in the Navy Seals would lead to a lucrative career saving people who would then go on to save millions of others. The generous remuneration was supposed to make up for the loss of a "normal" life once she'd signed up, but it actually financed her attempt at a normal life between missions.

She wandered along the waterside of Neoteric Wharf, feeling like she could breathe easier with each step. The area had replaced the once-thriving Fisherman's Wharf after it had fallen into the bay, and it was more open. Thanks to the introduction of the new building laws, the rest of the city and the newly carved coastline was now swathed in buildings that were a maximum of three stories. Just like Fisherman's Wharf had been, this area was the hot place to be, with restaurants, boutique shops, and coffee houses lining the streets, and Landry had made the place her home. It was just about anonymous enough to go unnoticed but still had plenty of women to keep her busy most nights of her vacation.

She stopped outside La Azucarera, the swish vegetarian restaurant on the ground floor of the building she owned, and tapped on the window. The little family were eating together as she knew they would be at this time, just after the lunch rush. They all looked up, then jumped out of their chairs and poured onto the street to pull her into a tight embrace. She'd never planned to make herself part of their lives, but events on one of her early vacations led to them practically adopting her.

Priscilla remained wrapped firmly around Landry's thigh even when her moms had released her. "We missed you, Lan Lan. You were gone long time."

"I've missed you too, sweet little P." She smiled down at the adorable kid. Landry couldn't explain to this little family that the cosmic time thread she used was an active energy string of a precise length, so any time she spent in the past also moved on in the future. But she *did* have to make excuses for her lengthy disappearances to this little family. "I had an important job to do, but I've only been gone four months." She ruffled the kid's short, blond hair, and Priscilla scrunched her eyes up and smiled a beautifully innocent smile Landry didn't see much of at work.

"Four months is like four years when you're three," Beth said and arched her eyebrows. She tapped a long fingernail on her watch. "*And* you're late. Your text said you'd be joining us for lunch."

"I got held up." Landry avoided Beth's unvoiced question. She was constantly mining for details on Landry's life but eluding her had become good sport.

"One day she'll find out what you do on these long business trips, you know? Take it from me, my wife never gives up on anything." Cait punched Landry's shoulder lightly.

"And *you're* damn glad I never give up on you." Beth slipped her arm around Cait's waist and kissed her cheek.

Landry nodded toward Cait. "Can she come out to play?" Like any fierce femme, Beth made all the decisions in their marriage, and Cait went along for the ride.

"Are you asking nicely?"

Beth looked at her the way Landry imagined had captured Cait's heart eleven years ago. If Landry didn't have strict rules about respecting relationships, she wouldn't hesitate to spend a few intimate days worshipping every contour of Beth's shapely body.

"I *always* ask nicely," Landry whispered, playing along.

Cait cleared her throat and stuck her head between the two of them. "The new coach brought a new point guard with him. Did you see the *Sports Illustrated* spread?"

Beth tilted her head in silent warning and nodded toward Priscilla.

"I've been away on business. I haven't been to the moon." Landry tapped the back pocket of her jeans. "I have two courtside seats for that exact reason. Block twenty-seven, right behind the team bench."

Cait bounced on her heels, and her eyes widened. "Beth...can you and the guys handle tonight? Josiah wanted extra shifts in the run-up to Christ—"

"It's the Friday before Christmas. We're going to be slammed, and you want to abandon us. Exactly how would you make that up to me?"

Landry shook her head, sure that Beth had anticipated Cait's plea and already worked everything out. She distracted herself by scooping Priscilla up and lofting her high above her head. The little girl giggled adorably.

"Landry and I will decorate Priscilla's room for Christmas," Cait said.

Priscilla grinned widely. "Lan Lan make my room all pretty?"

Landry lifted Priscilla higher, making her squeal in delight, though she wasn't sure why she had to do penance for Cait's enjoyment. "Sure." She lowered Priscilla, and she latched onto Landry's neck.

Beth gave her a mischievous smile. "She suits you."

"I'll leave parenthood to more responsible adults like you two, thanks." Landry wasn't interested in finding a partner, let alone raising a small human.

"Beth..."

Landry rolled her eyes at Cait's pitiful whine, but many a powerful butch squirmed under the thumb of their woman.

"Of course you can, baby. I knew you'd want to go, so I'd already told Josiah he could work tonight."

Landry laughed. "The games you married couples play."

"I'm sure they're child's play compared to yours," Beth said.

"You have no idea," Landry said and winked.

CHAPTER SEVEN

"Thanks for letting me drive this beast." Cait inched the Shelby forward in the inevitable game-day traffic.

"I didn't want to watch you beg twice in one day," Landry said.

"Hilarious."

Landry laughed then instinctively touched her ribs at the phantom pain making them ache. While they weren't injured any longer, her brain hadn't quite caught up to that fact.

Cait frowned. "Are you okay?"

Landry nodded. "I'm fine. Just an itch." She was grateful when Cait turned her attention back to the road. It hadn't been just an itch though. It had been a mistake that nearly cost her life and could've been catastrophic for her team. Mistake was too generous; her decision felt dangerously like weakness and far too close to compassion. Having her mom back in her life had taken the edge from her rage, but that shouldn't have made any difference. She didn't need to be angry to do her job properly. It was the opposite, really. She was always supposed to be cool under pressure, always able to make the right decision but instead, she'd allowed emotion into her thought process.

As Cait swung out into moving traffic, Landry thought about Foster's call that morning. Everyone knew Landry left the island early in the morning following a mission, but Foster had called anyway. She had a suspicion that Foster was concerned about Landry's mistake too; she probably wanted to make sure Landry knew she had her back. At least, that's what she hoped. She'd be devastated if her team had lost confidence in her and wanted a new extractor to lead them.

"Hey, are you okay?"

Landry glanced at Cait. "Sure. Why?"

Cait shrugged. "Seems like you're not really home yet, and you're still working in your head."

"I guess I am."

Cait nibbled on her lower lip but didn't say anything else. She never pushed about Landry's job, unlike her wife. After Cait had witnessed Landry in action when she'd needed some help, it seemed like Cait had decided she didn't *want* to know what their mysterious friend might be. CIA agent. Assassin. Spy. Whatever Cait thought, Landry knew she'd appreciated Landry's skills that night: skills that had saved her life.

Landry rolled her shoulders and pushed thoughts of work to the back of her mind. She came here to get away from Pulsus, not to analyze every second of her most recent mission. "Okay, pull me into the moment. Tell me how the restaurant is going. Has Beth created any amazing new recipes while I've been gone?"

Cait's smile lit up her face in that clichéd way that Landry had only ever seen in Hallmark movies.

"She's working on a special dessert for the Christmas menu, but I haven't been allowed to taste it yet." Cait pulled up behind the stacked traffic and tsked. "We've been getting busier too. The Wharf is the hottest place to be in the city right now. Property prices are hitting the roof. Sian, in the art gallery next door, pays four times our rent for half the space, and our lease is coming up for renewal. We're expecting the landlord to hike the price." She sighed deeply and shook her head. "We don't know if we could afford to stay here if that happens."

"Maybe they won't." Landry lowered the window and sucked in a breath of brisk winter air. Her little adopted family had no idea she owned the building and that she had zero intention of increasing their rent. "You should just concentrate on running the business and making as much money as you can, so you send your brilliant daughter to college. And it wouldn't hurt for you to go on a vacation occasionally. You need to enjoy your family while you can; you never know what tomorrow holds."

"You don't have to tell me." Cait inclined her head. "It's only thanks to you that I'm still here to be with them now."

Landry was thinking about her own dad rather than Cait, but she nodded anyway. "I'm just reminding you that life's short." Unless you worked for Pulsus, of course, and then you got to live decades longer than a natural life.

Cait swallowed hard, and tears edged her eyes. "Fuck. If you hadn't been around that night..."

"But I was." She nudged Cait and wiggled her eyebrows. "And it ended well for me; I hooked up with that hot cop who attended the scene. She was *filthy*."

Cait grinned. "I feel like you should share that story."

"Nah, you don't need to hear about my sex life."

"I don't *need* to; I just want to. Did she use her handcuffs?" Cait winked. "Did she stay in her uniform?"

Landry remembered every detail of that night. Her memories were like movies in her head that she could play back at will. With everything she had to do for Pulsus, those better times kept her sense of self intact. "She got out of her uniform before we were in her living room. There's something incredibly powerful about a woman who's that confident about being naked. Made me weak." Landry pictured all five feet four inches of perfection that was Officer Sanchez and smiled. "This is weird. It feels like I'm telling you a dirty bedtime story."

"Weird is good." Cait swung the car into an empty spot and turned off the engine.

Landry didn't answer and got out of the car to join the line of fans filtering into the stadium.

Cait caught up to her. "You were saying..."

She'd been annoyed earlier when Garrett wanted kiss and tell stories, and now Cait wanted the same. Her reputation had gotten out of hand. She stopped at the end of the line before security.

"Use your imagination."

"Come on." Cait shoved Landry's shoulder. "Tell me everything."

Landry gestured to the couple in front of them with a young son.

"Kid's gotta learn. He couldn't have a better teacher."

Landry was no role model in that department. She was always honest about not wanting anything beyond one night, and she was sure that wasn't the life Cait and Beth envisioned for their little girl. "Really? So I'll be the one showing Priscilla how to treat the ladies, will I?"

"You might be the one she comes to if she's having trouble getting hold of one."

Landry smiled. Despite the context, it was still nice that Cait thought Landry would be involved in their family for decades to come. She was as settled as she'd ever been and had no plans to leave Pulsus or San Francisco. Barring any more judgment errors like yesterday, she definitely wanted to be around for them, though she'd never make that promise. The only time she'd ever asked her father to promise to return safely, he'd stepped on an IED and was gone forever. She wouldn't make the same mistake with someone else.

After security, they grabbed game snacks and beers before taking their seats in time for the pre-game dap. The Warriors came onto the court with their new player, Jade Carter, nestled inside the group ready for the big reveal. They parted and gave a flawless execution of kick-ass capoeira, which ended with Carter being propelled into the air to perform a double backward somersault. The home crowd and even some of the away fans rose to their feet and erupted into ecstatic applause. Landry jumped to her feet and whooped along with the rest of the appreciative fans, then she dropped back into the plastic bucket chair. Tonight already promised to be just what she needed to kick off her vacation.

The team hit their warm-up drills hard, and Carter swished three-pointers and sank shots in the paint with graceful ease, illustrating the Warriors had gotten themselves one hell of a point guard. It didn't hurt that she was extremely hot either, with her olive skin, model-like features, and sleek physique. She danced around the other players with speed and agility like their boots were made of cement instead of leather. And she finessed the ball in a way that had Landry imagining those hands all over her body.

She half-turned to Cait while the teams took their positions for tip-off. "Did that article mention which team Carter played for?"

"The Knicks, I think. Apparently she didn't like the way the billionaire owner wanted to make coaching decisions."

Landry laughed and shoved Cait's shoulder. "Not her basketball team, goofball. Which team as in, who she takes to bed."

"This is what you get when you disappear for so long. I've only had food and baby conversation for four months."

"Aw, poor married wifey. So? What's her flavor?"

Cait shook her head. "Wow, aim high. You want to take a shot at the new MVP?"

"Not if she's straight." Landry pulled out her phone. "Forget it, I'll google her." In her periphery, she saw the Lakers on a fast break. Their number twenty-seven peeled down the right flank and tossed a baseball pass to her power forward. Carter flew in from nowhere and slapped at the ball viciously, propelling it toward Landry. She slipped her phone to her left hand and caught the ball in her right.

"Nice pickup. Wanna come down here and play?"

Jade Carter stood no more than five feet away, and the big screen displayed a close-up of Landry and Cait, whose mouth was open so wide, she could've caught the ball with it.

"With you or the rest of the team?"

Carter smiled and arched her eyebrow. "How about the team now and me later?"

"Give her the ball!" the crew chief shouted.

Landry tossed the ball to Jade, not really caring about the 36,000 pairs of eyes on her. "I'll just take the second option. I'll be right here after the game."

Jade's answering smile was brighter than the arena lights and ten times as hot as their 1000-watt bulbs.

Landry slipped her phone away. "Guess I don't need Google after all."

CHAPTER EIGHT

Slinging weights in the gym was a poor substitute for sex with Landry, but Foster needed the physical exertion to help her sleep. Between this and the Widow Jane, she hoped to keep her mind too exhausted to plague her mind with nightmares.

She was one hour into a planned four-hour session when Simson, another operative and another occasional fuck buddy, joined her.

"You done with that?" Simson asked, standing behind the Smith machine.

"Nearly." Foster completed her set then pushed the bar up on her final rep and rested it on the pegs.

"Your girlfriend left you all alone again while she screws around in the city?"

"Fuck you, Simson." Foster sat on a nearby bench.

"Wish you would. At least I acknowledge you exist." Simson loaded an extra twenty-pound plate on each end of the bar.

Foster tried to ignore the barb, but it slashed at its intended target and did the damage to her heart anyway. "Don't be jealous," she said. "It's not your fault she's hotter than you." She was having enough trouble figuring out her feelings; she didn't need Simson thinking she was right.

Simson snorted and began her squats. Simson wasn't ugly—plain was probably the best way to describe her—but she didn't affect Foster anything like the way Landry did. She still appreciated her strong body as she propelled the bar up and down, her powerful quads almost bursting from her skin. She was far bulkier than Landry, more of a bulldozer and far less agile, and because of that, she tended to go on missions where heads needed crushing. Foster knew Simson had brains too, the kind needed to be an extractor, but she'd told Foster she was happy being an operative, a foot soldier who followed orders and didn't have to make the tough decisions.

Simson completed her set and stepped away from the bar. She flexed her arms, which were the thickness of the average Pulsus science nerd's thighs, and grinned. "Don't tell me this isn't hot."

Foster shrugged. The adjective that came to mind was powerful, not hot.

"It's your loss, anyway. You barely fuck even when she is on the island. Why do you even bother saving yourself for her?"

Foster switched positions with Simson and lifted the weight onto her shoulders. She pushed up on her toes and stretched out her calves. "I'm not saving myself." Of course she was, and Simson was right that Landry was probably already sleeping with some anonymous long-haired beauty. She didn't see Foster as anything other than a friend she sometimes fucked.

Simson chuckled. "Prove it."

Foster stowed the bar. The rest of her day revolved around drinking Widow Jane and using the empty bottles for target practice; Simson could be a more interesting distraction. "What're you doing after this?"

"You." Simson grinned. "*After* I've done some grunt training. You should come watch. It'll be like foreplay," she said and winked.

They spent the next two hours generally trying to outlift each other, and Foster called an end to the session even though Simson had barely broken a sweat. They jogged to the training center, where a group of new recruits were warming up and sparring with each other. Simson had wanted Foster to be her co-trainer, but it didn't interest her. Plus, she hadn't been a mixed martial arts champion like Simson, who'd taken the MMA title five years in a row before she completed three tours with the Army. Now her main duty at Pulsus was training the extractors and operatives to fight.

Foster looked over the fresh recruits, playing a game with herself to spot the different forces they were from. Pulsus generally got their soldiers from the Army and the Navy Seals, so they came with some hand-to-hand combat skills, but the way wars were fought now meant those skills were rusty and underused. To do the things Pulsus demanded of them, they'd need the techniques Simson was about to teach them.

Simson made her way into the center of the melee, and the recruits fell into an instant silence. Delany smiled and took a seat on the bleachers. Simson's reputation clearly preceded her, and Foster could tell from the terrified expressions they were trying to hide that they'd already heard Simson's unique teaching method was to kick the shit out of them until they could adequately defend themselves.

Simson quickly set mismatched pairs—big versus small, women against men—and then wandered around the training area, barking expletives and degrading comments at the fighters and occasionally winking at Foster. She glanced at her watch and couldn't stop her thoughts from drifting to Landry, who'd be at that stupid ball game she couldn't wait to see. *Pack that shit up.* She blew out a short breath and tried to focus on the mini fights and guess the winners. More than once, she got it wrong, but mostly, it was pretty predictable.

Simson called them all back in then chose an ex-navy JAG for the exhibition bout she always ended her sessions with. Foster recognized the judgment jockey from the last induction group. He had a hot reputation, and Jenkin had pulled him in for an extractor position. She shook her head as he climbed into the ring with ill-disguised glee. Dumb fuck had no idea he was about to get pulverized. He was exactly the kind of rookie Simson liked to strip of their misplaced sense of invincibility.

Simson's first blow exploded his nose and sprayed her crisp white tank with his crimson blood. He stumbled backward, and she followed up with two uppercuts and a hook that sent him sprawling against the ropes. He looked dazed and already beaten, but he still lunged at her. She evaded his clumsy attack easily and slammed her elbow into his spine. He crumpled to the ground, and she kicked him in the gut and sent him skidding across the canvas into the corner. Simson stalked across the ring and grabbed a handful of his hair to yank his head up, then she delivered a series of knees into his ribs. He jerked like a puppet on her string until she tossed him across the canvas like he weighed nothing.

"You." Simson pointed to a skinny woman watching avidly. She was the victor in one of the mini bouts Foster had gotten wrong. "Get in here."

She swiftly did as instructed and cautiously approached Simson, who grabbed her shoulder and thrust her toward the JAG guy, who was being helped to his feet by a couple of other recruits.

"Show me what you've got what it takes to be like me," Simson said. "Finish him off then dismiss the class."

Foster recognized the look of adoration in the woman's eyes as she nodded at Simson, clearly eager to impress her. She strode across to the corner of the ring and let loose with a flurry of punches to his body and face.

Foster passed Simson a towel after she'd stepped out of the ring. "She'll go far."

Simson nodded and wiped the blood and sweat from her face. "Yeah, you're right. She's got a killer's instinct, and she never asks questions. Just follows my orders. She'll make a great operative."

Foster motioned to the JAG getting his ass handed to him by the woman half his size. "Are you harder on the recruits earmarked to become extractors?"

Simson tossed the towel at Foster's head and laughed. "I have to be. They come in here thinking they own the place just because they've been headhunted. I beat that out of 'em." She grinned as she watched the woman working the JAG over hard. "Besides, they're responsible for their team when they start running missions.

It's my responsibility to make sure they're ready for that."

As they turned to leave, the JAG fell to the floor, out cold. His conqueror paraded around the ring, and the rest of the class whooped and hollered.

"Your girl could always hold her own though. Top of the class. I never got to put a real beating on her, and I kinda regret that."

Foster winced inwardly. What would it be like to call Landry her girl? She pushed the intrusive thought away and forced herself to concentrate on the woman she was with right now, the woman who actually wanted to be with her. "That's why she gets paid the big bucks."

"What's she doing with all that money? Does she gamble?"

Foster opened the training arena door and waited for Simson to go through. "She bought property in the city so she can live a 'normal life,' whatever the hell that is, outside Pulsus." Foster trotted out the same shit Landry had given her when she'd asked the same question.

Simson grunted. "Normal? Has she bought a *normal* woman in the city too?"

"Like she'd need to pay for it." Foster clenched her teeth. Simson was pushing her buttons deliberately, trying to figure out the depth of Foster's feelings for Landry, but she wasn't about to give that information up. "Or that she'd only have *one* woman; she likes variety. I don't see her settling down. I mean, how do you even begin to explain the amount of time we disappear and can't have any contact?"

"Extractors are off-grid for a lot less time than we are."

"It's still time a partner couldn't speak to or see her. There's no job you can blame for that. Then there's the other women on missions. Who's gonna put up with that shit?"

"So she keeps it simple by fucking whoever she wants on the mainland, and you get the occasional leftovers like a stray dog." Simson stopped at a water station and took on some hydration.

"I guess you could put it that way," Foster said, holding back the desire to lash out at something. This wasn't a conversation she wanted to keep having with Simson. "Why are you so interested in what Donovan does anyway? Do you want her to fuck *you*?"

Simson laughed so hard, she almost choked on her water. "You know better than that, Foster. *I'm* the one who does the fucking."

"Which is why we don't work long-term."

Simson snorted and jutted her chin at Foster. "And yet, here you are: back for more."

Foster shoved Simson's chest. Jesus, it was like pushing a boulder. "You're a cocky cunt."

"Is that you asking for it?"

Foster looked at Simson and took in her incredible physique. It'd been a while since she'd given it up for Simson, and their kind of sex scratched a certain itch. "That's me asking for it."

Simson grinned. "I need to just swing by my place for a five-minute cleanup and—"

"A shave?"

Simson punched Foster's shoulder hard enough to make her take a step back. "You're pushing your luck, Foster. Did you not see what I did to that little snot in the ring just now?"

Foster smirked. "Please. That's your idea of foreplay."

Simson chuckled and put her arm around Foster's neck. "Good to hear you won't need warming up then."

Foster allowed Simson to pull her along the path toward her place. A few hours of mindless sex would get Landry out of her head for a while, at least. If only it could get her out of Foster's heart too.

CHAPTER NINE

SINCE LANDRY HAD LAST been at home, Cait and Beth had bought Priscilla a low-powered, remote controlled four-wheel quad so she could go with them on their weekend morning runs. Saturday mornings were family time, and Beth had insisted on accompanying Landry on the first run of her break. She slowed her pace to enable them to keep up with her, but Priscilla had no such trouble in her little vehicle.

She glanced down at Priscilla, and the hit of emotion that swelled her heart nearly knocked her off balance. How had she bonded so completely to this kid and her parents? And how did Beth not only know that but also encourage it, strangely ecstatic that her baby girl had formed another caring relationship independent of her and Cait? However this had come about, her connection with Priscilla baffled Landry. Her half-brother, Michael, had twins, but she had no interest in them at all, though any fledgling emotion had been dampened when one of the boys peed in her eye when she was trying a diaper change for the first—and last—time. Priscilla's attachment should be unsettling, but Landry found she was weirdly comfortable with it.

"I need a break," Beth said and dropped down onto the best bench in the Presidio, since it overlooked the bay. On a clear day, the very tip of Alcatraz Island's water tower was visible. "What are your plans for Christmas? This is the first time you've been home for it in the three years we've known you."

Landry didn't respond immediately, distracted by the thought that she finally had the home she'd never expected to have, and that she'd actually told other people her plans. With each piece of furniture and art she purchased and installed, her place had felt less like a high-class, minimalist hotel apartment and more like a real home. "I haven't decided yet," she said. Time was so important in her job that she liked to make it irrelevant in her "normal life," so she hadn't given the holiday a single thought. Nor had she considered the effect her presence or lack of it had on Priscilla and her moms. "Mom wants me to spend it with her and my half-brother's family." *And her lesbian lover, who is also my employer.* But she wasn't about to share that information, because Beth would undoubtedly have a hundred follow-up questions. Landry was slowly rediscovering the space in her heart where her mom and the notion of family had once resided, but her obnoxious brother, irritating wife, incontinent kids, *and* her cocksure boss were too much to endure in one sitting. And the thought of seeing her mom and Jenkin being intimate in any way made her nauseous.

"You have a half-brother?"

"Beth," Cait said, almost before her wife had finished her question.

Landry moved into a forward fold and touched the ice-cold tarmac. *Shit.* The personal information had slipped from her mouth so easily. She couldn't afford to get into the habit of being loose-lipped; that could be more fatal than her moment of weak compassion with Miguel.

"What?" Beth asked. "Landry will evade the question if she doesn't want to answer it like she always does. Won't you, Landry?"

Landry glanced sideways and nodded at Beth's astute assessment of the cat-and-mouse game they played when Beth dug for more details than Landry wanted to share.

"So, half-brother? Family? Christmas?"

Cait gave an exasperated sigh. "Maybe you should just leave her be sometimes."

"That's garbage, Cait. If I I did that, we'd never know anything about our mysterious neighbor."

Landry dropped into a set of push-ups. "Your lady has a point."

"She always has a point, and 'my lady' often sticks me in the ass with it." Cait sat beside her shivering wife and pulled her in close. She nudged Landry's ribs with her foot. "I'm trying to help you keep your shadowy secrets, Wonder Woman, and you're not helping."

Landry shifted to complete a set of one-handed press-ups. "I don't have blue eyes or black hair."

Beth laughed and gestured toward her. "You're not an emissary to the world of man either; you seem to be concentrating entirely on the female population. What does that make you?"

Priscilla, who'd been amusing herself feeding the squirrels, climbed out of her quad and up onto the bench, then laid across her moms' laps. She looked down at Landry and smiled sweetly. God, the kid was adorable.

Landry got to her feet and dusted the grit from her chilled hands. "You guys look like a Hallmark card."

"We model for them in our spare time," Beth said. "Half-brother? Christmas?"

"It's a long story for another day." A day that Landry wasn't sure she'd allow to arrive. "I haven't made any concrete plans, but I'm not really interested in spending the day with my annoying half-brother and his family for reasons I really don't want to talk about."

"Family *is* important, Landry. Even if they are annoying." Cait stroked Priscilla's hair from her eye, and Beth arched her eyebrow at her. "Obviously, I'm super lucky I don't have that problem," she said quickly.

"More garbage," Beth said. "If she doesn't want to be there, she shouldn't have to go out of some misplaced sense of duty."

Beth's forthright, take-no-shit attitude to life was one of the many things Landry liked about her.

"What about a sense of belonging?" Cait asked. "Everyone needs roots somewhere."

Beth sighed. "Baby, I love you. You know I do. But sometimes, you don't think before you start spouting." She tapped her own chest. "I was an orphan and lived in a children's home until I aged out. Where are my roots? Where do I belong?"

Cait clasped Beth's hand. "I'm so sorry, baby. I shouldn't shoot my mouth off." She kissed Beth's forehead. "Forgive me?"

Feeling slightly awkward at the show of unabashed emotion, Landry dropped to the ground again for a set of push-ups on her other hand. She'd hit thirty when she heard a stampede of feet pounding the tarmac. She looked up to see the entire Warriors squad, led by Jade Carter, jogging toward them. Landry continued to fifty before rising to her feet. It wouldn't hurt for Jade to see the stamina she'd missed out on by not hooking up with Landry after her game.

Jade motioned for her team to continue on while she paused and jogged on the spot a few feet from Landry. "This is a coincidence."

"Happy fates conspire." Sure, Jade was incredibly hot, but Landry wasn't about to go fan-girl crazy over her, especially after being shunned last night. That was something she wasn't used to and had no intention of *getting* used to.

"Sorry I didn't come back to you last night. The girls insisted we went out to celebrate the win."

Jade's gaze drifted quickly over Landry, as though sizing her up. The gleam in her eye suggested she liked what she saw.

"Your sixty-one-point debut deserved celebrating." In Landry's peripheral vision, Cait gawped in much the same way as she had the previous evening.

"It's a team thing; I wouldn't have scored that many without them playing out of their skin around me."

Landry nodded. Teamwork was something she definitely understood the importance of; she wouldn't be there right now without it. Without Foster.

"Are you going to introduce us?" Beth asked as she extricated herself from beneath Priscilla and came to stand beside Landry.

"I'm Jade," she said and held out her hand.

"She's the Warriors' new player." Cait joined Beth, holding Priscilla in her arms.

"I can see that from the training gear. I'm Beth. This is my wife, Cait, and our daughter, Priscilla."

Landry held her breath and waited for Beth's next move. She clearly wasn't as impressed with Jade as Landry and Cait were.

Jade smiled that dazzling bright smile again. "Your daughter's beautiful."

Priscilla giggled and nestled her face into Cait's neck.

"Thank you. So is our friend," Beth gestured to Landry, "and yet you left her waiting courtside like a fool last night."

There it is. Landry grimaced and stared at her feet.

Jade's eyes widened, and she kissed her teeth. "I was just explaining—"

"That you'd make it up by having dinner with her at our restaurant tonight."

"Baby..." Cait whispered.

Landry moved into the space between Beth and Jade, blocking the potential for it to turn into a battleground. "You'll have to excuse my friend. She's not well acquainted with subtlety."

Jade sidestepped Landry to face Beth again. "What kind of restaurant is it?"

"Vegetarian fusion. Would that be acceptable, or are you a meat-eater?"

Landry gave up. The war was on, and she and Cait just had to watch it play out.

"I'll eat pretty much anything as long as it's properly cooked and well presented."

Cait gave Landry an exasperated look and shrugged. There was nothing she could do to stop Beth when she was in flow, but Jade clearly didn't need any help.

"We've been a three-star Michelin establishment for nearly all three of the years we've been in business. *Everything* is perfectly cooked and exquisitely presented."

"And you're the head chef?" Jade asked.

"I am," Beth said. "You'll be able to make up for your transgression while sampling wonderful food."

"I can't tonight, but I'm free on Monday."

Landry sighed. They were doomed never to spend real time together; Beth didn't open the restaurant on Mondays. Maybe it was a good thing; taking her to the restaurant was too close to home, too close to Priscilla and the family.

"Shall we say seven?"

Landry kept her expression neutral; Beth was on the matchmaking warpath. She quelled the rising hint of panic at Beth's casual ease of inviting a complete stranger into their lives. Landry tried to look disinterested, half hoping Jade would decline the invitation. But it was only a half hope.

"I'm leaving early the next morning for an away game, so I have to be in bed by nine." Jade winked at Landry. "Could we eat at six instead?"

Landry couldn't decide if Jade was telling the truth or if she was just messing with Beth. Ordinarily, she could get a read on someone instantly, but her profiling abilities were non-functional around Jade. Her mind had already decided it was on vacation.

"That will be fine," Beth said. "I'll cook something low fat."

Cait ran her hand through her hair and shot another look at Landry.

"Carter!" someone from the squad yelled.

They'd circled back and were jogging on the spot thirty yards away.

Jade waved at them. "Thank you for the...invite. I'm looking forward to tasting your cooking, Beth." She glanced at Landry. "And I hope you'll have more to say that night."

She winked and sprinted away before Landry could respond.

Cait slapped Landry on the back. "I think that's the first time I've ever seen you tongue-tied."

Landry shoved her gently, avoiding Priscilla. "I wasn't tongue-tied. I couldn't get a word in edgewise because of *your* wife." She tolerated Beth's near-constant curiosity, but she'd pushed a little too far with this stunt.

"That's a strange way to say thank you, Landry," Beth said.

Landry flared her nostrils and bowed slightly. "I apologize, Beth. *Thank you* for railroading Jade into dinner."

"You're welcome. I've got a good feeling about this one," she said, clearly feeling no guilt for her intrusive intervention. "She's different from your usual conquest."

"Different?" Landry shook her head. "You haven't met any of my other 'conquests.' How can you possibly know if she's any different?"

"*You* were different."

Landry clenched her jaw, exasperated, but she didn't want to argue in front of Priscilla, so she sprinted off in the opposite direction from Jade at a pace none of the family would be able to keep. Maybe Jade *was* different and a world away from the women Landry usually went for, and maybe that was a good thing. But how had Landry been *different?* And what the hell did that mean if she was?

CHAPTER TEN

December 23, 2075

RIK'S PLACE WAS THE only bar on the island to get alcohol in a social setting. The myriad other haunts only served smoothies, fancy frothy coffees, and herbal teas. Jenkin catered to what her employees wanted, and most of them wanted the soft stuff. There was no Rik though; it was self-serve, and only a few battle-hardened operatives were regulars here, indulging in the wide range of top-shelf liquor.

"I'll get this," Simson said. "You get ice and some glasses."

Foster collected the items and sat in a booth toward the back of the bar, far away from the four other operatives betting on a slap fight. She whistled when Simson placed a bottle of Jefferson's Presidential Select on the table and slid in opposite her. Foster inspected the label. "You sprung for a 1990? What's the occasion?"

Simson pulled it from her grasp and poured a generous amount in their glasses. "I think what we did for eleven hours deserves celebrating, don't you?"

"Sure." Foster clinked her glass to Simson's, but honestly, she couldn't remember what they'd done. The hard workout and sex hadn't exhausted the deep white matter responsible for her dreams or given her a break from the new nightmares of her last mission. The two bottles of Widow Jane hadn't sent her brain into a stupor either, so she'd tried to stay awake and think about the work they did at Pulsus. That spiraled her thoughts in an entirely different direction, one with new possibilities for the scope of their work. Now all she had to do was make people listen and get them on board.

Simson took a sip of her drink and shook her head. "You look like shit, Jacqlyn. Didn't sleep because I wasn't there to spoon you?"

Foster knocked her glass back in one swallow and slid it across the table for a refill. "You know better than to call me that, *Sandy*."

Simson poured another couple of fingers and pushed the glass back to her. "I should kick your ass for that."

"But you can't. I'd ruin your reputation by putting you down." Just like Landry, Foster had been able to handle Simson's training. Neither of them were as big as Simson, but they were both faster, had more stamina and skill, and were almost as powerful.

Simson frowned. "Something wrong?"

"You don't want to know. We should just drink." She emptied her glass, and Simson refilled it again.

"You sure about that?" Simson nudged Foster's hand. "We've been through a lot together—seventy years at my reckoning—and I've always had your back. Right?"

"Yeah. You have." Every mission they'd done together, Simson had proven herself over and over to be the kind of soldier Foster wanted beside her in the heat of battle. And the things on her mind were demanding to be heard. Wouldn't Simson be a good sounding board?

"Jesus, Foster, if you can't tell me, who can you tell?" Simson asked then scoffed. "Or are you keeping it to share with Donovan?"

"Fuck, Sims, you're obsessed with her."

Simson gestured toward the mirrored beer ad hanging on the wall. "Me? You should take a look in that."

"I'm not the one who keeps bringing her up." Foster clenched her jaw and rolled the glass in her hands, fighting hard not to squeeze it so tightly that she'd crush it. Obsession could sometimes be a good thing, but she was beginning to wonder if her fascination with Landry was as dangerous for her health as the pack of outlawed cigarettes she pulled from her cargo pants' pocket. She lit one with the Zippo Simson had given her. The same

Zippo had saved Foster's life, stopping a bullet from a Chicom on the Laos mission. Despite the substantial dent in the body, it still worked perfectly. She could've hammered it out, but she liked the reminder. Things didn't have to be pristine to be fully effective, and she felt far from pristine.

Simson put a cigarette in the corner of her mouth, but she didn't light it. She tapped the Zippo. "Even when I haven't been able to stop things happening physically, I've kind of been there for you. That hasn't changed, Foster. What's bugging you?"

Foster took a deep breath. "We're soldiers. We're supposed to keep the shit inside, where it belongs, aren't we?"

"Sure. But when that means you're not dealing with it..." Simson twisted the lighter around and around on the table. "We both like to drink, Foster—it helps us cope—but lately..."

Simson didn't have to finish her sentence. After Landry, she was Foster's closest friend, and she would have to be blind not to recognize that Foster had been self-medicating a little too enthusiastically. Foster knew it too, but she couldn't stop it. Worse, she couldn't do anything about the root cause of her ever-growing reliance on alcohol, and it was beginning to consume her. The only thing she could think to do was refocus her energies and reconcile her escapades, but how was she supposed to do that when the next mission always required her to do more of the same? "I can't stop, Sims. Not unless things change."

Simson inclined her head and stopped fiddling with the Zippo. "What things?"

Could she get Simson on the same page as her without smacking her upside the head with the book? "We're at war, aren't we?"

Simson shrugged. "You could say that. I mean, no one knows it but us, so it's pretty one-sided. I see what you're saying though. What about it?"

Foster looked out the window and winced inwardly at the normalcy on their island bubble. Science nerds walking their dogs, workers collecting trash, operatives and extractors jogging in the park. "We do things…" She sipped at her glass. She trusted Simson, but she didn't want to be blind drunk when she was peeling open her brain for inspection. "We do bad things in the name of that war because we're told that what we're trying to achieve is for the greater good."

Simson nodded. "The end justifies the means."

"But like you said, this isn't a normal war led by a government. And it's not authorized by our president, by the head of any nation."

"Doesn't that make it better?" Simson asked. "Religion and politics aren't getting in the way."

Foster pressed her glass to her forehead, and the ice-cold condensation soothed her aching head a little. She took several long draws on her cigarette and followed the smoke as it curled toward the window. "Do you ever think about the orders we're following?"

"I don't follow blindly, if that's what you're asking. I'm following these orders until there are better orders. I believe what we're doing is for the good of humankind, but I don't like what we have to do to get there. That's what's bothering you? The bad shit we have to do?"

"Have you ever thought our focus might be too narrow?"

Simson threw some more ice in her glass and topped it up. "You want to do *more* bad shit? Now I'm confused."

Foster shook her head. "No, you don't get it. I don't want *us* to do more. I want the board to do more."

Simson hunched forward over the table. "Go on."

"The missions we've completed were a good start. They gave the science nerds time to iron out the kinks." She thought about the first mission, which resulted in Landry's mom being around to invent the regenerative tech. Without that, Pulsus would've gone through a lot more soldiers in the past three years. "But we should be thinking about bigger missions that could make bigger changes; we could be doing what needs to be done."

"What needs to be done?" Simson asked.

Foster took another sip and was able to appreciate the flavor of the over-priced bourbon. It reminded her of the pecan pie her grandma used to bake whenever her mom took her there to get them away from Foster's alcoholic father. She ate a lot of pecan pie. "Our focus should be wider. We save one person who changes the future, but we should be taking out whole drug cartels and the people who've been responsible for mass genocides."

"Won't that change too many things at one time?"

"So what if it does? Those changes won't be worse than letting those atrocities remain untouched. Look at our next mission: we're going to Nazi Germany to save a doctor who was close to curing cancer. That will save millions of lives, sure, but what if we went a few years further back and executed Hitler? We'd still save Doctor Cancer Cure, but we'd also save the one hundred million other people that died during that maniac's reign." Foster edged forward and grasped Simson's arm. Now that she said it all out loud, it made even more sense.

Simson rubbed her temple and narrowed her eyes. "Why have all this power and only get a fraction of the possible benefits?"

"Yes!" Foster squeezed Simson's arm. "The board is being too short-sighted. No one's telling them what they need to do, which is to make the big decisions to effect bigger outcomes. It might only take a few strategic missions before we don't need to go back at all."

And maybe then, Foster's nightmares would finally stop.

CHAPTER ELEVEN

RUNNING AROUND GOLDEN GATE Park on Monday afternoon brought back memories of Landry's mission to San Francisco in 1978 to save the rising politician Harvey Milk from being assassinated. He went on to become mayor and brought the gay rights movement forward nearly forty years, making San Francisco the first city to marry two guys in 1981. To get close to Dan White, Milk's would-be executioner, Landry had spent time jogging in the park with White's wife, Mary Ann.

Now, Sunset Boulevard was the park's new border to the Pacific Ocean. Visiting the past mostly made her glad of the future, but occasionally, it made her melancholy. Some things Pulsus hadn't managed to modify. Despite their constant search of their past, they still hadn't figured out if they'd missed someone who'd been on their way to solving global warming. No one in the present was anywhere near it, and the effects were seen in countries across the world: the once-beautiful city of Venice, Italy had been underwater for nearly two decades, and the United Kingdom was buried under a blanket of gray cloud so thick, it made air travel almost impossible.

She finished her run with a five-hundred-yard sprint to her apartment door and checked her watch. Would Jade show in two hours? Maybe she'd been too polite to refuse Beth's less-than-cordial invitation—or too chickenshit. Not that Landry would blame her for that; Beth had been her most fierce and formidable self when she'd thrown out the summons to Jade.

Landry undressed quickly and jumped in the shower. The hot water washed away her light sorrow, but that was replaced by a bad case of nervous tension creeping across her shoulders and into her neck. *You were different*. Beth's words had been a constant refrain in her mind for the past two days. She'd tried to ignore it and attribute it to Beth's blatant attempt to have her follow in her footsteps by settling down and having a nice family. As if the world's evils would be resolved if everyone just fell in love. Landry had more important things to do than fall in love, like saving the world one person at a time.

She ran the shampoo through her hair and realized she needed a haircut. The bangs she'd had to grow for Cartagena were getting out of hand, and the back of her hair touched the chain around her neck. That wouldn't do. She liked her neck shaved clean, loved the feeling of a woman's hand wrapped around it, the heat of the sun beating down on it as she ran. Longer hair made her sluggish. She'd have to find out how she might need it styled for the next mission Foster had already emailed her about. She didn't want to think about it yet though, so she hadn't replied. Foster wouldn't understand. They were close, but Landry liked the total separation on her vacations, and Foster was very much a company woman.

She turned off the shower and went to the walk-in closet without a towel, preferring to air-dry. She twisted this way and that to inspect her body in the full-length mirrors. "Not too weak now," she said, remembering all the taunts from her childhood. Landry had always been the skinny kid the bullies liked to mess with, and it wasn't until after her mom was killed that she resolved never to feel weak and helpless again. The women she hooked up with seemed to appreciate it too. There was nothing like that gasp of surprise when she lifted them up and carried them to bed. She had a feeling she'd need to do more than that to impress Jade though.

She sprayed her favorite cologne on her chest, stomach, and wrists before pulling on a pair of black briefs with a thick waistband and the matching muscle back sports bra, even though her muscled chest meant she really didn't need to bother with one. Then she looked over the racks and racks of the clothes she'd purchased over the past three years. T-shirt casual, shirt-smart casual, or evening smart? The girls didn't impose a dress code, but her dad was always impeccably attired when he took her mom on their weekly date night, and Landry figured he'd want her to be the same.

What would Jade wear? Landry had no idea what her style was, but she had no doubt that Jade would look stunning in whatever she wore, even if it was a paper bag, and Landry would enjoy thinking about undressing her and exploring every inch of her body. That wouldn't be tonight though, given Jade had already told her she needed an early night. Which meant Landry would have to make plans to see her again.

Again? When she hadn't even seen her tonight. That was unprecedented. One and done was her usual MO. Maybe Beth was right; maybe she was different.

Landry ran her hand along her extensive selection of color-ordered, button-down shirts, enjoying the soft cotton beneath her fingers. As she slipped on a plain scarlet red shirt, she could already imagine Jade taking it off. Jeans, belt, and boots followed, before she looked over her watch drawer. The occasion merited wearing her favorite, the Audemars Piguet with the black rubber band. It was the first gift her mom had given her in their *new* life after Landry had returned from the mission to save her. Her mom had bought Landry's dad an earlier model, but he always said it was too expensive to use. He died without ever wearing it. She wouldn't make the same mistake, but it was only for special circumstances, and tonight somehow fit that bill, Jade was a high-earning basketball player, and Landry didn't want to look out of her league sporting a Casio.

She fixed her hair and took one last look in the mirror before heading downstairs. She smiled when she saw Jade was already waiting at the bar. She looked up, and Landry faltered. It wasn't like she hadn't seen a hundred beautiful women smile, but Jade's was accompanied by something intangible that Landry couldn't name.

Whatever it was, it multiplied her outward appeal a hundred-fold.

"You live upstairs, and I still beat you here."

Landry glared at Beth, who stood beside Jade. Cait shrugged in sympathetic apology. "Is nothing sacred, Beth?"

"Plenty." Beth flashed that look most women would forgive her anything for. "You haven't given us all that much in the past three years, so our conversation has been pretty short."

Despite wanting to stay mad at her, Landry smiled. "Damn, woman. Someday you'll do something I can't excuse."

Cait slipped behind the bar and coughed loudly. "The usual?"

She nodded. Jade held a half-full glass of something blood red and orange. "Sex on the beach?" Landry asked.

"It's a little cold for that, and the coach wouldn't be happy if I called in sick."

Jade twitched her eyebrow, and something much lower on Landry's body twitched in response. "I was talking about your drink."

"Of course you were," Jade said.

"I'll head back to the kitchen and let you work on your apology, Jade." Beth gestured to her wife. "Cait will show you to your table," she said and swished away to the back of the restaurant.

Landry took her drink from the bar and held up her hand when Cait went to obey Beth's instruction. "I've got it. The window table on the mezzanine?" she asked without thinking. She always had the best table in the restaurant, but maybe it wasn't such a good idea to allow Jade into that space too. She was already in one of Landry's sanctuaries.

Cait narrowed her eyes as if she was thinking the same thing. "Sure. Let me know if you need anything."

"Thanks, Cait." Landry gestured to the floating steps in the center of the restaurant. "After you."

Jade shook her head. "After *you*."

Landry missed a half beat before she moved. "Are you desperate to check out my ass?"

"About as desperate as you were to check out mine."

Landry held Jade's gaze for a moment; her eyes were the color of blue-gray agate, and her intense look somehow rendered Landry a little off balance. She turned and headed up the steps, slow enough for Jade to appreciate the view but not too slow that she milked it. It seemed Jade was just as much an alpha in the bedroom department as Landry. That could make things... interesting.

When she got to the special table, she pulled out a chair for Jade, but she walked beyond it and sat in the one opposite.

"Beth tells me that you saved Cait's life."

Landry sat down and took a deliberately slow drink. "Really?"

"Really. You're quite the hero to them both," Jade said, clearly expecting Landry to fill in the blanks.

Landry cursed not getting down here before Beth could run her mouth. "It wasn't heroic or special. I'm sure you would've done the same thing."

Jade arched her eyebrows impossibly high. "Taken on four armed men and women single-handed?" She shook her head. "I would've called the cops. Sorry to disappoint you, but I bounce balls for a living, not heads. What do *you* do for a living that makes that nothing special?"

I time travel and sometimes have to kill people for the greater good. "I'm in a special military branch." That line generally evoked one of two responses: either the woman visibly swooned, or she'd begin to lecture Landry about conflicts before making a swift exit, so it was something she rarely admitted. Jade did neither.

"I'm guessing you're not a data analyst with skills like the ones Cait described."

Jade took a sip of her drink and caught an escaping droplet of juice with her tongue. The slow way she retracted it, along with the hungry look in her eyes, made it clear she knew exactly what she was doing.

Landry swallowed and refocused on their conversation. "The

story gets more impressive every time she tells it. The kind of people who attacked Cait aren't usually that dangerous for anyone prepared for them." She shrugged. "And they were drunk too. I was right beside them before they even realized I was there."

"Cait said your joke made her laugh, even though her ribs were broken. She didn't get a chance to tell me what you said."

Landry half-smiled, but there had been nothing humorous about that situation. "It wasn't that funny. I think Cait was just hysterical with pain by that point."

"Still, it's good to know you have a sense of humor as well as being deadly."

"It's essential with the work I do—the work I really can't talk about." Landry had said too much already. She could leave things to interpretation, but she didn't want to blatantly deceive Jade.

"The girls said you don't like to talk about yourself. You say you can't talk about your work. What does that leave us with?"

It didn't leave them with much at all. She tended to pick up women in loud bars where there was no need for deep conversation. "The girls can be melodramatic. Ask me anything that's not work-related, and I'll do my best to answer."

Jade smiled and drummed her fingers together, but before she could ask her first question, Beth came up the stairs with their first course.

"Chestnut, roasted butternut squash, and Bramley apple soup. Enjoy," she said and went back downstairs with only a backward glance and a wink.

"Tell me about your parents," Jade said, picking up a spoon.

"Straight in with the tough stuff." Landry tasted the soup before answering. "This is really good."

Jade inclined her head and said nothing.

Which version was she supposed to give? She had two realities with her parents, but she'd only really lived through one. "My mom's a genius in the medical profession. My dad died when I was thirteen, and she remarried. I didn't forgive her for that until I was a lot older. Now she's playing the happily married lesbian, and I don't know how to feel about that. Next."

Jade's laugh made Landry buzz weirdly, but she wanted more of it.

"Is that why you don't want to spend Christmas with your mom?"

Landry put her spoon down and took a swig of whisky. "Jesus Christ, what time did you get here? Sounds like you've already gotten the full story on me. Let's try small talk for a while; what's your favorite color?"

"Whatever color my team plays in." Jade winked. "How's this for small talk?" She pushed up the sleeve of her suede suit jacket and flashed her watch. "I have the ladies' version of your watch."

Landry ran her finger across the bracelet. "That's beautiful. It's a good sign that we have matching tastes, right?"

Jade smirked. "As long as you don't want to get matching tattoos, sure... Better?"

Landry nodded. "Better." They were both silent while they finished the first course. She stole occasional glances at Jade, already beginning to think this wasn't a good idea. Jade was insanely attractive, her mind was sharp, and she had a wicked sense of humor; she was more like someone Landry would enjoy as a friend. Sleeping together would spoil the chances of a friendship, wouldn't it? And a regular friendship might be exactly what she needed. It seemed like a natural progression in the normal life she'd been trying to build in the city. She'd let the cute little family into her life, and aside from Beth's nosiness, it hadn't been a disaster.

Cait's heavy footsteps up the staircase drew Landry back into the room. Cait removed the soup bowls and replaced them with the next course. "Angel hair pasta primavera," she said. "Beth said it'd be good for your energy at tomorrow's game."

The easy small talk continued about Jade's family, books they liked, and basketball, and though Landry was grateful for it, she also felt like she might be missing out on the possibility of something deeper.

Jade dabbed at the corner of her mouth with a silk napkin and smiled. "As wonderful company as you've been, Landry, I have to leave. The coach wouldn't be impressed if you kept me up all night."

"But would you be impressed?" Landry waved her napkin in the air. "Forget I asked. When are you back in town?" She reminded herself she was contemplating developing a friendship, not trying to initiate a one-night stand.

"Friday. After the game, I'm heading to the East Coast to spend Christmas with my family. There are a lot of us, so it's a big deal. And it's my nephew's first Christmas, so the whole family is super excited. You know how adults get around babies."

Landry laughed gently. "Not this adult. I don't get the fascination while they're just screaming shit machines. I get interested when they can hold a conversation using words with more than two syllables."

Jade wiggled her eyebrows. "That's another thing we have in common. If we keep going, we'll have the white picket fence and the whole shebang in no time at all."

She pushed her chair back and rose deliberately slowly, giving Landry a teasing view of her cleavage down her unbuttoned blouse.

"Do you want to get together Saturday?" Whether this was going to become a friendship or something else, Landry was sure she wanted to see Jade again.

"I have a game Saturday," Jade said.

"Of course." But maybe Jade didn't want to see her again...

"I'm free Sunday after training. We can go meet your mother."

Landry let out a sharp laugh. "Wow, your teasing knows no bounds, does it?" She began to get up, but Jade placed her hand on Landry's shoulder.

"No need to be all chivalrous. My car is ten feet from the door."

She leaned down and kissed Landry, deep and hard. Her hair caressed Landry's cheeks as she traced a soft line from Landry's neck and along the hollow of her throat before resting on her pecs. When Jade pulled away, Landry followed for more, but Jade pressed her fingers to Landry's lips.

"Patience, baby."

Landry cleared her throat and relaxed back into her chair. "I don't like waiting, Jade."

Jade pressed her lips to Landry's ear, her breath as hot as Landry's desire.

"You'll wait for me," she whispered huskily and sashayed away, her heels clipping the stairs rhythmically.

Landry let out a breath and shook her head. How was she supposed to resist *that* for the sake of a friendship?

CHAPTER TWELVE

December 27

"WE ADMIRE YOUR DEDICATION, Foster, truly we do. But the risks are too great, and there are too many calculations that we're unable to make to ensure any operation of that magnitude could be safe."

Foster's dislike for Carson, the chief experiment integration engineer, grew with every dispassionate word that came out of his mouth. She fought the strong desire to leap across the table and smash his head repeatedly against the wall. She stood at the far end of the boardroom, trying not to feel insignificant in front of the eleven high-level, high-intelligence people who occupied the rest of the table. Jay Jenkin sat at the head of them all, with Elena, Landry's mom, to her right. Foster's close relationship with Landry had meant that a quick conversation with Elena resulted in this extraordinary meeting being pulled together within the week.

Foster had presented her ideas for the development of their work in good faith, but now it was like she was on trial. She'd expected some resistance—change scared some people—but she hadn't expected them to dismiss it out of hand. They hadn't even taken the time to discuss it. "Aren't the risks worth it? Assassinating Hitler before his fascist policies gained traction would still save the doctor."

"Let's say we did that." Jolene Dudley, the chief environmental psychologist, tapped her pen on the table. "At what point in his life would you have us intervene? Right after his mother gave birth? Would you volunteer to murder an innocent baby?"

Foster threw her hands in the air. "Of course I wouldn't want to kill a baby, but we know there's no other path for him." She smashed her hand on the table. "There was nothing in his life that made him that way; he was just evil."

"We can't actually say that with one hundred percent certainty," Dudley said.

Foster scoffed. "Wouldn't that be worth finding out then?"

"But the earlier we murder him, the less impact he has on others, yes?" Dudley asked. "Or what if we ensure that his older brother, Edmund, didn't die? What if *that* was the life-changing incident that seeded his murderous anti-Semitism?"

Foster ran her hand through her hair and shook her head. "That's just guesswork. The energy and resources to run a mission that may or may not work would be a waste of millions of dollars. Assassinate the man before he becomes a decorated war veteran, before he develops his ideology. *That* would stop the ethnic cleansing before it even started. Without Hitler, World War Two would never have happened. It was the deadliest conflict in the history of the world, and you won't even *try* to stop it? Are missions like that not the whole reason Pulsus exists? Aren't we the monsters if we don't stop it happening when we have the power and the means?"

"I understand your perspective." Elena got up and joined Foster, sitting on the edge of the table beside her.

Elena placed her hand over Foster's, and she saw jealousy flash across Jenkin's expression. She didn't suppress a grin, despite the situation. Jenkin *should* be watchful; Elena was stunning and a more traditionally feminine version of Landry. Jenkin, however, was hard-faced, gray-haired, and had a God complex. Foster couldn't understand the appeal, but Jenkin had never been short of younger women fawning all over her. Elena was the only woman Jenkin had dated in her age bracket, as far as she knew.

"Foster?"

She blinked and refocused on Elena. "Yes?"

"I said that I understand your perspective, but we've only been established three years, and we hope to have many lifetimes of work in front of us." Elena gestured to the rest of the board members. "With the right leadership, we'll build a legacy that will outlive all of us in this room."

Something flickered across Jenkin's face which Foster couldn't place. They already had regenerative technology; theoretically, there was nothing stopping them from essentially becoming immortal. She shook her head. "I don't get your point."

"That we don't want to run before we can walk. The beauty of time travel is that we have all the time in the world to figure out if we can make the kind of changes you're talking about—safely—and with minimum negative loss or repercussions. We can run the kind of missions you're talking about in the years to come, and they'll still have the same effect. But right now, the board has already agreed its priorities and the next ten missions are either set or in the planning stage." Elena smiled and squeezed Foster's hand. "That's a lot of resources and no small amount of money. Time dilation to access the cosmic strings requires a metal that the earth only has a finite amount of, and we've already mined for and acquired all of it. Until we can replicate that ore or locate more of it elsewhere in the Universe, our ambitions are necessarily restricted."

Foster looked down at Elena's hand on top of hers; it looked so petite in comparison. "That isn't guaranteed though, is it? It's possible that you might never locate or create more of that metal, and that means every mission counts. You can't afford to avoid the big decisions and *hope* that you'll find what you need in the future."

"You're one of our finest operatives, Foster, and you've completed a lot of missions in your time with us. It's natural that you want to do more, given how much time you dedicate to each operation, but you have to trust us. And you need to be patient." She released Foster's hand and turned to walk back to her seat. "You need to continue to do your job and let us do ours."

Foster clenched her jaw. She hadn't expected Elena to blatantly patronize her. Their priorities were clearly very different from

Foster's, and they were short-sighted to be pinning their hopes of continuing their work on the availability of a metal they couldn't recreate or find more of. If they only had a finite amount of the ore required for missions, they should be prioritizing the ones that could have maximum impact, like assassinating Hitler. Foster wanted to be part of *those* missions; she wanted to effect bigger change right now. She couldn't wait forever. She *wouldn't* wait.

"What you do as an operative is incredibly intense," Lindsay Castillo, the chief clinical psychologist, said, "and it takes a mental toll. Perhaps you'd like to book time with someone in my team before your next mission."

Castillo sat closest to Foster and had looked the most supportive during her presentation. Now she understood that she'd misinterpreted Castillo completely. She was just wearing the sagacious therapist mask of empathy and unconditional positive regard. Nausea roiled in her guts at the thought. "Thanks, Ms. Castillo. Maybe I'll do that." *Or maybe I'll gouge my brain out with a wooden spoon.*

"We appreciate your input, Foster," Jenkin said, sounding genuine while still looking straight through her. "You're a valued member of Pulsus, and you're exceptional in your role."

Meaning, shut the fuck up and go back to torturing people for our version of the greater good. "Anything for the organization, Ms. Jenkin, you know that," Foster said, matching the sincerity of Jenkin's tone but without the feeling. They were blowing her off, and their logic was weak. She had to get out of there before she exploded. "Thank you for taking the time to listen." She gathered her things and headed out. But she pulled the door open a little too vigorously, and it smashed into the wall, leaving a handle-sized hole in the drywall. "Sorry." Foster shrugged and left the board to their broken wall and their broken principles.

CHAPTER THIRTEEN

December 29

JADE LEANED OVER THE pool table at the Warriors' team campus and hit an unbelievable shot, pocketing two balls at opposite ends of the table. With alternating views of Jade's chest and ass, the last hour had been a delicious kind of torture, but it had made it hard to concentrate on conversation. Landry's consideration of developing a friendship with Jade wavered in the face of temptation, and she was just about at boiling point.

"I don't know whether to be impressed or mortified that you didn't give in to family pressure," Jade said as she lined up another shot.

"Can you be both?" She'd hoped to avoid this conversation, but Jade wouldn't be dissuaded from pursuing it. "I gave in to pressure from my chosen family and spent Christmas Day with Priscilla and her moms. *And* I invited Mom to join us." Landry shrugged. "But she chose her lesbian lover and son over me. So maybe you should show me some sympathy instead."

Jade missed her shot. "Poor baby," she said and blew Landry a kiss.

Landry bit her lip. She didn't have the self-control to resist this woman, so why was she even trying? "Much better."

Jade came around the pool table and slipped her hand onto Landry's hip. "Have I told you how incredible you look in this shirt?"

"You did," Landry leaned into Jade's touch, "but you can tell me again."

"You look so incredible that I just want to tear it open and get a good look at all the muscle that's bunching underneath it." Jade pushed back and pressed Landry against the edge of the pool table.

There really was no point fighting it. Landry shook her head. "How about we start with a kiss?" She waited until Jade nodded, then she slowly ran her thumb over Jade's top lip before leaning closer to kiss her. Jade's softness was expected, but Landry didn't expect her tongue demanding access into Landry's mouth quite so instantly. She nibbled at it, and the kiss got hard and heavy until Jade broke away.

Jade ran her hand over Landry's abs. "Is that a six-pack you're hiding under there?"

"I'm not hiding it. You're welcome to take a look," she whispered and pulled her shirt slightly open.

Jade peeked inside it and sighed. "I'd love to see those ripple while you fuck me on this pool table."

Landry coughed and stepped back slightly. The kind of women she usually slept with weren't quite so forthcoming about their desires. Jade's directness was refreshing and welcome, but Landry needed a second to adjust. "I have a pool table at my apartment." That wasn't adjusting; that was a one-eighty.

A wickedly dirty look flashed across Jade's expression, as if she might share that fantasy. "Beth said you don't bring women back to your place. Are you making an exception for little ol' me?" She tugged on Landry's belt. "Is it because you're starstruck?"

Landry glanced away. "Beth shouldn't be loose-lipped. So you two are besties now, DMing every day?" She wasn't impressed with Beth acting like some crazy Cupid. Her prying into Landry's private life was usually irritating in a fly around a horse's ass kind of way, but Beth was taking it to a new level.

"No, this is all from Monday. That woman can get a lot of words out in a short space of time." Jade smiled. "Her heart's in the right place. She loves you and thinks you'll be happier if you settle down with the right woman."

"Is that what you think?"

"I think you're happy doing what you're doing," Jade said. "You're not looking for a soul mate."

There didn't seem to be an edge or any judgment to Jade's words. Landry took her shot and forfeited the game when she sank the eight-ball. "And what are you looking for?"

"I found out the hard way that this job makes it difficult to have a real relationship." Jade laid her cue on the table and sat on a nearby chair. "I'm playing, training, or traveling; I don't have time to give a woman the care and love she deserves."

Landry flipped a chair around and straddled it, facing Jade. "You found out the hard way?"

An easy-to-read sadness flickered across Jade's face. Despite her breezy attitude, she obviously had some difficult history.

Jade avoided Landry's gaze and took a long pull on her beer. "You're sure you want to hear about my heartbreak?"

Landry nodded. "If you're okay to talk about it, yeah."

"Promise you won't judge me?"

Landry laughed and shook her head. "I don't make promises. C'mon, spit it out."

"Fine. I met Hayley when I first signed for the Knicks and my career was really taking off. I was earning more in a week than I had in a year with my previous team, and she was definitely enjoying that aspect of being with me. We were together a year, and I thought we were good, but I discovered I wasn't giving her what she actually needed—other than the money." Jade tossed a handful of pretzel bites into her mouth and shrugged.

"Ah, crap," Landry said. "You're gonna tell me she was a closet hetero, aren't you?"

Jade laughed. "I could've handled that; it's not like you get to choose your sexuality, is it? No, that wouldn't have been her fault. Me coming home early to find her hog-tied on her knees with a dildo-brandishing butch buried inside her though? *That* was her choice."

Landry inclined her head and blinked, trying to stop herself from imagining Jade in a similar position on her bed. "That's a graphic description that'll stay with me."

Jade punched Landry's shoulder. "Deviant."

"Not deviant: open-minded," Landry said.

"It was a very damaging experience." Jade crossed her arms and sat back in her chair. "I'm emotionally scarred."

"Poor baby... Is that better?" Landry shifted quickly to avoid another punch. "Did you scar her in return?"

Jade giggled. "No, but I did fuck her up."

Landry chewed on the inside of her lip and tried not to laugh. "I really can't imagine that."

"Hey!" She swatted at Landry again. "I'm tough."

Landry gently tapped her fist to Jade's chin. "I can see that. You're a tough little baller."

Jade knocked her hand away. "You're mocking me because you're some super dangerous Navy Seal or something."

"Or something." Landry winked. "You know, I googled you after I heard you were joining the Warriors—out of professional interest, of course."

Jade rolled her eyes. "Of course."

"And I didn't see anything about you serving time for assault."

Jade gave a smug smile. "And you won't find anything, no matter how deep you dig."

"Because you killed them both and buried the bodies in Central Park?"

"No," Jade said. "Because I paid them both to disappear, and the team doctor fixed her up so there were no medical records."

"So you're not worried about them trying to blackmail you now that you're an even bigger superstar, because there's no evidence, and they can't prove a thing."

Jade tapped her nose. "Exactly."

She smiled, but her intense brightness faded, and that same melancholy crossed Jade's expression again. Landry pushed down the weird desire to comfort her with a hug. "And you haven't had a serious relationship since?"

"Nope." Jade shrugged and jutted her chin toward Landry. "Your turn. When was your last serious relationship?"

Landry inclined her head. "I've never had one."

Jade frowned. "*Never?*"

"My work takes me away a lot, and it always has. I'm sometimes out of the city for months, and," Landry paused, unsure just how much she should divulge but at the same time, sure that she wanted to trust Jade, "there's always the possibility that I might not come back at all." She searched Jade's face for a reaction, but all she saw was understanding and a hint of that sadness again.

"That must be lonely," Jade said and placed her hand on Landry's knee.

"I've gotten used to it." She couldn't say that she'd been alone since her mom died when Landry was seventeen. Sort of, since those memories were still stronger than the newer memories of a supportive mom her whole life. "I can't expect anyone to wait around for me, and I wouldn't want them to either."

"This conversation took a hard left to serious town, didn't it? Let's talk more about your estranged family and lighten things up a little." Jade chuckled and clinked her bottle to Landry's.

She laughed too, unable to recall the last time she'd been this comfortable sharing her personal life with anyone. It was something she didn't want to lose. "My relationship with my mom is complicated..." *Epic understatement.* "We want to be in each other's lives, but we're not quite sure how it's supposed to work. Me being away so much doesn't help. Tell me more about your family. It seems pretty much like yours is perfect."

Jade blushed a little. "I've been lucky. We were poor, but I never wanted for anything. Both my dads came from big families who struggled to feed and clothe themselves, but they worked damned hard. My dads wanted a big family too, but living on the poverty line made that difficult. They had me but knew they couldn't support a larger clan." Jade pulled out her phone and showed Landry a photo of two young-looking men and an adorable kid about three years old.

"Is that you?" Landry asked.

Jade nodded and flicked to a photo of the same couple looking maybe two decades older surrounded by Jade and five other kids. She smiled brightly. "That's my brothers and sisters. I started earning big while I was young, and my dads still had plenty of time to have the large family they always craved."

"That sounds like a lot of pressure for you, supporting the whole clan," Landry said.

"It's not like that. They've all made their own way and don't need my help." Jade touched her fingers to their faces. "I'm proud of every one of them."

Landry observed the centered calm that Jade exuded after talking about her family. "I can't imagine what that feels like," she said, then glanced away, not quite believing she'd said that out loud.

"I'm sorry. That was insensitive," Jade said. "It must've been hard without your dad."

"No need to apologize." Landry thumbed the condensation from her beer. "It sounds great, and I like hearing about where you've come from. Don't stop."

Jade shrugged. "There's not much more to tell. We get together for holidays, and birthdays when we can. Thanksgiving has always been my favorite; everyone getting together for no other reason than family, I love that."

"That sounds great, but I think you're greedy having two dads." Landry nudged Jade's shoulder. Her phone vibrated on the table, and a picture-perfect snap of Priscilla and her moms illuminated the display. Landry briefly considered not answering, but Priscilla hadn't been feeling well since Christmas, and Cait was worried she had a fever. "I'm sorry, I should take this."

Jade caressed Landry's tree tattoo, and the sensitive skin tingled under her touch.

"Go ahead. Your chosen family is important."

Landry nodded. Had they become more important than her blood family? That wouldn't be fair on her mom, and yet, Landry had chosen them over her at Christmas. "Hi, is every—"

"Are you alone?" Cait asked.

"No, I'm still with Jade. Why?" Landry looked across at Jade, once again struck by how unassumingly beautiful she was.

"We're at the RBG General Hospital with Priscilla... Beth isn't handling..." Cait sniffed. "Can you come?"

If Beth wasn't handling it, whatever it was couldn't be good. "Don't worry. I'll be there in twenty minutes."

"Landry. What if—"

"Cait, don't worry. Everything will be okay." Landry ended the call, regretting what she'd said. She couldn't know that and had no right saying it. "I'm sorry, I have to go."

"Is it Beth or Priscilla?" Jade asked, concern lacing her voice.

"It's Priscilla." Landry got up and threw on her leather jacket. "I'll call you tomorrow."

"Okay. Leave a message if I don't pick up; I'll be preparing for the game most of the day."

Landry nodded and kissed Jade's cheek, her mind already out the door.

Jade clutched Landry's jacket. "Drive safely. You can't help if you don't get there."

Landry frowned. "I do everything safely." She left the bar without looking back. If Jade knew what she actually did for a job, the way Landry drove would be the least of her concerns.

CHAPTER FOURTEEN

WHEN LANDRY GOT THERE fifteen minutes later, the emergency room was packed. She scanned the area and watched admin registration clerks darting from one person to another with neon clipboards, while teal-jacketed triage nurses trudged from one patient to the next, looking harried and exhausted. Beyond that chaos, she caught sight of Beth near a vending machine. Cait sat beside her, cradling Priscilla, who looked awful. It was far from the pretty picture she was used to seeing.

"Lan Lan," Priscilla said, barely raising her head before she nuzzled back down.

"Hey, little P." She gently stroked Priscilla's hair and registered the terror in Cait's eyes. "What's happening?"

Beth stood and almost fell into Landry's arms without words.

Cait looked up and smiled weakly. "Nothing's happening. We've been here for three hours. They're trying to say it's just a cold, and we shouldn't be worrying until the fever's run for more than three days. She hasn't been triaged yet, and they won't even take us through to the waiting area."

Beth raised her head from Landry's shoulder. "I know something's really wrong, Landry. She's my daughter, and I *feel* her."

Landry nodded. She didn't doubt it; her mom had said a similar thing more than once when Landry had minor injuries following missions. "Have you even been seen by a clerk?"

Cait let out an exasperated sigh. "That's another problem. They're saying our insurance might be invalid because the company has gone bankrupt, but that can't be right. Our payments are up to date. After the medical bills from that night..." Cait shook her head. "We changed insurers on principle. They can't be right."

"They won't be. Hospitals make mistakes all the time." Landry lowered Beth to the chair beside Cait, and she slumped into it. Cait squeezed Beth's hand. She began to stroke Priscilla's forehead gently while singing quietly to her.

Landry strode to the reception desk and cleared her throat.

The clerk, a middle-aged woman with a tired expression, looked up. "Can I help you?"

Landry glanced at her nametag and smiled as politely as she could manage despite the rage beginning to simmer. They were messing with Priscilla's health, and Landry's tolerance for that was, apparently, zero. "I hope so, Elaine. I'm with the Grayson family, and there seems to be a holdup. Will you clarify the situation for me, please?"

Elaine arched her eyebrow. "Are you family?"

"Yes. I'm the aunt."

Elaine glanced across to Cait and Beth and arched her eyebrow even higher. If she was skeptical about any family resemblance, she didn't care enough to argue.

"We've already told them that their insurance is no longer valid. The company went bust a couple of months ago, and we're not accepting any of their clients. I'm sorry." She looked across at the family again and shrugged. "I'm not sure why they're still here."

"They're still here because their child is sick." There was no time to argue the morality or ethics of the hospital's unwillingness to honor the family's insurance, so Landry pressed her thumb to the payment scanner. "We'd like to see a doctor now, please."

Elaine's expression brightened considerably when the machine flashed Landry's rhodium status. "I'll send the triage nurse over as soon as he's finished with that patient." She motioned to the short, skinny guy sitting beside a perfectly healthy-looking woman in her mid-twenties. "She just fainted at work. He'll be with you in a few moments."

Landry headed back to the family, and the triage nurse reached them at the same time as Landry.

"Would you tell me again what the symptoms are?" he asked.

Landry bristled at his gruff attitude.

"Of course," Cait said. "She's had a fever for nearly two days and—"

"It's probably just a cold, like I said." He sighed heavily. "Is this your first child?"

"And her eyes are bloodshot," Cait said, ignoring the stupid question.

"Has she been sleeping?" he asked, even more abruptly.

"No, the fever's been keep—"

"Then she's probably just tired. I'll put her on ES level four." He gestured behind him. "You can see we're extremely busy; you probably won't be seen for three hours, and you're probably wasting your time. You'd be better off going home and putting her to bed. She'll probably feel much better in the morning."

Landry balled her fists and then stretched out her fingers. If he said probably one more time, she'd rip his tongue out. She placed her hand on his clipboard and pressed it downward. He looked up at her, clearly assessing the threat level and deciding whether to hit the panic button or not. "She's an ES level two at the very least, and she'll go to the top of your list. You're 'extremely busy' with a whole host of drunks, DIFFCs, and DQs." She motioned toward Cait and Beth. "And these two aren't suffering from DPS. So we'll follow you to a consultation cubicle right now. Lead the way."

"And what are you? A doctor or a Jedi knight?"

"I was a doctor in the past. I don't practice any more, but I do work for people far more influential that a fictional religious cult." Landry smiled. "People who could buy and sell this hospital a hundred times over and not even blink."

He glanced around at the pit she'd astutely assessed and then nodded. "Okay, follow me."

Cait stood and bundled Priscilla tighter in her arms. "You were a doctor?"

Landry inclined her head. Mission prep counted, right? "Kind of. I trained for a while, but it wasn't a long-term thing."

The four of them followed the nurse along the corridor.

"What the hell did all those letters mean?" Cait asked.

"They're medical acronyms. Doctor slang, if you like. DIFFC is someone who drops in for a friendly chat and DQ is drama queen."

"What about DPS?"

Landry laughed quietly and put her arm around the still strangely silent Beth. "Dumb-parent syndrome. Parents who always think there's something wrong with their kid, or who think they know better than the medical professionals."

The skinny nurse motioned to a cubicle. "Wait here, please. The primary nurse will be with you shortly."

Cait laid Priscilla down onto the adult-size bed, making her look tiny and even more vulnerable.

Landry pushed away the thought that she could take Priscilla to the island and get her mom to fix her. "We need a doctor in here right now." She helped Beth into Cait's arms and marched out. It didn't take her long to secure a physician and primary nurse when she told them Priscilla's symptoms. "This is Dr. Stowe, Cait. She'll examine little P."

Dr. Stowe smiled at Landry in the way that usually preceded an intimate liaison, and she was happy to use her charm to get preferential treatment for Priscilla.

"Your daughter has a fever?" Dr. Stowe asked. After Beth nodded, Dr. Stowe touched Priscilla's cheek with the palm of her hand. "Nurse, take little Priscilla's temperature for me, please." She tapped the tip of Priscilla's nose gently. "The nurse is going to pop something in your ear, Priscilla, but don't worry, I promise she won't leave it there for long."

Landry's growing concern that the hospital staff were jaded and uninterested in their patients ebbed away with every second of this doctor's attention.

Stowe looked directly at Beth and Cait, who were hugging each other tightly. "Has she been complaining of any pains or aches?"

"She says that her hands and feet hurt," Cait said when Beth remained mute.

Stowe leaned over Priscilla. "I'm going to shine a bright light in your eyes, okay? Will you be brave for me?" she asked softly.

Priscilla nodded, and when she'd finished that, Stowe ran her finger over Priscilla's lips. Only then did Landry notice how dry and cracked they looked.

"Has she been drinking? Is she able to keep fluids down?"

Cait nodded. "Yes, she hasn't been sick at all."

"Priscilla, I need you to do something that your mommies tell you *not* to do," Dr. Stowe said. "Will you do that for me?"

The little girl nodded, her reddened eyes wet with tears and looking ever more vulnerable by the second.

"Would you stick your tongue out at me?"

Priscilla gave a little giggle, and Beth broke away from Cait to hold Priscilla's hand. Dr. Stowe nodded slowly and continued to nod when she inspected the thermometer after the nurse handed it to her.

"Okay, Priscilla, you're being super brave," Dr. Stowe said. "Do you think you can keep that up while we borrow a little bit of your blood?"

Priscilla looked up at her moms, tears edging her sore eyes.

Cait clasped her hand and smiled. "It's going to be okay. The nurse won't hurt you, and you can be brave like Lan Lan, right, baby girl?"

Priscilla glanced across at Landry then nodded. Beth pulled Priscilla's favorite cuddly bear from her handbag. "You can play with Oscar while they do that, okay?"

Cait closed her eyes briefly, and Landry met her gaze when she opened them. She nodded. They were clearly relieved that Beth had finally spoken again; a voiceless Beth was unnatural and unnerving.

Priscilla managed a weak smile and kissed the bear. "Oscar makes everything better."

Dr. Stowe turned to Beth. "We're going to need a urine sample too. Would you take Priscilla to the bathroom and help her fill this cup?" She gestured to the nurse, who pulled a lidded jar from a nearby drawer. "We'll be ready to take a blood sample when you get back."

"Of course. Priscilla, come with Mommy to the bathroom." Beth lifted Priscilla from the bed, held her close, and headed for the restroom.

When the nurse had left to gather what she needed to draw blood, Landry touched Dr. Stowe's arm. "Doc, it seems like you might know what's wrong with our girl. Do you want to share that with us?"

"Are you her mom?" Stowe asked and frowned.

"No, Doc, I'm her aunt. Cait and Beth are her moms. Do you have a diagnosis?"

Stowe shook her head. "It's too early to say without the test results."

"Please, Doc. Are we talking about something serious here?" Landry held back the fear racing up her throat and reined in her desire to shake the answers out of the doctor.

Stowe sighed and looked between Landry and Cait. "It could be something serious, yes, but I'm sorry, I want to make absolutely certain before I say any more." She put her hand on Landry's shoulder. "Please understand I'm not being obtuse, Ms. Donovan. I just don't want to worry anyone unnecessarily."

Landry put her hand over the doctor's and used the smile that often got her what she needed. "I get that, Doc, but please hurry. Little P is their life and their light." *And she brightens my darkness too.*

After Beth returned with Priscilla and the nurse took her blood, the next thirty minutes crawled by desperately slowly. The sense of impending bad news was pervasive and kept them mostly silent.

Dr. Stowe pulled back the cubicle curtain and gestured for them all to step outside, while two orderlies came in and set about moving Priscilla.

"Walk with me," Dr. Stowe said. "This is Dr. Burnett, a pediatric cardiologist. We need to take Priscilla to the fourth floor immediately to begin treatment for her condition."

"Cardiologist?" Beth faltered, and Cait supported her.

Stowe nodded. "Priscilla's blood tests showed an elevated erythrocyte sedimentation rate, and we found white blood cells in her urine sample. We believe Priscilla is suffering from a rare lymph node syndrome called Kawasaki disease. We need to treat her quickly to stop any possibility of coronary aneurysm or a heart attack."

Beth's legs buckled completely, and Landry stepped in to catch her from the other side to help keep her walking. The orderlies nearly ran into the back of them with Priscilla's bed.

"Will she be okay?" Cait asked, her voice trembling.

"The sooner we put Priscilla on an intravenous drip of gamma globulin and warfarin, the less risk there will be of heart problems."

"Not aspirin?"

"No, Cait. Aspirin is associated with Reye's syndrome in children, which can cause brain and liver damage. Priscilla is in safe hands, I assure you; Dr. Burnett is one of the country's leading cardiologists."

"I'll do an echocardiogram to check for existing aneurysms or any signs of heart disease," Burnett said. "But because you've caught the symptoms so early, you've vastly reduced that possibility. I just need to be sure. When I've finished tonight's treatment, you'll need to bring her back to me in three weeks for another echo, and you need to be on the watch for any changes in her extremities, any peripheral edema—"

"Maybe in non-doc speak," Landry said. Stowe smiled, and Landry noticed how beautiful and long her eyelashes were.

Burnet held up her hands. "Sorry. Please keep an eye out for swelling in her hands and feet, or skin peeling from her fingers and toes."

They stopped at the elevator, and Stowe pressed the button.

"How did this happen?" Beth asked.

"That's hard to say," Burnett said as they all got into the elevator. "Sometimes it's caused by an infection, other times it can be from exposure to an environmental toxin. It's a rare disease and often isn't caught early enough because symptoms are missed in combination with the fever. It's good for Priscilla that you're such observant parents."

When they reached the fourth floor, they emptied out onto the corridor in silence.

"Would one of the moms like to accompany Priscilla and me?" Dr. Burnett asked.

"I'll go," Beth said as she grasped Priscilla's hand.

Cait leaned over the bed and kissed Priscilla's forehead. "Be brave for us, beautiful girl."

"I will, Mommy." She held out her teddy to Cait. "You take Oscar, and he'll keep you safe."

Landry swallowed the ball of emotion suddenly lodged in her throat and glanced down the corridor, trying to clear her mind. She watched them wheel Priscilla away, and a wave of optimism rolled over her. The girls had acted fast enough to stop anything bad from happening, and Priscilla was going to be okay; she could almost feel it.

Stowe gestured down the corridor. "Let me show you to Priscilla's room," she said and headed off, with Cait and Landry following behind.

Cait sat beside the bed in the suite and waited for her girls to return.

Stowe motioned for Landry to join her outside. "You're not actually the aunt, are you?"

Landry wrinkled her nose. "How'd you guess?"

She looked Landry up and down. "There is *zero* family

resemblance to either of the moms."

Landry bit her lip. "Does that mean you're throwing me out?"

Stowe shook her head. "But I was thinking I might *ask* you out."

"Just thinking about it?" Landry thought about Jade. God, she was sexy, but then they'd gotten to talking and gone deep. She was so comfortable around Jade; she didn't really want to ruin that potential friendship by fucking her. But even if they did end up having sex, they both understood it was casual...which left Landry free to see the doc.

Stowe smiled and moved a little closer. "Yeah, just thinking about it because you might say no, and I'm really not used to that. I'm sure you know all about doctors and their God complexes."

"You don't strike me as a fragile woman with low self-esteem," Landry whispered and enjoyed the flare of desire in Stowe's blue eyes.

"I like a woman who knows her psychology," Stowe said.

"And I like a woman who knows what she wants and goes for it."

Stowe ran her tongue over her top lip. "So your answer would be yes?"

"If you asked the question." Landry nodded.

"Give me your phone." Stowe held out her hand, and Landry placed her cell in her palm. She navigated to contacts, pressed her thumb over Add, and her details uploaded. "Call me." She slipped Landry's phone back into her inside pocket and dragged her fingers across Landry's chest before she exhaled deeply and walked away.

Landry leaned against the wall and smiled. Her cell buzzed, and she pulled it out, half-expecting it to be the doctor. But the Warriors' yellow and blue team emblem of the Golden Gate Bridge flashed on the screen, indicating a text. She didn't believe in fate or signs, so why did it feel slightly wrong that she'd just encouraged the sexy doctor's interest?

CHAPTER FIFTEEN

December 31

"The hospital couldn't apologize enough for not taking our concerns seriously," Cait said. "They were so concerned about liability for a lawsuit that they haven't charged us for any of the treatments, which is a damn good thing, because they were right about our health insurance company—they'd gone bankrupt but were somehow managing to take our payments. That's money we'll never see again."

Landry smiled and patted Cait's back lightly. "Take a breath, or we'll have to call an ambulance to give you some oxygen."

Cait waved her away and turned back to Jade. "We could've been left with a bill we can't afford. Or worse," she swallowed and blew out a long breath, "they could've continued to refuse Priscilla treatment, and she would've developed heart disease."

Beth emerged through the kitchen's swing doors. She put her hand on her hip and shook her head. "Cait, I need you in here now."

"Oh, sorry, babe." Cait shrugged and grinned. "I'll be right back."

When she'd gone, Landry turned her attention to Jade. "Thanks for coming to this. I hope Beth's invitation was more polite than her last one."

Jade chuckled. "Let's say she made me an offer I couldn't refuse. New Year's celebrations at a restaurant with food this good is a match made in heaven for me."

"Still," Landry said and turned her glass of champagne around and around by its stem, "Beth's got her bow out, and she's aiming right at you."

"Don't worry, I'm wearing Kevlar." Jade ran her fingers along Landry's jaw. "I promise not to fall foul of Cupid's arrow and fall in love with you." She sat back and gestured toward the kitchen door. "Anyway, I'm more interested in that *amazing* story Cait just told." She raised her eyebrows. "I can hardly believe it, can you?"

As Cait had regaled Jade with her hospital tale, Landry had a feeling Jade wasn't convinced by it. Sometimes she was hard to read, but other times, it seemed she was an open book. Landry shrugged. "I don't know what to tell you. Hospitals are more terrified of lawsuits than they are of a COVID-58 variant. They got lucky, I guess."

Jade kissed her teeth. "That's the story you're sticking to, is it?"

Landry held up her hands. "I don't know what else to tell you. Don't you believe it?"

"No. Do you want to know what I think happened?"

Landry leaned back into the soft armchair and took a sip of her champagne. "Sure, I'll humor you. What do *you* think happened?"

"I think that you got there, and the girls told you about the insurance thing." She poked Landry's shoulder. "Then I think you flashed your financials and somehow convinced them to put little Priscilla on the top of their list. Maybe you used your charm. Maybe you were a little more forceful. Or maybe you were both. I think you got lucky with a great doctor, and I'm really glad about that. But then I think you spun an elaborate yarn to the girls, who were so relieved that their daughter was going to be okay that they'd believe anything...even something as fantastical as the hospital comping them thousands of dollars' worth of treatment."

Landry nodded slowly. "That's a fascinating fiction, and you've got an interesting imagination, but I don't know why you'd doubt what Cait told you."

"Maybe because you seem to be their knight in shining armor and their fairy godmother rolled into one very sexy package."

"Maybe you shouldn't tell me things like that." Landry took a bigger gulp of champagne and focused on the bubbles dancing down her throat instead of the way the restaurant lights sparkled in the translucent banded circles of Jade's eyes.

"Why not? That's normally how this seduction thing works." Jade wiggled her eyebrows suggestively.

"I've been thinking about me and you..." God, was she really going to say this? "I was wondering if maybe we could just try out the friend thing."

Jade blinked quickly then shrugged. "Don't friends build each other up with compliments? I googled it once, and I'm sure that's how it's supposed to work."

"I don't know," Landry said, both impressed and disappointed with Jade's easy acceptance. "I've only ever had imaginary best friends before, and they didn't talk all that much. I've—"

"You're a psycho!" Jade laughed. "*That's* why you don't want to sleep with me."

"You got it, because I'd have to be crazy not to want to sleep with you." Though she really, *really* did. "Anyway, as I was saying before your canyon-sized ego interrupted, I've had a vacancy for the best friend position my whole life, and I think you could be exactly the person I've been looking for." Should she say that it was because she wanted Jade around for more than one night?

"If that's where we're headed, you should also know that flirting isn't an acceptable aspect of friendships. You talk about a best friend like the lover you want to spend forever with."

"Lovers are easy to find. A best friend is someone who really gets you, and shares your humor and your views on life. That's much harder to find, and..." Landry bit her bottom lip. Best friends were supposed to be honest too. "And I don't want to ruin that by sleeping with you."

Jade frowned. "Most people look for those same things in a lover. It's a pre-cursor to a commit—ah, now I understand. You don't want that commitment."

Landry placed her glass on the table and nodded. "Neither of us can offer the commitment or time a stable relationship needs—and neither of us want that either—but we can be friends who see each other whenever we can. There'd be no expectations, which means we couldn't disappoint each other." She gazed into Jade's eyes and tried to will the attraction out of existence. "I really like you, Jade." Landry briefly closed her eyes; this whole honesty thing wasn't something she got to practice a whole lot. "I feel like we've made a connection, and I'd like to have you in my life, which is a new thing for me, as you've gathered from Beth. I'm learning to let people in, and it's taking some adjusting to find a balance between work, which has been everything to me for years, and a real home life." She glanced at her empty glass and wished it would refill with a hundred-proof bourbon. "A normal relationship like Beth and Cait have isn't possible for me. Every time I go away, I might never come home, and I don't want to put anyone through that."

Jade looked thoughtful. "I hear what you're saying. I haven't wanted anything more than casual since 'Dildogate.'"

Landry almost choked on a sharp intake of breath. "You have such a beautiful turn of phrase."

"Thank you, kind sir," she said and waved her hand theatrically. "I'm a ball player whose career could end every time I get injured on the court. And I know I'm not going to be the player I am right now forever."

Landry nudged Jade's high heel with her boot. "You've got plenty of good years in your sneakers."

Jade smiled, but her sadness was obvious. Her reasons for staying away from long-term relationships came from heartbreak whereas Landry's came from locking her heart away by necessity.

"Right place, wrong time," Jade said.

There was more than a little irony in that, but Landry didn't comment.

"Seriously though, I don't know what you do, and you're clear about not being able to share that. I respect that, but maybe your career isn't forever either. If we build a strong friendship, maybe someday we can be more than that. But—"

"But if we have sex now, we could destroy that possibility altogether." And she didn't think Jenkin would authorize a mission for Landry to go back in time for a do-over. "Friends with benefits is a myth. Somewhere down the line, someone's heart opens up, and everyone ends up getting hurt."

"That'd be you, obviously." Jade winked.

Landry laughed. "Sure it would," she said. "I love my job and the difference we make. If I was in sales, or if I was a celebrity like that old movie star Elodie Fontaine...if I did any other job in the world, this whole situation might be different, but—"

"But it isn't." Jade touched Landry's face softly. "I get it. I really do. And I'm blown away that we can be this honest with each other. So let's be friends and keep having fun whenever we're in the same city, okay?"

"Sure." Landry topped up their champagne and then raised her glass to seal the deal. They toasted just as Beth and Cait headed out of the kitchen toward them.

This was the first New Year's Eve Landry hadn't worked since college, and she was determined to enjoy it despite the tinge of melancholy that edged its way into her soul. Her father had drilled into her that work took precedence over everything else, and there'd never been more worthy work than what she did for Pulsus. Having Jade in her life as well as the girls and Priscilla gave her something to cherish when she was home, and her missions gave her immense purpose, so she had the best of both worlds. The girls joined their table, and small talk soon turned into laughter. The balance she'd been pursuing was finally coming to fruition, and Landry couldn't remember when she'd been happier. Maybe this time, it could last.

CHAPTER SIXTEEN

January 3, 2076

"How was the mainland?" Foster asked.

"It was...interesting," Landry said after an awkward moment of silence. Foster looked like she'd hadn't slept in two weeks, her hair was greasy, her skin looked dry, and her nose was beginning to develop the telltale signs of alcohol abuse. Her clothes looked crumpled, like they hadn't seen an iron since she'd bought them, but she did seem to fill them out with more muscle, so that was something positive.

"Interesting?" Foster bumped Landry's shoulder. "How so? Are the tourists getting kinkier?"

"I didn't really see any. I spent a lot of time with the new point guard for the Warriors. She's..." Landry searched for an adequate adjective. "She's different."

"Different how?"

"In every way." She thought about ending the conversation there. Foster was her closest friend on the island, but she was a jarhead. All brawn and no heart. That had never been a problem before, but maybe this was the kind of mom and daughter chat that she could now benefit from.

"You sound soft." Foster gave a low chuckle. "Are you sweet on this baller bitch?"

Landry tensed at Foster's disrespect. She rolled her head, and her neck cracked. "Don't be stupid. We're just friends; she's part of me trying to lead a normal life away from this circus."

Foster sneered. "I don't know why you're so obsessed with that idea. The mainland doesn't have anything you can't find here, even the unending supply of fresh meat."

"Jesus, is that all you think I do on vacation?"

"From the stories you've told me in the past, yeah, that's exactly what I think you're doing. What's up?" Foster shoved her again, a little harder this time. "Have you been boosting the estrogen?"

Landry gritted her teeth. "Have you been boosting the steroids?"

"What if she has?"

Landry half turned and nodded at Simson as she joined them in the briefing room. Simson put her arm around Foster and shot a quick glance at Landry. It seemed like she was marking her property. "She doesn't need 'roids, and I'm a big believer in doing things naturally."

Simson scoffed. "Yeah? Then what're we all doing here? There's nothing natural about interfering with the past."

Landry tightened her jaw. She'd never thought much of Simson; she seemed to take way too much pleasure from knocking the new recruits around. "It was a specific reference to building muscle, Simson, not rebuilding the world. And if you don't like what we're doing here, you can always leave."

"Huh, can I though?" Simson chuckled without humor. "Has anyone actually left this island?"

"Shut up, Simson." Foster shrugged Simson's arm from her shoulder. "I haven't been pumping steroids, Landry. You don't have to worry about that."

Simson narrowed her eyes and frowned. It seemed like their dynamic had changed and their friendship had grown over the past couple of weeks, though it seemed more fractious than it should be.

"She's been working hard in the gym getting ready for the next mission." Simson squeezed Foster's bicep and grinned before looking back at Landry. "What have *you* been doing?"

"It's called a vacation for a reason. The idea is *not* to work."

Foster glared at Simson, confusing Landry even more. What

the hell had been going on while she'd been off-island?

"If we don't get away from this bubble every time we get the chance, there's a danger we would drift into more harmful ways to cope," Landry said, looking directly at Foster as she began to realize that maybe that was exactly what was happening with her. It wasn't unusual that Foster hadn't left the island—Landry was the anomaly there—but it didn't seem like Foster had done anything with her vacation other than drink and spend time with Simson. And Landry was certain that Foster could find better friends than that sadistic asshole.

"You get away from the 'bubble,' but I reckon you fucking hundreds of random women could be seen as a harmful way of coping too." Simson glared at Landry. "Especially for them."

"Everything I do on the mainland is consensual." She shouldn't be rising to Simson's bait, but there were pockets of people gathering outside the room to observe this play out, and Landry didn't want anyone thinking she was some sort of misogynist.

Foster elbowed Simson away and stepped between her and Landry. "Anyway, about this mission."

Landry tucked away her concern about people's perceptions of her and focused on Foster. "Do we know any more about it than the details you sent me?"

"Not really." Foster jutted her chin. "Good to know that you read my comms after all."

"Of course." She'd had just enough time to skim it on the train on the way back to the island.

Foster raised her eyebrow as if she wasn't convinced. "Well, I've been polishing up on my German."

Both extractors and operatives had to be multilingual, which wasn't hard with the dialect implants that the time nerds had invented. But with its harsh, angular words and hardening of the final sound of a sentence, German wasn't Landry's favorite language. She wasn't sure if it was the phonetics or the association with Hitler and how he'd used the language to generate so much hate.

The director of mission operations, Pamela Diaz, entered the room with someone Landry didn't recognize. He was a prime example of Hitler's master race with his blond hair and blue eyes, and an obvious choice for this mission. Diaz's presence indicated the briefing was about to begin, so they all took their seats and sat at attention.

Diaz set her briefcase down and positioned herself at the head of the table. "Good morning, people. How are we all?" Before anyone responded, she continued, "This is Eugene Griffin. Foster and Simson, this is his first mission. I expect you to teach him well." She motioned for him to join his new team.

Griffin nodded, and Simson kicked out a chair for him to sit beside her.

"Our target is Bina Chernick, aka Dr. Chaim Galitz. Our research shows her living in Cologne from 1933 to 1939, where she'd secured her residency at University Hospital. Hitler had just come into power, and within months, began reversing the liberation women had experienced under the Weimar Republic. When she realized the only way of continuing in her dream as a doctor was to masquerade as a man, Chernick falsified her paperwork and medical degree, and began living her life as Dr. Chaim Galitz from the age of twenty-seven. Bina was thirty-six years old when she disappeared."

"So the Nazis killed her for being deviant?" Foster asked. "What does that have to do with us? How has she gotten on our radar?"

Landry looked across at Foster, who seemed unusually agitated about the mission choice even though Diaz had yet to fully explain it.

"Patience, Foster, I was getting to that. Her secret life was discovered in 1939, and she was shipped off to the women's concentration camp, Ravensbrück, where they forced her to become part of the experiments they conducted there. Soon after her arrival, she continued her research into carcinomas, and a friendly female guard, Ilsa Blumstein, smuggled her research journals out of the camp for safekeeping. Chernick wanted them sent to the States, where she believed her work could be followed up. Blumstein was dismissed from the camp in 1943. She was no longer able to cope with the brutalities she was witnessing and refused to be part of them." Diaz glanced around the room. "Unfortunately, she didn't manage to get the journals out of the country, but she did keep them safe in her attic for decades. In 2044, Blumstein's great-granddaughter came across the journals and took them to an auction. Jenkin bought them back when she was in her twenties, already thinking in terms of time travel. It turns out she was definitely on to something, but our scientists haven't been able to pick up the threads or decipher much of the code she was writing in."

Foster scoffed. "I thought we had the finest minds of several generations here. If they can't follow her work, maybe it's total crap, and we're wasting our time *and* a valuable mission."

Landry frowned at Foster's outburst. Simson looked serious and nodded, as if agreeing with her. What the hell had Landry missed?

"We're ninety-two percent confident that the data is going in the right direction, and the board believes it's worth the risk."

Foster shook her head and pushed back in her chair, but she made no further comment.

"As I was saying, we need to extract Dr. Chernick from Ravensbrück and relocate her to the States, so she can continue her research. Given the requisite environment, we believe she'll find a cure to eighty-five percent of cancers."

"What if her research doesn't pan out?" Foster asked. "What if we rescue her, and she dies of cancer a few years later."

Maybe she was right. When the board chose these missions, she knew they calculated the risk, but this one did seem like a long shot. "We follow the orders, buddy. Like you said, there are finer minds than ours making decisions based on knowledge we could never hope to have." Landry frowned when Foster grunted and rolled her eyes.

"We know the Nazis were using her to help with their research, so why would they kill her?" Griffin asked.

"The last entry in Chernick's journal is on the seventh of July 1942," Diaz said. "They were expecting a visit from Josef Mengele. We believe he experimented on her, among the hundreds of others he mutilated in the name of science. There was extensive mention of Chernick in Mengele's diaries that were found in Sao Paulo in 1985. Hitler had given him strict instructions to discover why Chernick tried to live like a man. He wouldn't accept the simple sociological explanation. It seems that he believed she was mentally ill, and he was desperate to determine the differences in her brain that made her that way in order to prevent it from ever happening again. It was part of his plan for the master race."

Landry raised her hand to catch Diaz's attention. "Why can't we just extract her before she was taken in 1939?"

"I'm afraid we can't do that. Her journals show that she didn't get to a key position in her research until after she was imprisoned in Ravensbrück. It might be that inspiration struck her *because* of the work she had to complete there. We can't risk extracting her until the last possible moment, to make sure she's where we need her to be in terms of her research."

"Is it a simple raid, or have you got something more elaborate in mind? Like, what year are we going back to?" Foster motioned to herself, Simson, and Griffin.

Landry could hear something new in her voice. *Tension or nerves?* Operatives spent so much more time in the past than she or her fellow extractors ever had to. Maybe it was getting old.

Diaz rolled up her sleeves and steepled her fingers. "We're sending you back to 1938. Griffin will infiltrate the SS and become part of the guard to be assigned to Ravensbrück." She opened her briefcase and removed three slim folders, giving one each to Foster, Simson, and Griffin. "You and Simson will secure positions in the prison service at a workhouse for prostitutes. When Hitler initiated his action against the 'work-shy,' prostitutes were targeted and taken to the camp. That's when your career path will open up for you, and you'll apply for the new jobs at Ravensbrück in 1939. Griffin will be well placed to ensure you get in. You'll have to be fully embedded in the Nazi party to get this detail, and it will give one of you time to establish a trusting relationship with Blumstein. We need to come away with the doctor's diaries as well as the doctor, and Blumstein is the keeper of those journals."

Foster took her file but didn't open it. Usually, she was eager to find out who she was going to be. It seemed this was one mission Foster wasn't looking forward to. Landry cursed herself for not encouraging Foster to get off the island with her. She clearly needed some real downtime.

"So no smash and grab?" Foster asked.

"The camp is guarded by over eighty personnel," Diaz said. "We can't send more than six through the time circle, and that would be too small a team to break in, secure the doctor and exit successfully. This isn't your first rodeo, Foster. You know we have to minimize disruption."

"So we should avoid starting families while we're there?" Simson asked and chuckled. "You know, to minimize disruption?"

Diaz arched her eyebrow. "I'm sorry, did I take a turn into the wrong room? Am I briefing new recruits? You know how this works. Did the previous mission fry your brains, or are you just trying to mess with Griffin?"

Landry glared at Foster. "Sorry, Ms. Diaz, they're just being juvenile. If we have to get there before Mengele begins experimenting on Chernick but after she's well into her research, when do I go in, and how?"

"We've calculated that early June 1942 will be sufficient for your entry, Donovan. You'll be a carpenter and plumber by trade but also an habitual criminal."

Landry nodded. "And what kind of crime have I habitually

committed?"

"We found records of a German version of Bonnie and Clyde who were never caught." Diaz pulled another folder from her briefcase, opened it, and placed it in front of Landry. "Donovan, meet Truda Stark. This is her background and her papers. You're going to borrow her identity for a few weeks. You'll jump and hide the people retrieval unit as usual, then you'll need to get yourself arrested."

"People retrieval unit?" Griffin asked.

"Yes." Diaz frowned. "The PRU for short. It's the unit Donovan will use to bring you all safely back to the future. Have you not read your time-string manual?"

Griffin nodded, but the vacant look in his eyes told Landry otherwise.

"Perhaps you should revisit it before you leave," Diaz said, clearly not convinced. "Anyway... Donovan, when the police have finished with their interrogation, they'll send you to Ravensbrück. Your criminal background will get you the green triangle. Foster, you'll then be able to make Donovan the block guard where Chernick has been placed." She turned her attention to Landry again. "Your trades will make you useful to them, so you won't end up in the sand pit unless someone targets you."

"The sand pit?" Foster asked.

"Yes. It's where they made the prisoners shovel sand from one pile to another for no other reason than physical torture; it was particularly unpleasant in the summer heat. And there are some awful accounts of a sadistic game called abdecken. You'll want to avoid that too; the guards made prisoners tunnel underneath soil piles until they caved in and buried them alive. If they were lucky, their friends would be allowed to pull them out." She pulled out a book called *If This Is A Woman* and slid it across the table to Landry. "This is full of the tales of torture, degradation, and inhumane experimentation that occurred at Ravensbrück. At the very least, it will disabuse you of the notion that women are incapable of the barbarity we usually associate with men."

"I read it in college when I was studying European history. It haunted me for months." Landry shuddered. "Every human being can be just as proficient as the next in committing atrocities. Gender is irrelevant."

"Indeed it is." Diaz offered a tight-lipped smile. "You'll need to get close to Chernick and make her your friend or... Do whatever it takes to gain her trust."

"No problem," Landry said, ignoring the quiet scoff from Simson.

"Whatever you do, and however you do it, the four of you must extricate the doctor on the eighth of July, before Mengele's visit and after her final journal entry."

"That all seems pretty straightforward. I'm assuming we all just need to update our dialect implants, and then we can get moving. When's the jump date?" Landry much preferred missions with minimal prep and no lengthy training programs.

"Yes, that's right. You'll need skills implants for carpentry and plumbing for that era," Diaz said and then focused on the three operatives. "You're all soldiers, so this should be simple for you. Professor Castillo has recommended that you all visit her department prior to mission start. She also wants you to check in with the environmental psychology team, so they can prepare you for what you might witness while you're there. You jump Monday."

Landry imagined prep would involve watching black-and-white film and photo slideshows of the horrific cruelties that were emblematic of Hitler's reign and the subsequent World War. She was concerned for Foster, who didn't seem to be herself. As a guard, she would have to be party to the merciless acts of "malicious pleasure." Landry glanced back at the book, remembering the account of a female guard at Ravensbrück using the skins of prisoners to make a lampshade. After her trial, she was executed by hanging but showed no remorse. Landry sighed deeply. No amount of time with Professor Castillo and her team could ever heal the kind of mental wounds sustained from exposure to that. But this was what Foster had signed up for; and her ability to infiltrate and assimilate made her the best operative Pulsus had. She'd handle it, just like she'd handled all their previous missions. Landry was sure Foster would be okay. She had to be.

CHAPTER SEVENTEEN

Foster closed her eyes and tried to sleep for most of the environmental briefing. It would be hard enough to perpetrate those heinous acts over the next few years; she didn't need to watch the torture-porn too. Instead, she slipped into thoughts of her disastrous attempt to make the board see sense. She hadn't known that the resources to make time travel possible were finite; that made her suggestion to concentrate on the bigger missions even more relevant, even more important. But they refused to see it. So be it. She'd regroup and figure something else out.

She had to.

The board's way of achieving the greater good weighed her down with disturbing demons and grotesque visions, and even the thought of a drink when she got back to her apartment wouldn't quiet them. Simson was clearly ready to be a part of her plan, which was great, but she needed Landry; she'd know what to do and how to change the board's mind, starting with her mom. And her mom had Jenkin's ear. That might work.

Foster tuned back into the briefing to discover it was almost over. When it was, she left without talking to anyone and headed back to her place.

She should be practicing her German and ensuring the implant had taken, but her thoughts were consumed with Landry's city adventures instead. Who the hell was Jade fucking Carter? And how was she different? Different from Foster? How was that a good thing anyway? Running up and down a court shooting hoops for thousands of dollars didn't really compare to what she and Landry did for a living. Civilians had no clue how to live with someone in the service. Sure, they *tried* to understand, but military people were different, and a skinny-ass baller could never hope to keep someone like Landry happy and grounded.

And what the hell was with Landry's maudlin sentimentality? Was she thinking of giving up on Pulsus and settling down for the normal life she was always so eager to get back to after missions? The utopia Landry seemed so enamored with wasn't all she hyped it up to be. They'd given up on any semblance of a civilian life when they signed up for the military, and then they doubled down when they joined Pulsus. They couldn't have it both ways, and Landry needed to accept that and live with it, just like Foster was trying hard to.

She'd never seen Landry so touchy either. Simson had made a sport of baiting Landry over the past three years, but she never rose to it. Today though, Foster wouldn't have been surprised if Landry had punched Simson...which was exactly what Simson wanted. Foster needed to curb that behavior. It was like Simson was trying to claim Foster as her property, and that was never going to happen.

Fuck this love shit. Why couldn't Landry see who was right in front of her if she wanted to be in love? Foster had been there for years, ready and waiting like a dog for a bone. Two weeks of sex with Simson had done nothing to cure Foster of that obsession. They'd be perfect for each other; why couldn't Landry see that? She grabbed a bottle of whisky and pressed it to her lips. Just for a second, she was strong enough not to open her mouth and let it slide down her throat. But she needed it. One hit would wash away these thoughts and let her concentrate on her plan...

Pulsus needed a push in the right direction to change the way they thought about missions, and Foster had to figure out how. They were jumping back to 1938, a full year before the beginning of the war. Did that give her enough time simply to assassinate Hitler? Simson would support her, but Griffin was another matter. Was he malleable? He was freshly graduated from the Pulsus training program, and in itself, that was like indoctrination. It might be too soon to turn him. They'd separate soon after they jumped though, so maybe she didn't have to concern herself with him. If she and Simson could kill Hitler in 1938, the Second World War simply wouldn't happen, and they could spend a few years traveling around Europe before returning to Landry's jump point. She'd explain everything: how they'd saved millions of people, how they'd stopped Hitler's demonic Third Reich. Landry would be impressed, wouldn't she?

She took another swallow of whisky as she thought about how hard it would be to get close to Hitler. There had been countless assassination attempts; how could she ensure they succeeded where everyone else had failed? And if they did fail, only Griffin would be there when Landry made it in 1942, and no one would know what'd happened to her and Simson. No, she needed time to research Hitler's movements, to formulate a plan, and that was a luxury she didn't have. She pushed away the bottle. It was a suicide mission that would change nothing. There had to be another way.

A short rap on the door disrupted her ruminations. "Foster? It's me."

Foster scanned her apartment, assessing whether or not she could invite Landry inside. God, she'd let things go. The place needed a damn good clean. If she was going to lead Pulsus to a new era, she had to get her shit together. She opened the door slightly. "What can I do for you?"

Landry frowned. "You could start by letting me in."

Foster shook her head. "It's pretty fucking messy in here. Let's go to Rik's instead."

"I don't think that's a good call this close to a mission, do you?" Landry asked.

Was that concern in her voice? She usually wasn't reticent to share a few drinks... "What's the harm? The jump is two days away."

Landry sighed. "Can I come in or not?"

"I told you, it's a dump." Foster motioned to the chairs on the front deck. "Let's just sit outside."

Landry shrugged and lowered herself into a seat. "Okay."

"I'll get drinks. What do you want?"

"Coke."

"With bourbon?"

Landry shook her head. "Just ice."

"Cool." Foster closed the door behind her, not willing to let Landry see inside. She hadn't quite realized how she'd let it deteriorate, and it reeked of stale sweat and cigar smoke. She sniffed her armpit, and the stench nearly knocked her out. She didn't have time for a shower, so she grabbed a fresh sweatshirt from the closet and pulled it on.

She went to the kitchen, put a few chunks of ice in the only clean glass in the house, and filled it with soda. Then she filled a coffee mug with bourbon and headed back outside. "Your mom wasn't happy about you not joining the family for Christmas," Foster said and sat beside Landry. She had an absurd thought about the two of them shooting the shit from similar chairs when they were in their eighties, watching the world go by from a porch behind a white picket fence.

"Did she tell you that?"

"She didn't have to," Foster said, knowing Landry disliked anyone talking about them as a family. "Your mom's an open book."

Landry leaned back in her chair and put her glass on the table beside her. "Did you go see her?"

Foster shook her head. "We bumped into each other the day after Christmas, and she told me about it. You would've had to be blind not to see she was upset. I think she'd been crying."

"I doubt that. Unless sentimentality came with her new lesbian persona."

Foster couldn't understand Landry's apparent anger. She'd been given a second chance to have her mom, but she wasn't making use of it. Foster would've given anything to have a mom like Elena. "You have a problem with your mom liking the ladies?"

"I've got a problem with all of it," Landry said. "My first mission was to rescue my mom so they could fix the physical effects of the whole time-travel thing together. Now I'm wondering if it was so Jenkin could seduce her, or if they were already fucking before Mom died, and I had no idea."

Foster took a long drink before answering. "They *were* working on time travel together before your mom died. You know that for sure. Elena was the only one who could invent the regenerative tech. And she doesn't seem like the kind of woman who suddenly decides she's gay. Maybe you just didn't want to see it, but what if they were and you didn't know? So what? It's not like you make a huge effort to spend quality time with her, is it? You can't have it all ways. Either you want to be part of the family, or you don't."

Landry pushed up from her chair and leaned against the deck railing. "It's not as simple as you make it sound. I've got two memories of my life, and they're always competing against each other."

Seeing Landry so confused almost made Foster itch, but that inner discord hinted that she might understand what Foster was going through too. And if she did, maybe she'd be open to hearing Foster's thoughts on how Pulsus should be operating. If Landry was with her, maybe they could convince the board together. "Why don't you talk to Castillo about it?"

Landry laughed. "She thinks they fix you, but they don't. Not really. The brain is too complex an organ and can't be manipulated as easily as they think it can. Sure, they can fix our bodies, but our minds? That's another thing entirely."

Foster could hardly believe what Landry was saying; she was mirroring exactly what Foster was thinking. Maybe Landry could convince Elena to let the two of them do a trial mission—assassinating Hitler would be something they could achieve together. When they got back, the positives would be clear, and how much easier was it to kill one bad guy than to save one good guy? Foster nodded. "I can't rid my mind of the things I've had to do on past missions. I have nightmares, crystal clear visions playing in a loop, and I wake up in cold sweats. Most nights, I'll do anything I can to avoid sleep."

Landry gestured to the mug Foster held. "Is that why you're drinking so much?"

Now Landry's impromptu visit made sense. "What do you know about my drinking?"

Landry inclined her head slightly. "C'mon, we've always been honest with each other, haven't we?"

No. How could they be? "Sure."

"Buddy, you look like hell. Your face telegraphs your drinking habits, and you're walking around in clothes that look like you slept in them for a week. And Jesus, you stink."

"Maybe we should call a halt to honesty. That was brutal." Foster raised her mug to drain it, but Landry's judgmental glare stopped her.

"Is it just the nightmares? Or is something else going on? You're only spending time with Simson, and she isn't the best choice for company."

Foster scoffed. "At least she's around." She wanted to retract the words, but it was too late. Guilt-tripping Landry hadn't worked for Elena, so why would it work here? "Forget I said that. Look, Simson is easy to be around, and the sex is great." She glanced at Landry, hoping for a flare of jealousy, but there was no reaction at all. "I don't need to socialize with big groups of people, you know that."

"Sure I do, but the alcohol and your appearance? We've always enjoyed a drink—it takes the edge from what we do—but there's something deeper going on with you." Landry pushed away from the railing and sat down again. "I know you're never going to bare your soul to one of Castillo's crew, but it seems like you've got something on your mind. And...I'm kinda bummed you're not talking to me."

Now or never? Foster sighed. "Do you ever stop to question what we do?"

Landry frowned, and she shook her head. "No. Why would I? It works... Do you doubt that?"

"No, of course not. I know we're making a difference, but..." Foster swallowed hard against the desire to keep quiet, to stay safe. "But I think we could do more. Like our next mission: we could just go back and kill Hitler. Nazi Germany will never exist, so the doc gets to continue with her research, and sixty million people live. Can you imagine the lost potential in that many lost souls? Who knows how many missions we could save ourselves with one simple change."

"Doesn't that present a bigger problem?" Landry asked. "A huge change in the population like that could have a huge effect on the future—on *our* past. A mission like that could have colossal implications even the board couldn't imagine. Jenkin has Jewish ancestry; if her family wasn't forced to flee Europe, she might end up not being born. Then Pulsus wouldn't be created, and everything we've already done post-1938 would be undone. We could complete the mission and not be able to come home because there'll be no portal on the island." Landry rose and paced the deck. "We'd no longer be there to help... And it's not just that. Great minds see things in a way other people can't. Like this doctor: she had the way forward to cure cancer, but it was in her mind, and no one else since her has had thought processes exactly the same. That's why even our nerds can't follow her journals. You can't hope to navigate the inside of someone else's brain, especially when they're fucking geniuses."

"There's got to be more we can do, Landry, and in a different way." Foster slammed her mug on the table. "I have to live with the things I do for Pulsus *between* missions. No amount of time with Castillo could take that away. I've racked up ninety *years* of mission time, and I don't know how much more my brain can take—they weren't built to withstand that kind of wear and tear." She picked up her mug and knocked it back.

"So the drinking *is* about trying to numb yourself?"

Foster sighed. "You don't know what I've had to do, Landry. And what about going into a concentration camp this time? You think I'm gonna be serving those women three-course meals and running hot baths to soak their aching bodies? Fuck, no. I'll be herding them into the gas chamber; I'll be whipping the ones who fall down exhausted and starving on their work duty; and I'll be choosing women to undergo sick experiments." She shook her head and gestured at Landry. "Then you'll come in, kill a few Nazis, and extract the good doctor. Your conscience will be clear." She relaxed back in her chair, a little lighter for voicing her concerns. If anyone could empathize with her, it was Landry, and if she empathized, maybe she'd also be able to see that Foster's vision *should* be the future of Pulsus.

Landry placed her hand on the arm of Foster's chair but didn't touch her. "Changing the way we operate won't help the memories you already have, and—"

"No, but it'd stop the onslaught of more, wouldn't it?"

"I guess it would," Landry said. "And I do know what you've had to do, and I totally get the nightmares. You wouldn't be human if those things hadn't affected you. Maybe you should take a longer break. Get off the island and build some better memories."

"Maybe...if you'd do it with me." She leaned closer to Landry, hoping for her to match the move, but she pulled back.

Landry laughed lightly. "It's not about me though, is it? We can't fuck your issues away."

Foster rolled her emotions back, recognizing Landry clearly wasn't ready for them. "Isn't that what you do when you're on the mainland?"

"No," Landry said. "I've told you a hundred times that it's about having a taste of a normal life; it keeps me sane." She patted the arm of Foster's chair. "Look, we both know you won't talk to Castillo or one of her cronies; we're soldiers and talking about our feelings isn't what we do. So take an extended vacation and recharge. I can clear it with Jenkin. What you do matters just as much as what I do, and we need you. Buddy, you're an operative because you've got the emotional resilience for the work, but you're burned out right now. You've done mission after mission with no real break in between. You never leave the island, so how are you supposed to recharge and recover? And I need you to recover. We're the best team Pulsus has, and I couldn't do it without you."

That admission was unexpected. "You're right. I'll take a break after this mission, and maybe I'll try the mainland too. Would you help me find a place?"

Landry clamped her hand on Foster's shoulder and squeezed. "Of course, buddy. Anything you need."

What she needed was for Jenkin and the others to realize they were doing everything wrong. She'd work on Landry when they got back. With Landry on board, Elena would follow, and then Jenkin. Everything was going to take a little more time than Foster anticipated, but it *would* happen. Foster was sure of that.

CHAPTER EIGHTEEN

January 6, 2076

"How's your German?" Landry's mom asked.

"Mein Deutsch ist perfekt. Wie gehts dir?" Landry responded in a perfect Berliner accent as she entered the jump room.

"I'm fine. I would've been better if you'd spent Christmas with us," her mom whispered.

Landry caught the bitterness in her voice but ignored it and shook her head. Her mom knew she didn't like to discuss family issues anywhere near her work colleagues.

Foster, Simson, and Griffin were already there. They were dressed and styled for the era; Griffin sported a horsehide motorbike jacket Landry immediately coveted. His hair had been styled with a Prussian crew cut, shaved to the skin two inches above his ears with the remaining blond tuft on the top of his head parted on the right. Foster and Simson wore high-waisted wool trousers with turn-ups, simple linen blouses, and boots with a stubby heel. Their hair had been lengthened with extensions to suit the period and were styled with smooth, swept-back rolls. Foster just about pulled it off, but it made Simson look even more hard-faced. Landry had a suspicion she'd fit in well and even enjoy herself at Ravensbrück.

"That blouse really sets off your green eyes, Foster," Landry said.

Foster punched Landry's shoulder. "Fuck you. You got lucky getting to butch out in your carpenter-cum-cargo pants and man shirt. You're gonna get a rough ride when you land in our KZ."

"You're just jealous, *Sieglinde*." Landry hooked her thumbs onto the three-inch-wide leather belt holding up her men's pants.

"You'll need to forget you know that name or you'll blow her cover," Simson said as she adjusted her belt.

"Really, *Johanna*, is that how this works? That must be where I've been going wrong with all those other missions I've already successfully led." Landry rolled her shirt sleeves; she wasn't in the mood for more of Simson's snide attitude. "Is there anything else you want to teach me?"

Foster stepped in front of Simson as she came at Landry. "Leave it. She's just fucking with me."

"That's exactly what I have a problem with," she muttered quietly.

That explained why Simson was being more confrontational than usual; her relationship with Foster had gotten serious. She had nothing to be jealous of. Landry and Foster were just friends, and that's all they'd ever be.

"T minus ten minutes. Time for you three to go down to the jump platform." Elena motioned to the door. Simson shot a glare at Landry before heading out, closely followed by Griffin.

"Stay safe." Landry grabbed Foster's forearm and pulled her into a bro hug.

"I'll be fine." Foster clapped Landry on the back. "You watch your step. Be careful when you're getting arrested; it's not like those thugs need a reason to end someone."

"I'll see you at the camp."

Foster smiled, but there was no hint of it in her eyes. "I'll see you back here in four and a half months."

"It'll fly by, buddy. Then we hit the mainland and get your head cleared."

"Sure," Foster said and walked away.

Whatever Foster was going through, they could fix it together when they got back. But with four years of exposure to Nazi Germany, Landry just had to hope it wouldn't be too late. The three of them left for the jump platform, leaving Landry with her mom.

"Please be extra careful with this mission, Landry. You can't afford any mistakes before you enter the camp."

"Thanks for the vote of confidence, Mom." Landry laughed gently, but the memory of Cartagena was still fresh. She didn't need her mom *and* Foster reminding her that even the smallest of slips could result in her death.

Her mom put her hands on Landry's shoulders. "You know what I mean, pumpkin. This is not the kind of time you can... Well, you can't be *you*."

Landry was glad they were in the debrief room, and that nobody could hear them. She'd never live *that* nickname down. Her mom's use of such an endearing term made her discomfited and yet comfortable at the same time. "I'll be fine. I know what I need to do, and I know when I need to tone *me* down."

"I know, baby, but you seem...distracted. Usually, you're so focused pre-jump, but I noticed that Simson managed to irritate you. She often tries, but I've never seen her succeed...until today." Her mom pulled out a chair and sat directly in front of Landry. "Is there something you want to talk about?"

This was the kind of moment Landry had to get used to, had to lean into and use now that her mom was back. "I don't know... You think I'm distracted?" She'd been too focused on Foster to think about Jade, but maybe Jade was on her mind a little. "Can anyone else see that?"

"Of course not." Her mom looked at her intently. "You wear a great mask for everyone else, but I'm your mom, and I can tell when something's bothering you. I can't quite figure out what it is without you talking to me, but I can feel you're not quite right."

Landry broke the intense stare and looked at her feet. "I think I'm developing feelings for someone. Beyond the usual, beyond sex..." She let the words sink in, not for her mom, but because she was admitting it to herself for the first time. "We're trying to just be friends, but..."

"Is it Foster?"

"God, no. We *are* just friends."

"Who fuck occasionally."

"Mom!"

"What? I can't say fuck?"

"Not about me, no."

"So if it's not Foster, who is it? Has a new recruit caught your eye?"

Landry exhaled slowly. "Her name's Jade Carter. She's a basketball player for the Warriors." She saw something in her mom's eyes, but it was too fleeting to name. Disappointment? Resignation?

"Baby, you know I support your choice to have a life outside of Pulsus, but can't you fall for someone on the island? Wouldn't that be easier?"

"Because I have a choice? Did you have a choice when you fell for Jenkin?" Landry didn't hide the contempt in her voice, but her mom's expression made her wish that she had.

"Is that why you didn't join the family for Christmas?"

"We haven't got time for this, Mom. You said yourself that I need to get my head straight for the jump." Landry moved to rise from her chair, but her mom grasped her wrist, and she stayed put.

"We're making time. That's what we do here."

Landry sighed. *This mom-daughter thing is a pain in the ass.*

"Is my relationship with JJ the reason you didn't come home for Christmas?"

Landry shook her head. "Your son's house isn't my home."

Her mom arched her eyebrow. "Stop being pedantic and answer the question. Is it?"

"It wasn't the only reason, but yeah, it was part of it. I need my space from everything to do with Pulsus, and you know that." As soon as the words were out of her mouth, she heard how weak her excuse sounded. It had been one day of fourteen.

"But this is the first Christmas you've been around for three years." Her mom took Landry's hands. "It would've been nice for us to spend it together."

"Nice for you maybe, but not for me." She pulled her hands away. "What is it with families and the pressure to do what makes other people feel better instead of what you really want to do? Did *you* enjoy it? Was it everything you hoped it would be?"

"Don't do that. Don't get angry and turn this on me. Why is it so hard for you to be part of our family? Your brother and his family made—"

"He's not my brother, and he never will be." Landry jumped up and stalked across the room, getting as far away as she could without leaving.

"Are you still angry about me remarrying?"

Landry clenched her fists. This wasn't the prep time she needed before a jump. "Dad was barely lukewarm in his grave."

Her mom stood and went to the door. She turned around and looked at Landry, her stare cold and hard. "You have no idea who, or what, your father really was."

The door slammed behind her, driving her mom's parting words hard into Landry's consciousness.

"Donovan, please report to the jump site. T minus twenty minutes to activation."

The speakers reverberated in the darkened, sparse debriefing room, and her mom's words echoed in Landry's head. When they'd gone into the room, it had been two hours before her jump, to give them time to recalibrate the machine and refresh the consumables after Foster's jump. She estimated their mom-daughter chat had taken less than fifteen minutes, so she'd sat there in the dark for over an hour in some kind of shock. Her parents' relationship had been perfect, hadn't it? They hadn't given her any reason to doubt that. Sure, her dad wasn't there a lot because of his job, but her mom had never complained. *What the hell did she mean?*

There was a sharp knock at the door before it was pushed open and one of the time nerds peered around the corner, somewhat gingerly. "Donovan?"

She stepped toward them. "Ich komme." For now, she needed to push her mom's cryptic statement aside and focus on the job, which was already proving difficult with thoughts of her friendship with Jade and Foster's issues swimming around her mind.

"This is a tough mission, Donovan. Good luck."

"Thanks, Micky," she said and walked beside them toward the operations landing.

"This is personal for a lot of us," Micky said. "I wonder if we could've done more with this one."

That's what Foster thinks too. She put her hand on Micky's shoulder before they entered the jump room. "We do what we can, Micky. We can't make wholesale changes when we have no idea what the consequences will be. You're a techie; you know that better than any of us."

Micky inclined their head. "People on the mainland think time travel isn't possible at all. We don't know what we can or cannot achieve until we try." They shrugged. "Just be careful, Donovan. You're our best extractor. You lead the way for many of us, and we can't lose you. It feels like there's a lot more riding on this one." Micky didn't wait for another response, but they opened the door and motioned for Landry to go in.

She saw her mom on the operations platform but didn't acknowledge her. Micky handed her the PRU, and Landry tucked it into the inside pocket of her leather flight jacket. She climbed the short ladder to the jump platform and waited for the countdown.

"T minus thirty seconds."

Landry wanted to look back at her mom but restrained herself. Micky's worry about her not returning had made her a little uneasy. What if she didn't make it back this time? Every mission was a risk. There was always a strong chance of failure if something went wrong on the other side. It hadn't bothered her until now.

Until Cartagena.

Until Jade?

CHAPTER NINETEEN

November 9, 1938: Berlin, Germany

FOSTER, SIMSON, AND GRIFFIN emerged from the jump spot, and the wormhole closed behind them. Unlike the time thread the extractors used, theirs dissipated, stranding them there for the next four years. She closed her eyes briefly to stave off the nausea. She never liked to dwell on the knowledge that unless the extractor showed up, there'd be no way of getting home.

It was hard to believe the country was less than a year away from invading Poland and setting in motion the world's most lethal military conflict to date. They'd jumped to Grunewald Forest in West Berlin—far enough away from the city that their time entry wouldn't be detected but close enough to make the walk there relatively easy—and had entered on the edge of the Havel River. Surrounded by conifers, birch trees, and shrubs, Foster took a deep breath of the fresh, natural air. It was peaceful and beautiful, a far cry from where they'd all be tonight, taking part in Kristallnacht, the night of broken glass, to announce their allegiance to the Führer. Griffin would head to the Fasanenstrasse Synagogue to carry out Joseph Goebbels's destructive orders, justified by the assassination of Hitler's ambassador to France by a seventeen-year-old German Jew. Foster and Simson would join the general populace on the streets, raiding homes and destroying shops. The air she'd be breathing tonight would be full of smoke and fire.

She looked across to Griffin, who was busy puking up what seemed to be the entire contents of his stomach into the clear waters of the river.

Simson laughed. "Didn't they tell you not to eat before a jump?"

"The first jump is always the worst," Foster said. "The speed and bright lights mess with your eyes. It gets easier."

"Butch up, Griff," Simson said.

Griffin spat out the last chunk of his breakfast. "Thanks for the sympathy." He moved farther along the river and away from the vomit to rinse his mouth. "If it feels like that every time, I'm not sure I want to go back." He wiped away the excess water with the sleeve of his jacket. "So we go our separate ways now?"

Foster squatted down and laid out a map on the floor. "You do. We're heading for the train lines. We're about six clicks west of platform seventeen. We'll catch the train to Berlin, and you get to walk. Head north-northeast for five clicks, and you'll hit the B2. Stick to that road all the way into the city for another ten clicks. It's thirty degrees, so keep a swift pace or you'll freeze. You should be in Berlin in less than three hours." She folded the map and handed it to him.

"I guess I'll see you in a year or so then." He took a step back but seemed slightly hesitant to leave them.

"If we don't bump into you tonight and everything else goes according to plan, that's the idea. Are we good?" Foster could see a hint of anxiety in his eyes. It had been so long, almost a century in real terms, that it was hard to remember how her first jump had affected her.

"He'll be fine." Simson ate up the ground between them with three large strides and whacked him hard across his back. "Won't you, Christoph? This is what you've been training for, what you joined us for. Trust me, there's nothing more exciting than going it alone on the first mission." She shoved him hard in the chest. "Now get moving. We can't risk being seen together. Go make some nice Nazi friends, drink lots of German beer, and try not to get killed."

Griffin nodded and walked away. He took one quick look back and waved.

"Your methods of motivation are questionable," Foster said.

Simson laughed. "But they work, so who really gives a shit? He's ready, or he wouldn't be here. This'd be a tough mission for a novice, but he's ex-CIA. Deep cover like this will be a walk in the park."

"Time to go catch a train then, sister."

"Sister." Simson scoffed. "Dumb fucking luck. Next time we mission together, I want input on our cover story. How are we supposed to fuck without getting accused of incest?"

Foster shook her head. "We won't be fucking. You'll just have to satisfy yourself for the next four years."

"You know that not's happening. I'll have to find myself a nice plaything at the Magic Flute Dance Palace, and then a hefty little guard when we get to the camp."

Simson was clearly trying to make her jealous, but Foster didn't have it in her to feel that emotion for now, and especially not for Simson. "It's comforting that you've researched the important things for this mission. I'm glad it won't get in the way of your raging libido."

"We're going to be here for four years, Foster. I'll bet you a thousand dollars you take a few lovers."

Foster inclined her head, conceding Simson's point. Four years was a long time not to have sex with anyone but herself. At least lesbians weren't persecuted here quite as overtly as gay men were. The Third Reich decided it was too difficult to differentiate between social affection and true lesbianism, and regardless of sexuality, all women could still do their Nazi duty by giving birth to more Aryan babies. That was one thing she *definitely* wouldn't be doing in the next four years. "I'm not taking that bet; the odds are slim."

Simson laughed. "That's the Foster I know."

"So, Johanna, my heavier and much uglier sister, let's go find lodgings in Berlin and employment at the workhouse. Maybe a prostitute can be your first conquest."

"I've never had to pay for it, and I'm not about to start, Sieglinde."

"Then you can teach them how to give up sex for free."

Simson grinned. "The next four years are starting to look a little brighter."

Foster's mind flashed to the images she'd seen and the texts she'd read over the past couple of weeks. Once they hit Ravensbrück, there'd be nothing bright about their lives. To look after the doctor, they'd have to be stationed in the medical facility, where part of the job would be selecting prisoners for experimentation and shipping out body parts to the Race Hygiene and People's Biology Research Institute.

Foster could only hope that Landry's cover held up to scrutiny. Otherwise, she'd end up being one of the guinea pigs. But if it was ever a choice between the mission and Landry's well-being, she'd save Landry every time.

CHAPTER TWENTY

June 2, 1942: Tollensesee, Neubrandenburg

LANDRY KNELT IN THE sand and leaned against the trunk of the impressive tree that stretched fifteen meters over the Tollensesee River before its end branch dipped delicately into the water. The effect of the faint clouds veiled thinly over the rising sun and the still lake created a perfectly lit reflection. It would've made a beautiful canvas against the stark brick wall of her living room, maybe opposite the pool table.

She pushed the distracting image away and refocused on the mission. Saying goodbye to Cait, Beth, and Priscilla had been more difficult than usual. Not because she was getting soft, as Foster had accused her, but because she might see the effects of a successful mission closer to home. Cait's first partner, Theresa, had died of cancer, and Landry had to deal with the possibility that she might return to a completely different scenario in the unit beneath her apartment. With Theresa never getting cancer, would she be Cait's wife? Or would Beth and Cait still have met and be spending their lives together? Priscilla was Beth's biological daughter, but would she have had a baby without Cait? And would she still have gambled on the restaurant business? The thought of not having that family in her life was physically painful, and their parting had been all sorrow and no sweetness, and she couldn't say a damn word about it.

Landry knocked her head gently against the tree trunk. If she didn't concentrate, she'd end up dead. She stood after the slight nausea from the jump had worn off. That was something that never changed, no matter how many times she did it. She focused on finding the perfect place to hide the PRU while they completed their mission and spotted a hollow halfway along the branch dipping into the river. She slipped the small black rubberized unit into its watertight housing and climbed the tree. She edged along the branch, and it bowed slightly under her weight, making it dip deeper into the water and form ever-increasing circles.

When she got to the hollow, Landry stuck three fingers into it and dug out the fungi, careful not to let any drop into the water. She took the waterproof bag holding their passports and other mission papers from her pocket and placed them into the hole. She shoved the PRU in after them and pushed it all deep enough into the hole so that she could just reach it with her index and middle finger. Then she replaced the fungi and patted it back down. Confident it looked as though she'd never been there, she retreated to the shore. She took one last look at the age-old tree to ensure it was imprinted on her memory and began her five-kilometer trek along the path toward Neubrandenburg.

Just over an hour later, Landry circled the city's outer walls, looking for a place where she could be discovered. She'd read about these walls and seen photographs of its four Brick Gothic city gates. They survived the assault by the Red Army that would take place at the end of this deadly war, and they still stood in 2076. The timbered Wiek houses built into the wall had been converted and were restaurants, museums, and wineries in her time, but now, people loved them as their homes.

As the sun rose and the temperature hit the sixties, she stowed her leather jacket over her satchel and stripped to her tank top halfway through the trek. When she got close to civilization, a woman hanging her washing eyed Landry suspiciously from one of the house gardens outside the perimeter wall. She became slightly conscious of her conspicuous appearance, pulled her shirt on and tucked it into her carpenter pants. Given that the woman was airing only dresses, Landry figured that she lived alone or her husband had joined the army. Either way, she was probably lonely, and Landry could exploit that. The three-story house looked rundown and in need of a coat of paint. The garden was overgrown and clearly hadn't been tended in a while. She strode toward the woman, smiling, before stopping at the closed gate. "Could I trouble you for some water?" Landry asked in German. A few silent moments passed while the woman took her time looking Landry over. She said nothing but went inside and emerged with a glass of a murky-looking liquid.

"Come inside," she said finally, stepping a little closer.

Landry smiled and closed the gate carefully behind her after entering. She took the proffered glass and knocked it back. "Thank you."

"Why have you come here?"

"I'm looking for work," Landry said. No need to complicate things with an elaborate tale.

"What kind of work?" The woman retrieved her glass, and her fingers brushed lightly over Landry's hand.

"Anything physical. I'm a carpenter and a plumber."

The woman's eyes darted to the left and right. "I cannot pay you, but I can give you lodgings. No doubt you need a place to stay."

No, she needed a place where she could draw attention to herself and get arrested. A garden on the outskirts of this town fit that bill, and a Nazi patrol would pass by soon enough, on the lookout for anything out of the ordinary. "For a few days, perhaps. What work do you have?"

"I'm told it is man's work, but there are no men around anymore. They have all gone to join Hitler."

She extended her right arm in the air, but her "Sieg Heil" lacked passion and commitment. Landry frowned, fully aware the straight-arm salute had been appropriated from the USA's early pledge of allegiance to the flag, enforced in schools when racism and segregation were rife. "I can do just about anything a man can do."

The woman looked Landry over once more, a little slower and perhaps more appreciatively than the first time, before a smile began to form on her lips. "My name is Margret."

"Truda." Landry offered her hand. "What can I do to help?"

"Truda." Margret shook Landry's hand as she rolled her name around her mouth as if she were tasting a fine wine. "You can start by rebuilding that wall. You will find everything you need over there." She pointed to a dilapidated building beside the house. "I will make lunch in a few hours. You might want to avoid the midday troop unit by busying yourself in the shed. If there is trouble, you are on your own."

Landry nodded and thanked her again before turning to gather some tools. The wall was close enough to the main road for her to be noticed without making an obvious scene.

All she had to do now was wait.

CHAPTER TWENTY-ONE

December 13, 1940: Ravensbrück

A HUNDRED YARDS OUTSIDE the camp walls, in a perversely idyllic setting amidst pine trees, Foster sat on the edge of Ilsa Blumstein's bed in their shared villa. The moon bounced off the still waters of the Schwedtsee Lake and cast a soft light into the room. Were it not for the fresh and grotesque memory of transporting ten dead, but still warm, bodies of women to the ovens of the Fürstenberg crematorium a few miles from the camp, Foster might have thought she was on vacation in a national park. The murdered women she'd helped to move brought the death toll to just under forty for the year. In her first year there, four women had died from relatively natural causes. If she didn't know exactly what the future held for this camp, and that 90,000 women and children would be killed here over the next five years, she might have thought the place wasn't so bad. But Hitler's Jewish Solution was just beginning, and her job here would get far worse when the mass murders began next year.

For now though, the camp was just a prison, and Foster was working her way into Dr. Chernick's small inner circle of four trusted prisoners and this female guard. She pulled the thin cotton sheet back to uncover Ilsa and caressed the curves of her breasts. She smiled as Ilsa raised her body from the bed, urging her to explore.

"Please..."

Softly spoken as she was, Ilsa made the German language sound almost romantic. Ilsa being gay had made getting close to her a piece of cake. Foster suspected it was the reason Ilsa had ended up smuggling Dr. Chernick's research journals, fueled by the sisterly connection of their shared sexuality.

"Aren't you worried you might be caught?" Foster asked. She needed Ilsa to be concerned for her own safety, so she'd accept Foster's help. When Landry came to complete the operation, it would be important for Chernick to know that Foster was on her side, and Ilsa was her way in.

"It's just research. Bina tells me she's working on a cure for cancer. If she's on to something but never gets out of here... Maybe someone can continue with her work if I can get them to the right person." Ilsa wrapped her hand around Foster's neck and pulled her down to kiss her. "You can help me. You can protect me, my strong guardian angel." Her other hand gripped Foster's bicep, barely wrapping even halfway around.

"Protect you with these?" Foster flexed, and Ilsa moaned appreciatively. "We must be careful. How many journals do you have already, and where are you hiding them?" Foster moved from Ilsa's mouth to her nipple and sucked one between her lips.

"I have just one. And I'm not hiding it. It's in plain sight on the bookcase in the reading room." She gasped as Foster nibbled lightly with her teeth. "They have no reason to search our living quarters. I provide her with the same journals I buy from Fürstenberg, so they blend in with my own."

"Such a clever girl." Foster continued downward, kissing Ilsa's ribs and stomach. She made a mental note to buy some identical journals, so she could replace Chernick's when they left. When Landry got there, and they began the doctor's extraction, Foster would have to secure the books to take with them to the States. Getting Chernick out was only half the problem. Getting her halfway around the world to her university hospital was another dangerous element of the mission. But at least in that part, Foster would only have to kill the bad guys.

"I'm wasted here, but my law degree means nothing in Hitler's world."

Foster sighed, glad she hadn't been born into this time, this place. Women had been blamed for taking "men's jobs" and corrupting the morals of the country. As soon as Hitler had taken power in 1933, women were fired or barred from most professions, and access to universities was restricted. She and Simson had been present at the failed assassination attempt in Munich in 1939. She could've helped them succeed. She could've put an end to all of this, and women could've continued to follow a more liberal path. Ilsa could still be a practicing lawyer. "I'm sorry, Ilsa." Her sympathy was genuine, even though her interest in Ilsa wasn't. But there were worse ways to spend an evening. She pushed Ilsa's thighs apart and settled between them. She lightly blew hot breath onto her swollen lips, and Ilsa raised her hips to meet Foster's mouth.

"Don't be. I'm not. I would never have met you if I was still a lawyer in Berlin, would I?" She placed her hand on Foster's head and gently pressed her down. "Enough talking, sweet Sieglinde. Please make me come...again."

The desperate need in Ilsa's eyes was clear. Foster began with soft kisses and ran her tongue along from the tip of Ilsa's clit. Ilsa moaned as she tenderly wrapped her fingers in Foster's hair. Her delicate touch was something Foster simply wasn't used to. With Landry and Simson, the sex was hard, fast, and hot. It delivered much but promised little. Without saying a word, Ilsa demanded that Foster make love to her. Being wanted this way was new but not unwelcome. The problem was, Ilsa wanted Sieglinde Thalberg. She had no idea who Jacqlyn Foster was, and if she did, she'd want nothing to do with her.

Foster took a deep breath and centered her concentration. Ilsa had to feel her there, physically and emotionally. Even though they'd only been having sex for three weeks, Ilsa knew when Foster's mind wandered. And it wandered often. Ilsa would stop whatever they were doing, look into Foster's eyes, and ask, "Where are you?" The only way to stop it from happening was to be fully present.

She grasped Ilsa's thighs and pulled her deeper. She circled her clit soft and slow, just the way Ilsa had taught her that she loved. Ilsa took one of Foster's hands and pressed it over her breast. She ran her finger over Ilsa's nipple, mirroring the movements of her tongue. Ilsa groaned and began to raise and dip her ass as she approached her orgasm. Foster felt Ilsa's throbbing increase, felt the pulsing of her pleasure. She gripped Foster's hair just a little tighter as her grinding became more frantic. Foster kept the rhythm of her tongue and finger in strict synchronicity, knowing that the combination would soon have Ilsa riding out her release and yelling into a pillow to subdue her animalistic cries.

"Perfect...please...don't stop."

Foster couldn't resist a smile. "Don't stop" was a plea she liked so much more than "please stop." She squeezed her eyes shut tightly and refocused again. Now wasn't the time to be thinking about anything other than the present.

Ilsa's climax was fast approaching. She released Foster's hair and took hold of the headboard, gripping it so tightly, her knuckles whitened. Her thighs held Foster in place, though she had no intention of moving. Ilsa pushed her hips up hard, thrusting herself into Foster's mouth. She turned her face into her pillow and suffocated her scream, desperate not to wake her sleeping colleagues in neighboring villas.

Foster remained there until Ilsa's throbbing subsided, and she released her. She pulled her into her arms and covered her with the sheet to keep her warm. Ilsa nestled her face into Foster's neck and murmured her gratitude before quickly falling asleep.

Foster looked up at the ceiling. She fixed her attention on the uneven brushstrokes and counted them, hoping it would help her fall into an uninterrupted sleep. She was kidding herself. All she could really see in the shapes were other prisoners in the crematorium, sweeping out the remains of their friends from the ovens. She'd only been there just over a year, and it was another eighteen months before Landry would show. Foster took a deep breath and let it out slowly, cooling the sweat on her body. *How many more innocent people will I have to kill in that time?*

CHAPTER TWENTY-TWO

June 2, 1942: Neubrandenburg

LANDRY ONLY HAD TO work a few hours before two police officers in gray-green uniforms strolled into view. The heat of the noon sun, coupled with the strenuous work of wall-building, meant she'd stripped down to her tank again, so she knew she'd attract their attention without really having to try. A woman with her physique wasn't inconspicuous in this time, and in a town this small, she expected the police knew everyone by name.

"Where is Margret?"

Landry could tell from his fancy plaited epaulettes he was a major, while his colleague was merely a sergeant. "I believe she's inside. Do you want me to get her for you?"

"I will see for myself."

The officers came through the gate and marched to the door, eyes narrowed and questioning. The major stepped inside without knocking, while his sergeant stood guard, watching Landry as she continued her work. He lit a thin cigarette before sitting on a metal garden chair with a clear view of Landry, trying his best to look menacing as he took slow, deliberate draws of his smoke.

Margret appeared in the doorway with the major, just as the sergeant finished his cigarette and flicked it Landry's way. She looked panicked and terrified. Her blouse was torn, and her hair and makeup disheveled. Landry tossed the stone she was moving to the ground and advanced toward them. "What happened, Margret?"

"Your papers. Show them to me." The major stepped in front of

Margret and held out his hand.

His sergeant stood at attention, obviously anticipating trouble. Landry sneered. "Why?"

He flicked a backhanded slap at Landry's face. The move was so obvious, she saw it coming almost in slow motion, much like a fly sees any human movement, but she didn't move to avoid or block it. She let his leather-clad hand connect with her cheek and lip, and her head snapped to the right.

"I don't need a reason."

The sergeant pulled the Browning GP-35 from his hip holster and leveled it at Landry's face as she turned back to them.

She spat out blood at the major's feet and smiled. "Auditioning for the SS?" Landry briefly saw the shock on Margret's face before the major struck her again. The sergeant grabbed Landry's throat and shoved her against the wall of the house. The rough brick grazed her face, and as his gun pressed into her temple, his stale breath invaded her nostrils.

"Margret. Her bag."

Landry blinked, trying to signal to Margret that it was okay, and she should do as he asked. She hesitated for a moment before disappearing from view to retrieve her satchel, and the sergeant forced Landry into the seat he'd previously occupied. His sweaty hand gripped her neck, and his gun still nestled at her temple. The major snatched Landry's bag from Margret, and he tossed it on the table in front of her.

"Is there anything in here you shouldn't have?"

The sergeant cuffed Landry's head hard with the butt of his gun when she failed to answer, and she closed her eyes to fight off a threatening lack of consciousness. "I'm sure you'll find something you think I shouldn't have."

The major smiled widely, revealing yellow, tobacco-stained teeth. "Spoken like a true criminal. What is your name?" He opened Landry's bag and emptied the contents across the table.

"You don't want to ruin the surprise."

He nodded to his sergeant, and he slammed her head against the table. She saw stars, and a growing blackness seeped into the outer edges of her eyes. When he pulled her back up with a handful of her hair, the major had found what he was searching for.

He opened up her papers to inspect them. "Truda Stark. I think you will join us at the station to see if there are any notices for a Truda Stark. Perhaps there, we will persuade you to be more forthcoming."

He nodded again to his lackey, and the sergeant quickly secured Landry in handcuffs. He pulled her from the chair by her neck and shoved her forward toward the gate, while the major quickly refilled Landry's bag with her few belongings, mostly collected from empty houses and cars on the way from her jump site.

"Margret."

"Yes, Major Oster?" Margret's voice trembled.

"How long have you been harboring this...woman?"

"She stopped by here this morning, looking for work. With Dierk away, I needed some help. She said she could fix the wall."

Oster grasped Landry's shoulder. "Is that right, Stark? Did you offer to do the work of this woman's husband?"

"I did. She doesn't know me, and I don't know her. I'm just passing through."

Oster smiled as he picked up her leather jacket from the half-repaired wall. "Not anymore. You'll be staying while I get to know you." He half-grinned, half-sneered. "And that could take some time."

***

Days passed. Nights dragged. In the dark, concrete cell, the screams of fellow inmates echoed around the walls and filled her ears. When it was her turn, Landry was hauled from the floor, stripped down, and beaten with rubber clubs until her consciousness crumbled. Ice-cold water pulled her back to a vague awareness of her surroundings, only for them to begin again. They never asked a single question.

Oster visited after each torture session to ask if she was ready to give up the location of her husband. Landry had no information to help them in their search. And since the real Truda Stark and her husband were holed up somewhere, she just had to hope they wouldn't be discovered.

On what was maybe her sixth or seventh day, Oster entered Landry's cell and dragged her to the door. The distinctive sound of multiple, synchronized gunshots echoed along the dark, narrow corridor.

"Your days as a criminal are over, Stark. It would be better for you to tell us where he is. Then we can pack you off to a comfortable women's prison, and you will serve your time. We have no more patience for your resolve. Talk to me now, or say your last words," he said and gestured outside.

Landry looked away. "I don't know where he is. We were in Hamburg three weeks ago after a job went wrong, and I woke to find him gone. I cannot help you." Landry turned to face Oster, careful to portray the fear he wanted to see in her eyes. "If I knew anything, I would tell you. I don't owe him anything, least of all this." She motioned to her bruised and battered body.

"I want to believe you, Truda, I do, but you've been nothing but obstinate since you crossed my path."

"I was angry. My husband had just left me, and I was... frightened." Landry could see him processing, and his grip on her arm loosened slightly. "If I knew where he was, I'd tell you. I can't take this anymore."

He released his hold on her completely and stood. "Richter. Scherer."

The two guards appeared around the edge of the cell door. "Sir?"

"Prepare Stark for transport."

One of them looked down at her with what looked like concern. "To where?"

"Ravensbrück. Gather her things."

Score. "Thank you, Major Oster. For sparing me, thank you."

He smiled, smug and self-congratulating. "I'm sure they will find good use for you there, Truda. Perhaps you might emerge a reformed woman."

Landry nodded, looking as contrite as she could manage considering she wanted to shove him in front of his own firing squad. *Phase one complete.*

CHAPTER TWENTY-THREE

September 23, 1941: Ravensbrück

FOSTER WAITED FOR THE new intake about to arrive at the small railway station in Fürstenberg. Over five hundred Polish women packed on a train, some from the infamous Lublin Castle, with no idea where they might end up. Foster bet they were thinking that no matter where they were traveling to, it couldn't be any worse than where they'd already been held and tortured.

You couldn't be more wrong.

Foster had volunteered to head up the team collecting the women. She needed a break from the invasive viciousness of the camp. She and Simson had just returned from a recovery party for a repeat escapee, a Romany woman called Katharina, for whom the four-meter walls of this hellish prison were too much to bear. Strauss, the camp commandant, ordered her fellow cellmates to beat her to death with the legs of their cell chairs.

Foster had tried to look beyond the slaughter. The stench of vomit from the prisoners as her starved and delirious cellmates continued to pound Katharina's limp, bloodied body into the mud, temporarily replaced the smoky soot of freshly cremated bodies. Ilsa had slipped away from the edge of a group of prisoners, her hand clamped over her mouth in an obvious attempt to stop being sick herself. Simson seemed to look on dispassionately, and Foster wondered if any of this affected her, or if she managed to stay completely remote and removed from it. If she did, Foster needed some tips on how to do exactly the same. There was another ten months of this before they would bust out with the doc. The nightmares were getting worse, and the violence was conquering her.

The smoke from the engine was visible before the train appeared.

Vogt smacked her across the shoulder forcefully. "I bet these bitches think they're coming to a vacation camp. We'll show them, Thalberg."

Foster nodded and smiled with enough sadistic enthusiasm to satisfy the camp's most notorious female guard. As the train slowed, Foster took the opportunity to study the twenty-year-old Erika Vogt. The soft waves of her hair fell onto her shoulders lightly, 1940s movie star-style, but that was in complete contradiction to her hardened face and her brown eyes. Foster wasn't a religious person, but it was easy to see there was evil in those eyes. Unadulterated. Pure and deep. And it was being allowed unchecked access to vulnerable souls, allowing her to play out any sick and twisted fantasy she so desired. In her knee-high socks, checked shirt, and sweater vest, she could've been mistaken for a school matron. But what the prisoners saw—what Foster saw too—was a tyrannical beast.

The train doors were pulled open, and women of all shapes, sizes, and ages tentatively emerged. Vogt yelled orders in German, ordering the prisoners to line up in rows of five. Her Alsatian, Buster, costumed in his dog jacket replete with the SS logo, strained at the leash and echoed her orders with deep-throated barks. She and other guards struck out at the stragglers with plaited whips and threatened to flog them if they didn't get in line fast enough. Foster saw Ilsa helping the older prisoners from the train and onto the platform, gently organizing them into the group. Her compassion was utterly outweighed by the other guards' wretched behavior.

Foster would be sorry to leave her behind but was marginally comforted with the knowledge that she would be dismissed from the camp the following year, unable to cope with the deteriorating treatment of the prisoners and unwilling to participate in the ever-increasing brutalities. She would miss the worst of it, but Foster decided that when they jumped home, she'd find out what happened to Ilsa Blumstein after 1943. If she were in charge of this operation, maybe she'd just take her home with them. Maybe Ilsa was her antidote to Landry, and if she took her back to 2076, they could have a life together. Ilsa wouldn't have to witness any more of this, and Foster wouldn't have to perpetrate it either.

She pulled her attention away from Ilsa and watched as the bewildered and confused prisoners did as they were instructed, and Vogt soon had five lines of one hundred women each ready to march...to their death. Foster tempered the thought that it might not necessarily be true. They had a one in three chance of not being exterminated or dying from disease or exhaustion and surviving until they would be liberated in three years' time.

Foster looked along the mass of women, some in rags, some in finer clothes, and others with bags of their possessions, unaware that they would be stripped of them once they were within the cold, callous walls of the camp. An uneasy hush overtook the cacophony of barking, shouting, and crying as Vogt began to lead the prisoners on the one-mile march to Ravensbrück. Foster slowed her pace so she could walk alongside Ilsa. She was becoming reliant on Ilsa's softness to balance the pitiless cruelty she had to exhibit and live with on a daily basis.

"That woman makes my skin crawl," Ilsa whispered quietly. "How can one so young be so vile?"

"Maybe she had a tough childhood, and this is her way of working through that."

"Don't joke, Sigi. Your childhood was tough, and you're not being a sadistic monster to these poor women."

Foster bit her lip. In building her cover story with Ilsa, she'd told her way too much of her real life. There was something so authentic about Ilsa that Foster found it hard to lie to her any more than was absolutely necessary. "Things are changing around here, Ilsa. Maybe this isn't the place for you anymore."

Ilsa had served her purpose in the mission. Getting close to her had resulted in Chernick trusting Foster. She now had access to Chernick's journals and had already smuggled two out of the camp and into her villa. Foster couldn't see what the harm might be if Ilsa got out of here earlier and with a little more of her innocence intact, though her absence would make the mission a whole lot lonelier.

Ilsa grimaced and shook her head. "Do you want rid of me so you can move on to that new guard, Jennell Decker?"

Foster cocked her head and smiled. Decker was typically Aryan—crystal blue eyes, hair as blond as sunshine, legs up to her ass and beyond. Even if Foster wasn't busy with Ilsa though, Simson had already decided she was having the first shot at bedding her. "Why would I, when you're the most beautiful woman in here?" She nudged Ilsa's shoulder gently. "I'm worried about your state of mind. This place...it'll infect you. It could taint you for life. I don't want to see your spirit dulled."

"You're sweet, but I have no intention of leaving you here on your own. You're not immune to the effects of this place either, no matter how tough you are."

Foster didn't respond. She *had* no response. Ilsa had more of a grasp of Foster in three years than anyone else had in her lifetime. She might know Foster under a different name, but there was no denying, Ilsa *did* know her. "I'm going to circle around the back and make sure there're no stragglers. I don't want to see another Katharina incident."

Ilsa took a deep breath, as though she might be stopping herself from being sick again. "That was—"

"Don't think about it," Foster said and put her hand on Ilsa's shoulder.

The rest of the march was uneventful, and there were no attempts to escape the throng. Most of the women were political prisoners, and the resolute determination in some of them was blatantly obvious. She hoped they held on to it; the ones who did had the best chance of beating the odds and survive this place.

As the gates were opened, they passed the welcoming sight of well-kept flowerbeds in front of the SS headquarters. The blooms seemed so out of place, so vibrant and colorful in a place that sought to draw the life and individuality from all of these women. Vogt and her posse herded the new prisoners into the yard, and it was made clear they should remain still while they waited to pass through administration. Foster saw the attempts at communication between existing and new prisoners and ignored them. Other guards did no such thing, and a few strategically placed strikes of their whips put an end to it.

Four lines of five were called forward to enter the bathhouse. As they did so, they were robbed of their possessions, which were then tossed dismissively into a pile on the floor. Moments later, existing prisoners retrieved armfuls of the goods and headed to the clothes store to number and file everything. It was all such a waste of time. Most of these women would never see their things again, and most of them would die here with nothing but a prison-issue uniform, an arbitrary number, and a triangle of colored felt.

Foster escorted them into the bathhouse and ordered them to strip. The male SS officers stood languidly against the wall, watching and laughing amongst themselves. Foster recognized it for the sick power play that it was. She knew they had no sexual interest in the women—they saw them as filthy and beneath them—but their polished performances were designed to increase the inescapable feelings of vulnerability and helplessness.

Invariably, they succeeded.

After the women stripped, the bathhouse guards took over, forcing them into chairs and shaving their heads. It reminded Foster of being a grunt in the army, the first-stage initiation process of leaving your vanity behind to become part of a team, of something bigger than yourself. But this was about dehumanization and uniformity, destroying individuality, and was the first step in breaking the women's spirits. Foster found the next stop in the production line particularly unpleasant, but if she were seen to not be taking an active part assisting the bathhouse guards, her cover would be jeopardized. So she forced them to stand with their legs apart while they were inspected and shaved. In years to come, women would do this as a choice, but all Foster saw were rows of naked women looking strangely prepubescent. The sight sickened her, but she looked on as impassively as she could manage.

Simson strode purposefully toward her, and Foster was glad of the acceptable distraction. It was the first time they'd been able to speak since they'd returned from finding Katharina. *Katharina.* Simson had told her she should only refer to the prisoners by their last name, or better yet, just their number. Foster believed otherwise. Katharina would be a name and an experience she'd never forget, and Foster's mind would never relinquish the graphic images of Katharina's death, even if she wanted it to.

"How was the march in?" Simson asked.

"Same as usual. Nothing special."

"It was probably a good thing you got that detail. I ended up supervising the disposal of fourteen seventy-six. That was some messy, fucked-up shit."

Even with the German accent, Simson still managed to sound as American as apple pie when she spoke to Foster.

"I think the commandant succeeded with his message. I can't see anyone trying to escape after that." Foster blinked away the visceral image of the half-crazed inmates venting their anger, frustration, and fear.

"I saw your girl disappear around the medical block during the punishment. It's no wonder she ends up being dumped from this place. She hasn't got the stomach for it."

"Isn't that a good thing? I've told her she should consider leaving."

Simson raised her eyebrows. "Are you trying to convince her to leave before history says she's supposed to? What about her part in the mission?"

"She's served her purpose." Foster tried hard to sound dispassionate about Ilsa but wasn't sure she succeeded. "Chernick trusts me, and I have the journals in my villa."

"The villa you share with Blumstein. What if she took them all with her, like she does when she's supposed to leave in forty-three?"

"Then I'd convince her to leave them with me so I can keep them all together. I'd handle it."

Simson held up her hands. "I'm not doubting your ability to handle anything. I'm just wondering if this is you starting to work in your new way, as opposed to the way Pulsus wants us to work."

"And if it is?" Foster didn't mind Simson questioning her motives. It would clarify where she stood, and if Foster would be able to count on her.

"If it is, then you know I'm with you," Simson said. "I think you've got it right, and if they'd let you handle this mission the way you wanted to, I wouldn't have had to watch a hundred pounds of female flesh stuffed into three refuse sacks and thrown into a dumpster like it was leftovers from a frat party."

Foster balked at both the image and the metaphor but was pleased Simson had pledged her allegiance. When they jumped home, she'd do as Landry had asked and find a vacation place on the mainland. She'd play along, but ultimately, her goal was to secure Landry's buy-in. Together, they'd reform Pulsus and get it working how it should be. These kinds of small-scale missions wouldn't be part of that future, and maybe, just maybe, Foster would finally get to sleep peacefully again.

CHAPTER TWENTY-FOUR

June 6, 1942: Ravensbrück

LANDRY HAD BEEN TRANSPORTED with six other prisoners from Neubrandenburg in the back of an army truck. She'd managed a whispered conversation with a British woman called Adelita, who'd told her she was suspected of being a Special Operations Executive. Landry knew better than to ask her to confirm their suspicion, particularly with the two male guards itching to pounce on any crumb of information they might be able to take back to Major Oster.

As soon as they were pulled off the truck and into the camp square, a female guard singled out Adelita, and Landry saw Griffin, disturbingly striking in his SS uniform, march toward them. She quickly scanned for Foster and Simson, but they found her first, and Simson stood beside her. She said nothing, but Landry followed the line of her gaze to see Foster standing next to the woman she recognized as Ilsa Blumstein. It looked like their part of the mission was proceeding as planned.

"Adelita Lake, meet Erika Vogt."

Griffin's perfect German accent was impressive. Four years of going native had exceeded the dialect implant's capabilities immensely, and he blended in perfectly.

Vogt thrust the handle of her whip into Adelita's stomach. She doubled over, and Vogt struck her across the back, knocking Adelita to her knees in the mud. She tossed a piece of chocolate onto the ground. "Like a dog, scum."

Landry shifted an inch forward, but Simson pushed her forearm across her chest, blocking her path. "Stay put or you'll end up in the ovens. There's no place for your heroics here."

Landry unfurled her clenched fists and went to turn away. If she couldn't help, she wasn't going to give Vogt the satisfaction of an audience.

Simson stopped her again and whispered quietly, "I told you, stay exactly where you are. There's no version of this that ends well for you if you do anything other than stay put."

The guard placed her boot on Adelita's back and pushed her toward the candy. Adelita reached to retrieve it, but the guard kicked her hand away. "Like a dog."

Adelita looked to Landry, her eyes wet with tears and shame. She turned back to the chocolate and picked it up with her mouth.

"Filthy Juden-lover." Vogt laughed and motioned for Griffin to help her up.

Adelita stood, and Landry hoped her little show had convinced Vogt she was no threat, let alone a spy.

"Why are you in my country?"

Adelita looked puzzled, and Vogt backhanded her. She fell against Griffin, and he held her in place with his hands wrapped around her upper arms.

"Why are you in my country?" Vogt asked again.

"I do not understand," Adelita said in a perfect Berliner accent. "I was born here."

Vogt snarled, and Landry she was a barely controlled dog herself. She slapped Adelita three times, but Griffin's grip stopped her from falling to the floor.

Landry moved against Simson's arm, intent on intervening, but Simson shook her head.

"She's not the mission."

Landry took a deep breath. Inaction wasn't something she was comfortable with, especially when she could do something to stop it. But Simson was right, and going off-book would only result in mission failure.

"Are you or are you not a British spy?"

Adelita shook her head slowly. "No. I am a proud German. I don't know why this is happening to me."

Vogt stepped to Adelita's side and hit her in the stomach with the whip handle. She crumpled to her knees, but Griffin pulled her back up.

"This is happening because you are a British spy. You have been caught, because you're stupid enough to think you can outsmart us." Vogt nodded to the ground, and Griffin kicked Adelita to her knees. He pulled out his pistol and pressed the barrel against her neck.

Landry closed her eyes. There was only one ending to this scenario, and she couldn't do a damn thing about it.

"Confess, and I'll spare you."

Adelita shook her head. "I'm not who you think I am."

Vogt smiled. "I was hoping you'd say that."

She walked behind Adelita, wrapped her hand around Griffin's, and her index finger caressed his trigger finger as though she were caressing a lover. Landry wondered how far he'd been forced to go to be accepted as an SS officer.

"I will ask you one more time, for the sake of leniency. Are you a British spy?"

Vogt rested her other hand on Griffin's bare neck, and the two exchanged a quick glance that only lovers would share. Adelita took a final look Landry's way and gave her a slight smile. *Goodbye.*

"I am not."

Vogt smiled, sadistic and satisfied, as she squeezed Griffin's trigger finger. The bullet tore through Adelita's neck and throat and hit the ground before she did. Death was instant. Three of the women beside Landry vomited at the sight of sinew and blood. Their political activism clearly hadn't prepared them for this.

"What about the rest of you? Are there any more spies among you?"

Landry clenched her teeth. She wanted to rip this woman's

throat out with her bare hands.

Vogt came into Landry's eye line and stopped directly in front of her. She consulted a piece of paper. "Truda Stark. A career criminal. You've misplaced your husband? How careless." She snickered. "I'm sure he'll turn up somewhere—probably on the end of a German bayonet."

Landry said nothing and kept her expression blank. She couldn't give this bitch anything to go on. She was nothing more than a power-crazed psychopath, and Landry couldn't risk the mission by engaging with her now. *But she lives through this.* Landry recalled the file. Vogt escaped the camp before the Red Army got there, and she lived as a fugitive in Argentina until she was in her sixties. *Every mission has collateral damage.* They did their best to minimize the impact of their presence, but some people just had to die.

"You are also a carpenter and a plumber. They are not usual trades for a woman."

It was tempting not to respond again. There was no question, after all, but it obviously wouldn't take much to make Vogt strike out. "I wanted to make sure I could take care of myself if there was no man around."

Vogt nodded and looked slightly impressed. "We can make use of your talents here, you can be sure of that." She placed her whip handle under Landry's chin and forced her head up slightly. "No use wasting someone like you on the road gang, shifting soil and sand for no good reason."

She and Griffin laughed again, and Landry couldn't miss the sexual undertones of Vogt's statement, nor the lustful look in her eyes. The Angel of Death chose her partners from both sexes, even having sex with some prisoners before sending them to the crematorium. Landry hoped she could keep her at bay. She'd had to do some unsavory things with some unpleasant people, but she wasn't sure if she could be the plaything of this twisted bitch. An image of Jade surfaced involuntarily. She wasn't sure if she could be anybody's plaything anymore. *For the mission...* "I'd be happy to do whatever you need." The words burned her lips as they escaped her mouth, and she hoped to god it wouldn't be her that Vogt *needed*. It'd take gargantuan control to keep from wrapping her hands around Vogt's throat and squeezing the sadistic life out of her.

"Thalberg, take our new inmates to the bathhouse and get them more appropriately dressed."

Simson nodded. "Yes, ma'am." She grasped Landry's elbow and pulled her away. "Looks like you got away with the shit duty," Simson whispered when they were a few steps in front of the following prisoners. "Bet you were hoping to keep your pants. It's gonna be hard to keep a straight face with you wearing a dress."

"You're wrong if you think you're rocking that skirt and sleeveless sweater look."

Simson shoved Landry into the bathhouse. "Have fun."

Landry was quickly relieved of her leather jacket and the rest of her clothes, which were tagged and bagged with the same prisoner number they gave her. Griffin would have to get those back for the rest of the mission once they had the doc and were on their way out. There was no way she was going outside of these gates in a dress.

Having her head shaved didn't bother her. It was just like being back in the Seals. When they roughly shaved between her legs, she remembered the time when her dad had brought back crabs from a tour of duty, and everyone in the house had to lose their pubic hair. Landry had been mortified, because at ten, she'd only just started to cultivate a little bush that made her feel more grown up. She'd overheard an argument, and her mom accused her father of sleeping around. Her father was adamant he'd caught it from sharing towels with the guys in his company. Landry had always assumed his innocence, but after what her mom had said before the jump, she wasn't sure of anything to do with her father.

She was handed a dress with a green triangle, while the others who'd come with her received either red or black. Ravensbrück was originally built for the political opponents of the Nazi regime and so-called asocials, such as beggars, lesbians, and prostitutes. Landry didn't know what made Hitler decide to destroy thousands of women, but how well he succeeded was something she really couldn't get a handle on. Most of the guards in this place claimed to just follow orders but were personally responsible for ending the lives of thousands of women. Maybe Foster did have the right idea. If the mission had been to assassinate Hitler, none of these women she stood with now would be in this place, let alone die before their time.

Her thoughts were interrupted when a fellow prisoner handed her a blanket. It was topped with a set of crockery and basic silverware, a toothbrush and paste, a chunk of soap, and a towel that would barely qualify as a washcloth, another element of the camp to further humiliate the women. She was ordered to wait while the rest of them were given their rations before being led to their block.

Inside the block were rows of three-tiered, wooden bunk beds, and each unit was approximately four feet long. When the camp was built, the beds were meant to sleep one woman; now, each housed four. As she filed down the narrow corridor between the beds to her bunk, Landry tried to make eye contact with every woman. Hundreds of shaved heads, sunken faces, and starved bodies melded into a vision of one woman. Malnutrition, disease, and overwork. Landry was suddenly grateful for her position as extractor. She only had to be here for six weeks, comforted with the knowledge that if all went according to plan, they'd escape. How did these women, who looked at her now with compassion and sympathy, hold on to those sharp shards of desperate hope? How could they continue to believe that good would triumph over evil when the screams of their tortured friends hung in the air all day long?

And how was Foster coping? She'd promised to begin carving

a separate life on the mainland after this mission, but what if that turned out to be too late? What if the atrocities she had not only seen but also had to perpetrate here left wounds that could never heal? Landry should've done more. She could've talked to her mom or Castillo, and they could've delayed the mission while Foster got the help she needed. She was an integral part of the team, and Landry had failed her.

She placed her blanket on the cot and stacked her stuff on the tiny empty shelf built inside the beds. A gaunt woman looked up from the bed she would be sharing with Landry and two of the other new prisoners. There was hope in her eyes, and Landry found herself wanting to feel that same hope, more than ever before.

CHAPTER TWENTY-FIVE

June 16, 1942: Ravensbrück

"The doctor needs guinea pigs, Sieglinde," Vogt said. "Mengele will visit next month, and I've promised him results."

Foster nodded and swallowed the rising nausea at the thought of what Vogt was asking her to do. "Do you have parameters?"

Vogt smiled, and Foster was once again struck by how apt her moniker was. How could someone so outwardly beautiful be so dark and evil on the inside?

"Good question," she said. "Older than twenty and younger than forty. Not fat, but not skinny. Healthy, but not the healthiest." She wagged her finger. "Otherwise, with how quickly the doctor goes through the little pigs, there will be no one left to do the hard work around the camp."

"No problem," Foster said and left Vogt's office to head to the blocks. Among the more sadistic guards in the camp, this gruesome duty was considered a coveted detail. But Foster would happily swap it with any one of them, Simson included, because she seemed to be handling this mission far better than Foster was. Simson had managed to get herself some action with an attractive guard and consequently had stopped bugging Foster for sex. And she was acting as if they weren't perpetrating some of the worst atrocities in human history. Whatever Simson's coping mechanism was, Foster wished she could share it.

The dreams that already haunted her were competing for show times with new visions of the vile acts she'd been involved in over the past three years. For appearances and the sake of formality,

Ilsa kept her own room in their shared villa, but each evening, Ilsa unmade her own bed before joining Foster in hers. Every night, Foster woke with her tank soaked in sweat, shouting and shaking, and Ilsa wiped away the sweat from her face with a washcloth and held her tight, whispering that everything would be okay.

But everything *wasn't* going to be okay, unless Foster acted. Unless she did what she felt she had to do.

She acknowledged Griffin standing guard at the main entrance to the admin building and made her way toward Block F. Now that Landry was safely here, Foster had no doubt that they'd complete this mission. She hadn't been prepared, though, for the rush of emotion that had swept through her when she saw Landry again. There were so many moving parts in these missions that if anything went wrong, the whole thing could fall apart, so when their extractor showed up, the relief was palpable. But Foster had felt something far more powerful than that when Landry stepped off the train.

Maybe she could settle her disquiet by counting down the days to the seventh of July. She kicked some gravel from the path as she did the math: twenty-two days until the team left this shitpit of a prison and began their trek back home. Part of her was looking forward to seeing what New York looked like in 1942; it had been one of her favorite places to visit between army tours. But she was also impatient to get back to 2076, to kickstart her plans and organize missions with far wider reach. *With me at the helm.* It would have to be that way, and Landry would see that too. The board lacked imagination, ambition, vision. Mission by consensus was clearly ineffective. Pulsus needed a strong leader, someone able to make the tough decisions, and Foster now saw she was the person they needed.

It was six a.m. when she collected two female guards to accompany her into the block. At this hour, the prisoners knew why she was there. Most of the women refused to look at her, but others, mainly the women with a red triangle, met her gaze then stared straight through her. Foster admired their strength. They were telling her she meant nothing to them, and that she, or any other guard here, could commit any number of egregious misdeeds against them, and they would never break. She'd seen that same look in Landry's eyes on a mission where being captured and tortured had been an integral part of the plan.

Foster scanned the women as she navigated the tiny walking space between the bed rows. She and Simson had discussed who they'd choose if either of them were given this detail. "Pick numbers, like an unlucky lottery," Simson had said. "Don't look at faces. And remember that it's already happened anyway. Don't think you're changing history, because you're not. You're just doing your job." But Foster had to look like she was putting some thought into it, like she was enjoying exercising her power, and perhaps even punishing prisoners who'd broken rules. It was like a warning system—mess up, and you'll end up on the doctor's tables. Doing anything less would raise suspicion.

There was no easy way out; she had to choose five women to undergo excruciating operations with no anesthesia. She reminded herself that this was the easiest, and least conspicuous, way of getting to Chernick. And *she* was the mission. Foster strode alongside the beds and pointed at five women who matched Vogt's requirements. In the end, she tried not to think too much about it. She couldn't use the lottery method Simson had suggested, so she tried to see the characteristics rather than the woman and convinced herself that would have to be enough.

Foster led the way to the medical block, while the two other guards flanked the five prisoners. They shuffled behind her, their ungainly wooden clogs clomping noisily on the pathway. The rising sun cast a beautiful light across the lake. Surrounding them with beauty was another pitiless way of penalizing the prisoners, but Foster wanted to believe that it kept the women's hope alive, that one day, freedom would come, and they'd get to swim in that lake. Foster shook off the unfamiliar romantic notion—it sounded like something Ilsa would say—and refocused to prepare herself for the horrors of the medical block.

Dr. Chernick, their target, greeted the prisoners in Yiddish, and Foster all but saw the unspoken words exchanged in their looks.

"Thank you, Fraulein Thalberg," Chernick said. "Dr. Drescher has asked for your assistance to restrain the...test subjects."

Foster could see how hard it was for Chernick to vocalize the terminology she'd been instructed to use. She imagined the words forming a wooden chunk in the doctor's throat. "Just me?" Foster motioned to the guards with her.

Chernick nodded. "Just you, Fraulein."

"Have fun, Sigi," one of the guards said, laughing as they exited the building.

Foster closed her eyes briefly at their contempt for human life. As more time passed within these high concrete walls, guards like Ilsa dwindled.

"The doctor would like you to strap down the...subjects...to those tables."

In the next whitewashed room, there were five medical gurneys, replete with ankle, wrist, and neck cuffs. Drescher, the camp "doctor," hummed a jolly tune as he prepared his tools. Foster motioned for the prisoners to go into the room, and they did, quietly and calmly, as if they were going to see their own doctor for a routine checkup. She gestured to the tables. "Select a table and get up on it."

Again, they did as they were instructed. Foster began to secure the restraints on the closest woman to Drescher.

"Good morning, Sieglinde," Drescher said, apparently devoid of any misgivings about what he was going to do.

"Morning, Doctor. How are you?" Foster hated herself for matching his light and breezy tone.

"Marvelous, actually." He held up a sharp steel implement and polished it enthusiastically. "I feel at my most inspired at this time in the morning. I have a feeling we're going to have a breakthrough with this batch," he said and nodded toward the tables.

Foster fought the urge to react against his dismissive and dehumanizing language. "I'm glad to hear that. It's good that you've found a way for them to be useful to society." Foster swallowed hard, the acid lie burning her lips as it emerged. She avoided the stare she could feel from Chernick.

"Absolutely. I tried to join the army, but my eyes aren't up to scratch." He tapped the glass on his gold-rimmed spectacles. "This way, I get to help our boys in the field."

"What are you doing differently this time around?" Foster had seen the large wounds inflicted on the many women who'd died on these tables, and she would rather slice her ears with a razor blade than hear his answer, but she had to appear intrigued.

"You saw the previous experiments, yes?" He peered at Foster expectantly, and she nodded. "Follow me."

Drescher led her to a smaller room. The three-foot by six-foot wooden tub in the center of the space was filled with severed arms and legs, floating in God knows what. All of them had wounds between six and ten inches long and up to two inches wide. Had Chernick been forced to separate the limbs from the rest of the victims' bodies?

"These are some of the last batch," he said and prodded a couple of the gashes with a pair of long tongs. "We tried to simulate lacerations similar to those sustained by our boys from bayonets and bombs, but they were too clean. You can see that even now the flesh hasn't putrefied, although the formalin has helped in that respect. And so..." He crooked his finger, indicating her to follow him back to his table of tools.

Foster sighed deeply. The new women lay there, perfectly still, making no attempt to communicate with each other or with Chernick. Why didn't the fifty thousand women currently in the camp rise up and riot? Some would die, of course, but there weren't enough guards or bullets to kill them all. The question plagued her as much as her nightmares.

"This is what I'm going to do differently, Sieglinde." He slipped a latex glove on, carefully picked up a shard of glass from a small pot on the table and held it aloft for inspection. Similar pots contained collections of dirt, sawdust, splinters of wood, and rusty nails.

"You're going to...?" She played along, but she already knew exactly what Drescher had in store for these poor women; she'd seen it in the videos pre-mission.

"I'm going to slice the subjects open and introduce each of these into a deep incision to mimic the environmental situation of our soldiers. Very rarely are the medics seeing clean wounds. It seems they always have some foreign body or other in there." He replaced the glass shard then flicked at one of the wrist cuffs on the adjacent table. "That's why I need them secured to the tables. We need to let the injuries fester for a suitable amount of time before beginning treatment, so the subjects must stay here for the duration of the experiments."

Foster nodded, feigning interest and admiration. "That's impressive, Dr. Drescher. How will you empty their bladders and feed them if they're not to be moved from the tables?"

"That's where she comes in," he said and gestured dismissively at Chernick. "She'll fit the bags for nature's call." He nudged Foster. "And empty them, of course! I couldn't have you or other guards doing that. She'll also feed and water them."

He smiled brightly, and Foster returned it with an enthusiasm she didn't feel. The women weren't plants; they were human beings. Drescher would be hung for all of this in 1946, but that wasn't nearly enough punishment for all the suffering he gleefully caused.

"Then I'll get on so you can begin." She returned to the gurneys, and one by one, secured their ankles wide apart and strapped their wrists so they could barely move. Putting the neck cuff on was the hardest. Each of them stared at her, as if they were looking deep into her soul for some shred of decency, something that would stop her from doing this, that would make her release them. But they couldn't see the truth behind her dispassionate gaze. She pushed the coarse blue-and-white striped dress up from the ankle of the final woman as Chernick appeared beside her.

"I have to perform a laparotomy. I'll need your help." Chernick took a pair of scissors from an adjacent table. "Alicja...be brave."

Foster tensed. Now the woman had a name. She was no longer just 7533. Simson's coping advice became even more useless. Acid burned at the back of Foster's throat as she helped Chernick perform the operation on the prisoners. After they finished just before ten a.m., Drescher instructed Chernick to furnish Foster with some paperwork to take to the commandant, so she followed Chernick back into the front area of the med block. Chernick gathered the required paperwork and slid a tan leather journal amidst the stack of folders.

"You are keeping them safe, yes?" Chernick asked when they were out of Drescher's earshot.

"Of course. When you get out of here, you'll be able to continue your research. Maybe even in America." She couldn't risk telling Chernick about their planned rescue, but Foster wanted to give her something to hold onto.

She smiled wryly. "There is no escape from this place. I will die here."

Foster shook her head. "You don't know that for sure."

"It's only a matter of time before Mengele comes for me. I lived a strange version of a life before they caught me and put me in here. I'll soon be on one of those tables, with my scalp removed and quacks poking around in my gray matter. And you will hold my only legacy."

Her prophetic words stopped Foster from responding. That *had* been Chernick's fate before Pulsus discovered her journals, one of which Foster had in her hands right now, but they were going to change all that. It didn't really matter what Chernick believed. She and Landry would rescue the doctor from that fate and set her on a path to rid the world of cancer. *If only you knew how important you're about to become.*

CHAPTER TWENTY-SIX

June 18, 1942: Ravensbrück

AFTER RETURNING FROM THE morning count, Landry sat on her bed with her daily bread and coffee ration. It wasn't Starbucks, but it was hot and full of caffeine. And the bread was barely a snack, providing hardly enough energy to walk around, let alone work the day in the sandpit, like a lot of these women would have to. What she wouldn't give for a stack of pancakes topped with bacon and maple syrup, followed by a double protein shake.

Simson entered the block, and the women hurried to get out of her way. Landry had discovered that Simson had established quite the reputation around the prison. She wasn't in the same league as the Angel of Death, but she certainly wasn't known as a compassionate guard like Ilsa Blumstein. Foster, on the other hand, was known to be firm but fair, despite Vogt's apparent desire for Foster to be her lieutenant. Landry hoped she was staying away from the truly dark dealings of the camp, but she'd been assigned to the medical block, and they'd all been briefed on what happened there. Landry was marking the days to their escape from this place for Foster's mental health as much as for Dr. Chernick's rescue.

"Stark," Simson said, blocking the light from the door with her considerable form. "Vogt wants you in her office. Follow me."

Landry pushed the last piece of stale bread into her mouth and washed it down with the thick black liquid. One of the first things she wanted when they jumped back would be a chai latte to wash away this particular taste memory. She was focused on home comforts to help navigate this mission in a way she never had been before, and Jade was a constant visitor in her dreams.

She stood and adjusted her dress. Landry missed her jeans. Not only did she feel near-naked and incredibly vulnerable, but the dress was also impractical for the work she was doing. Her knees were skinned and bruised, and she felt the constant need to tuck the dress under her ass when she bent over. The only thing that made her feel a little normal was the hefty leather tool belt she collected when she was given her work duties each day. It looked a little incongruous around the waist of her dress, but its weight provided a small sense of security.

Landry followed Simson silently out of the block. When they were alone on the path toward the main admin building, Simson gave Landry a quick rundown of where she and Foster were with their part of the mission, including the journals and the doctor.

"How's Griffin? He made Adelita Lake's execution look run-of-the-mill."

Simson shook her head. "Vogt took a shine to him the moment he got here, and he's having to fuck her when she's not busy fucking the prisoners. He's worried his dick might fall off because she's so fucking toxic, but he's handling it. He's doing his job well, so you don't need to be concerned about him disappearing into his cover."

"It's his first mission," Landry said, "and we're relying on him to get the weapons and the vehicle we need. You're sure he's good?"

"It's his first mission with *us*. He's not a wet-behind-the-ears raw recruit: he's ex-CIA, remember? You read his file too; he was in deep cover with the Villanueva gang for six years *and* developed a drug habit to cement his place with them. Griffin is solid. So, yes, I'm sure he's good."

Landry sighed and nodded. "Okay. Are they sharing a villa? That'd make getting out on extraction night a problem."

"The duty rosters are set for a month in advance, and Griffin and I are on night watch on the seventh. Foster won't have any trouble getting away from Blumstein; she often takes late night walks."

When she can't sleep because of the nightmares. "Tell me you'll be able to get hold of my clothes."

Simson chuckled. "I don't think so. Everything's labeled and itemized but getting it from the store to our villas would be too difficult. Foster's secured some other clothes for you." Her jaw clenched. "No doubt she knows your size."

Landry didn't rise to the bait. "As long as I don't have to stay in this getup a minute longer than necessary, I don't care if it's three sizes too big. Has Griffin secured access to the transport keys yet?"

Simson nodded. "He'll grab the keys to a Kübelwagen before we go on shift at twenty-two hundred hours."

"Then you'll feign illness, and Griffin will take you to the medical block. I'll already be there, and that's when we swap you for Chernick. Griffin drives her out of here, picks up Foster and the journals, and heads up to the rendezvous point. You and I escape over the far wall, trek through the forest, and meet them at the rendezvous point."

"Sounds nice and easy when you say it fast like that."

Landry nodded. "Like clockwork."

Simson opened the front door to the admin block and followed Landry up the stairs to Vogt's first floor office. Simson knocked and opened the door.

"Stark, I have a job for you. Sit." Vogt motioned to the chair in front of her desk.

Simson shoved Landry forward and pressed her into the wooden seat in front of the desk.

Vogt came around and sat on her desk, so her crotch was in Landry's eyeline. "You may go about your duties, Thalberg."

"Yes, ma'am."

Simson left, closing the door behind her, and an unpleasant mix of unease and aggression swept over Landry.

"Some glass needs to be replaced in the medical block," Vogt said and parted her legs.

Landry maintained eye contact. "I can do that. Do you already have the supplies, or would you like me to provide a list of the things I need?" Landry had become just as much of an expert in fending off unwanted attention as she had in faking interest in women for the sake of a mission. The problem here was that if Vogt decided that's what she wanted, Landry wouldn't be able to do a damn thing about it without jeopardizing the entire mission.

Thoughts of Jade raided her mind. *How would she feel if she never saw me again?* Landry usually only concerned herself with her own well-being and that of her team, and she lived by the philosophy that if her time was up, so be it. That had never made her reckless with her life, but now that she'd met Jade, a latent motivation to cheat death surfaced. But she couldn't allow that to make her cautious and less effective. Was there any way to make it a new strength? An overwhelming drive to get home alive might motivate her to be more creative.

"We have what you need." Vogt pushed herself away from the desk and circled behind Landry, then put her hands on Landry's shoulders. "But you have something I need."

Landry took a deep breath and tried to relax every muscle that had contracted in revulsion the second Vogt touched her. "And what might that be?"

"I need your carpentry skills. I want a large bookcase in my villa. It looks like I'll be here for a while, and I want to be comfortable. My place should feel like home. And what is a home without books?"

"A poorer home," Landry said, relief bleeding from her pores, though she'd never figured Vogt as a reader. Would she be making shelf space for the complete works of the Marquis de Sade? "When would you like me to start?"

"I'd like to see some designs first." Vogt walked back to her chair and sat, before pulling out some loose-leaf papers from a top drawer. "Here are the measurements for the wall I'd like it to cover. I want it to feel like a grand library, with wall-to-wall books." She handed Landry the papers and two pencils. "Come back to my office when you need to sharpen them."

Landry took the proffered items. "Do I get to work on this during the day?"

"No, this is extracurricular. When I'm happy with the designs, you can let me know what supplies I need. When I have them, you'll be working at my villa every evening until the job is satisfactorily complete."

Vogt smiled widely, and there was a flicker of flirtation in her eyes that made it clear Landry might not be safe from her desires after all. But if she dragged out the design process and if the supplies took enough time to be sourced, they'd be gone before she had to step inside Vogt's lair. "Then I should get on with the glass job?"

"Yes, you're free to go."

Landry folded the papers in half and put them in the front pocket of her dress before getting out of the chair. "Thank you, Fraulein Vogt." She retreated from the office and closed the door behind her. Outside, she took a deep breath of fresh air. Vogt's office had been stifling, and it smelled of something that caught in Landry's throat. *Death?* She remembered reading about Vogt and her lampshades made of prisoners' skins. She closed her eyes and mentally scanned the inside of the office. Yep, in the corner of the office as she'd turned to leave, next to the wingback chair beside the small bookcase: a lampshade made of human skin.

Landry shuddered and went to collect her belt and tools. Being assigned a job in the medical block was fortuitous, giving her the perfect opportunity to get close to Chernick. Landry had to discover whether the doctor would cooperate with the rescue, or if she might complicate matters by not coming willingly. Landry couldn't fathom why Chernick might want to stay, but it was a possibility she had to eliminate or identify without raising her suspicions.

Ilsa Blumstein called Landry forward to skip the line. She walked past the long line of women waiting to collect shovels to shift soil and sand all day. For the sake of those women, she hoped the guards wouldn't be interested in playing their sick games today.

Blumstein handed Landry a tool belt, along with putty, nails, and three panes of glass. "Do you need help with the glass?"

Landry smiled. "I'll be okay but thank you."

Blumstein's softness and the gentle way she addressed the prisoners was a stark contrast to the woman she'd just been forced to spend time with. It was surprising Blumstein had withstood it here quite as long as she did without cracking. For Chernick's sake and for anyone ever afflicted with cancer, it was lucky she had. Without Blumstein, this mission simply wouldn't be. Landry picked up her supplies and turned away. It was almost unkind that Blumstein would never know the unique contribution she was making to the development of a cancer cure.

Landry walked quickly to the medical block and introduced herself to Chernick.

"Ah, our new handyman," Chernick said. "Or should I say, handywoman?"

Landry put the glazing panels down and extended her hand. "I've been called both. My name's Truda Stark though, Doc."

Chernick shook Landry's hand firmly. "I saw you when you came in. It looked like you might've been living like I once did."

Speaking of Chernick's time living as a man might speed up the friendship process. Still, she feigned surprise. "What do you mean?" She took a quick look around; Drescher was nowhere to be seen, so they could both speak freely.

"It's the reason I'm in here. I pretended to be a man."

"Really? For how long?"

"Six years. When Hitler made it clear that the only position women should be in was beneath a man on a bed, I had a decision to make. I falsified my papers and secured a seven-year residency at UHC in 1933. I was so close to finishing it." She looked almost wistful.

"How was your secret discovered?" Landry asked.

"Listen to you with all the questions." Chernick touched Landry's arm. "What about you? How did you end up here?"

"I apologize, I didn't mean to pry. I was arrested in Neubrandenburg flying solo after my husband left me in the middle of night."

"Oh." Chernick pulled her hand back. "I'm sorry. I assumed—"

"That I was a lesbian?"

Chernick looked guilty and chastised at the same time. "Yes. Now it's my turn to apologize for stereotyping you."

Landry laughed and shook her head. "No need to apologize. You're right. We all do things we might not want to in order to make our life easier."

"Indeed, and speaking of which, perhaps you should start on your work before Drescher returns."

"Sure. So where are the broken ones?" Landry didn't push. She'd already gotten further with Chernick than she'd expected. She would take her time with the windows and make it last the rest of the morning.

"The first one is in here." She put her hand on Landry's shoulder. "But you should prepare yourself for what you'll see."

Landry nodded and followed her. She knew that nothing, none of the videos or photos or accounts she'd already seen and read, could prepare her for what was in this room. The smell of rotting flesh was the first thing that hit her though as she stepped through the doorway. She gagged and had to take a second to breathe past it, so she didn't vomit.

Chernick lifted a hypodermic syringe and a bottle of yellow liquid. "I need to quickly give them these injections before Drescher comes back."

"What is it?"

"Homemade anesthesia. These women need something to ease their suffering. Can you imagine being opened up like this and have to feel *everything*?"

Landry looked at each of the women, and they stared back,

glassy-eyed and hopeless, used and broken. Then, instead of turning away, she tried to bear witness to what was being done to them: the open wounds all over their bodies, the foreign objects forced into those wounds, the infections clearly present, and the colostomy bags and catheters. Landry had been tortured numerous times on Pulsus missions, but she couldn't begin to imagine what this felt like. "You're taking a risk, aren't you? What if Drescher discovers what you're doing?"

Chernick inserted a needle into the arm of one of the women. "I don't care. I have to do *something* to help."

Chernick began to address the full colostomy bag situation, so Landry began her own job.

Drescher arrived moments later, and Landry worked on two of the three windows accompanied by a symphony of screams. If that was their level of pain even with Chernick's homemade anesthesia, she couldn't imagine how it would feel with none. She didn't manage to renew her conversation with Chernick, so she slowed down to an amateur degree until he stopped for lunch.

"Chernick, photograph and catalogue the wounds," Drescher said, dropping a pair of gloves into the trash. "Then extract the infection seepage and add it to each subject's tube. I'm going for lunch. Enjoy your bread."

"Yes, Doctor."

He picked up a journal that looked similar to the photos she'd seen of Chernick's and quickly left the building.

"Join me for lunch?" Chernick offered up a chunk of bread, her own rations for the day.

Landry nodded. "I'll join you to chat, but I won't take your food. I've already eaten mine."

"You must share. I get double rations for working in here. Please..."

Landry smiled and accepted the torn-off bread. "So what made you do it?" She really wanted to know. If she'd been a Jew in Germany when Hitler took power and his genocide began, she would have been one of the first out of the country. "You could've sought refuge in Britain, or America even, and continued to practice as a doctor there. Why stay here and risk...everything?"

Chernick stared at the ceiling for a long moment. "A strange mix of a stubborn streak and a desire for freedom, I suppose. I wasn't about to let a tiny man with a bad haircut and a penchant for shouting hateful rhetoric stop me from pursuing the career I'd worked so hard for. And being a man gives you a freedom you simply can't experience as a woman. And I'm patriotic. I love my country, despite its current leadership. We can be a great country, a supportive one, helping others. We'll make up for this in years to come."

"I like your passion and commitment," Landry said. "There's talk of the research you're doing here, and that you've got two guards helping you. Do you think they could help you escape?"

Chernick's eyes widened, and she glanced at the door. "Then people should stop talking, or I might end up dead. But escape? Absolutely not. The last escape attempt ended very badly. That's not something I'm prepared to face." She shuddered as if it was happening right in front of her again. "And anyway, who would look after these women if I left here? I wouldn't escape even if it *was* an option, which it's not." She leaned forward and placed her hand on Landry's knee, her eyes full of concern. "You should think very carefully if that is your goal, Truda. Very carefully indeed."

Chernick's response complicated the rescue. They'd have to sedate her for the swap with Simson and put her unconscious into the jeep. "But what about your research? Don't you want to complete it?"

"Of course I would, but I believe I've left enough clues for others to follow." Chernick tapped her nose. "Another doctor would be able to pick up the threads and continue...from wherever I have to leave it."

Landry picked up on the hint of melancholy in Chernick's voice. "What if they can't? The minds of no two geniuses think the same way. And I hear you're looking at a cure for cancer; scientists and doctors have been trying since the early nineteenth century and have gotten nowhere." And they were still no closer a hundred and thirty years later. "Don't you owe it to the world to complete your research, if you were given that opportunity? You're helping a few women here, sure, but cure cancer and you help millions, not just now, but in the future."

Chernick nodded slowly. "You make a salient point and, might I say, very eloquently for a career criminal."

"There's more to me than that, Doc." *And you'll soon find out how much more when we bust you out of this hellhole.*

Chernick smiled. "Charm and intelligence being just two of those things. I'm sure you were a hit with the ladies before you were married."

"My husband and I had an agreement. Our marriage was one of convenience for both of us, so it didn't really stop me." Landry winked. "Which reminds me, you never answered my question about how you ended up in here."

Chernick's expression darkened. "There was a nurse. She was such a pretty little thing, all bouncy brunette curls and brown eyes. I'd been so careful to that point, going out of town to discreet lesbian bars to meet others like me. But she flirted with me mercilessly, and I thought maybe I could get away with it if we only ever had sex in the dark. If I never let her touch me. If I never fell asleep afterward and always went home alone." She sighed deeply. "It worked that way for a little while. But we ended up in her apartment after I'd pulled a triple shift one night. I was exhausted, but she wouldn't take no for an answer." She balled her hands together tightly and rested her chin on them. "I'm sure you can guess. I fell asleep, and she woke before me. I'll never forget that look of disgust and disappointment."

Landry put her hand on Chernick's shoulder firmly. "She reported you?"

"Yes. I tried to explain, but she wouldn't listen. She kept

screaming that I'd lied to her, over and over, that I'd betrayed her, and she'd be tarnished for life because of what I'd done. I bolted from her apartment to my house and tried to gather a few things in an attempt to run. The SS arrested me at the train station; stupidly, I had no women's clothes to reverse my disguise. I was here within the week, after a short and terrifying spell of senseless torture at the local Gestapo office." Chernick held her ribs, then she wrapped both arms around herself. "That left more than physical scars."

Landry nodded. "Torture always takes away a little piece of you, and you have to fight to get it back. Maybe surviving this place and continuing your research can be your way of doing that."

"Yes, Truda. Perhaps you're right."

Landry put her hand on Chernick's shoulder and squeezed gently. *I'm definitely right.*

CHAPTER TWENTY-SEVEN

July 7, 1942: Ravensbrück

"Is this a special occasion I don't know about?" Foster asked as she stood in the kitchen doorway and watched Ilsa slicing a loaf of bread. She'd come home from her afternoon shift to find the table set, replete with candles, fancy napkins, and wine glasses.

Ilsa had turned the second reception area into a dining room, so that she could entertain her colleagues, but she soon found there were few of them she wanted to spend more time with than was absolutely necessary. Apart from Foster. It seemed she wanted to spend every spare moment with her, and though being wanted that much had taken some getting used to, Foster had not only adapted, she'd also come to enjoy it.

"It's been eighteen months since we first slept together." Ilsa stopped slicing and pointed her knife at Foster. "I think that's worth celebrating, don't you?"

She held her hands up in mock surrender. "If I don't say yes, are you going to chop me up with that knife?"

Ilsa laughed. "No, silly, I'm teasing. Would you open the wine?"

Foster approached her from behind and gently swept aside the hair from her neck to kiss her bare skin. "Can I do this first?" She slipped her arms around Ilsa's waist and pulled her close.

"You want to skip dinner and move straight to dessert?" Ilsa whispered.

The atmosphere dialed up a notch, making Foster wish this wasn't their last night together. But did it have to be? Could she convince Landry that it was a good idea to take Ilsa back with them? She shook her head at the ridiculous thought. There was no way Landry would allow it, and she was in charge of the number of time strings they accessed to travel home. Who would they leave here? "I'd take three courses of you over food any day of the week."

"You're such a charmer, but dinner's up first. I need to talk to you."

Something akin to anxiety gripped Foster by the throat and squeezed. She was hoping to get through tonight without any deep conversation. She wanted to spend the evening being as real as she possibly could. She pulled away and caressed Ilsa's butt before picking up the wine bottle and opener and going into the dining room.

"How was your day?" Ilsa asked.

Foster smiled at such an ordinary question. Maybe this was what Landry was always talking about. Maybe this was the normal she was striving toward. "I saw Chernick, and she gave me another journal. And I managed to avoid Vogt all day; that's always a good thing." She pulled the cork, poured two glasses, and took them back into the kitchen. "She's decided my sister is a better bet for her lieutenant, and I think she's on to something. Johanna's not been the same for a few weeks now. I feel like I don't know her anymore."

"What do you mean?"

Foster took a sip of wine before answering. She had to set this up perfectly, because her plan for keeping Ilsa safe after the escape depended on it. "She's acting strange and spending a lot of time at the medical block. She talks to that handywoman all the time too, but I'm not sure if that's because Vogt has a thing for her too. I heard she's designing some bookcases for Vogt's villa, and I reckon her carpentry skills aren't all that she's after."

Ilsa prepared their plates and gestured to the dining room for Foster to follow.

"So what do you think is going on? Does she know about the journals we're smuggling out for Bina?" Ilsa's brow furrowed.

"No, I haven't told her about those. It's best if you and I keep that between us." Foster sighed. "Something's going on, I'm sure, but I can't figure it out right now."

Ilsa speared a potato, dipped it in the white sauce on the steak, and chewed it slowly. It was something she did when she was figuring out how to say something. She was so innocent and transparent, so easy to read.

"So, you've got something you want to talk about?" Foster asked before popping a piece of steak in her mouth.

"Do you love your sister?" Ilsa asked.

"She's my sister. I don't really have a choice." Foster shrugged. "What are you asking?"

"You came to the camp together. Have you always been close and done everything together?"

Foster laughed and shook her head. She wasn't sure where Ilsa's line of questioning was going, but it was feeding nicely into her plan. "God, no, that was a coincidence. We answered the same ad without even talking to each other about it. We'd barely seen each other for years."

"So if she—or you—decided to leave the camp, you wouldn't have to do it together?"

"No. We've always led very separate lives. We wouldn't really miss each other. Still, I don't get what you're asking."

Ilsa took a big gulp of her wine like she was hoping it might give her some liquid courage. "I've been thinking about what you said to me a couple of weeks ago, about this place infecting me and breaking my spirit. I think you're right." She took Foster's hand and tenderly stroked each finger in turn. "I want to be someone, to *do* something. I don't want to change like other guards have. I don't want to keep seeing the awful things going on around here and come to accept that behavior as okay." She withdrew her hand from Foster's and briefly hugged herself. "It's *not* okay. What they're doing to the women in that lab is *not* okay. And I can't do anything about it other than hope we lose the war soon and someone else stops it from happening."

"You're thinking of leaving?" Foster continued eating. Had she misjudged their relationship? Did Ilsa feel nothing for her?

"I don't want to go alone... I want us to leave together before we both become tainted by what's happening here."

Ilsa took Foster's hands in hers and squeezed them gently. She looked deep into Foster's eyes, and Foster could see the longing... and the love. Ilsa *loved* her. For the first time in her life, she was truly loved. Her breath caught in her chest like it had been hooked on a line. *Love.*

"Sigi, will you come with me so we can start a new life together?"

Briefly, Foster considered the proposition. It wouldn't be hard to stay here tonight. The team would only wait at the rendezvous point for thirty minutes, then protocol meant they'd leave her behind, and they'd assume that something bad must've happened. They couldn't come back for her, so they'd be none the wiser.

She dismissed it almost as quickly as she considered it. *This doesn't have to be goodbye. This doesn't have to be forever.* Foster could come back once she'd taken control of Pulsus. She could return on this exact night, one hour after the rendezvous time with the team. She wouldn't jeopardize this mission, and Ilsa would never know the difference. Foster would have a couple more years on the clock, but it probably wouldn't be noticeable; she could even use the curatio tank to drop those years. If she went with Ilsa now, they'd have maybe thirty good years together. If she stuck with her own plan, they'd both be all but immortal once she took Ilsa to Pulsus. Ilsa wanted to do something special with her life, and Foster could give her that. She'd even be able to tell Ilsa that she'd played a vital part in ridding the world of cancer.

For now though, she had to play along. "What about Chernick and the journals?"

"We take the five we have and give them to scientists in England. We can use them as a bargaining tool to get into the country. Or maybe America; I've always wanted to see Hollywood. We can't do any more for Bina. There's a rumor that Mengele is visiting the camp soon. They say he's coming for her because of how she lived before she was arrested. So how much more research could she do?"

Ilsa had obviously spent a lot of time thinking about it, and Foster mentally kicked herself for sowing the initial seed in her head. *No, I'm thinking about this all wrong.* If Foster played this right, when she returned after the mission, Ilsa would have her bags packed and be ready to go. "Are you sure that's what you want?"

"I'm positive. And I'm positive I want you to do it with me. I love you, Sieglinde. I started to fall the moment I saw you, and you sealed it when we had sex for the first time."

Her eyes twinkled mischievously, dragging Foster into her enthusiasm and emotions. "Then I guess we'd better start making plans."

Ilsa grinned widely and embraced Foster. "Is that a yes? That's a yes, isn't it? Oh, I'm so excited, Sigi. I can't wait to get out of here and start anew."

Foster pulled Ilsa into her lap and kissed her hard. She looked so beautiful and full of verve that it made Foster even more determined to pull this off. She needed to be inside Ilsa, to be all over her. She wanted to possess and be possessed by her. In the time they'd been together, Ilsa had made her see that she could be happy without Landry. Foster was still in love with Landry too, and she somehow needed to rid herself of those feelings, but Ilsa gave her the strength to do that. Ilsa was so completely different from Landry that Foster almost couldn't believe what she felt for her.

Foster checked the wall clock. "I have to make love to you." It was after eight already, and Landry's plan would be in motion at ten thirty. Foster had to be at the rendezvous point by midnight, and she was traveling by foot. But she also had to finish up her plan to keep Ilsa safe. That only gave them two more hours together before Foster had to leave her behind. But not for long. Foster thought about her plan, the human casualty of which was already in the woods wrapped in garbage sacks and recently invented duct tape.

"So take me to bed."

Ilsa's words were like gasoline on the smoldering fire of Foster's need. She slipped one arm beneath Ilsa's knees and stood.

"Your strength does *so* impress me," Ilsa whispered in Foster's ear.

"Then this will really impress you." Foster walked up the staircase with Ilsa in her arms. This was goodbye sex for Foster, but Ilsa had no idea. If everything went well, in Ilsa's reality, she'd only be without Foster for an hour. But for Foster, this encounter would have to sustain her for months, possibly longer.

Foster gently released Ilsa to a standing position by the side of the bed. She slowly undid the front buttons of Ilsa's dress from top to bottom and slid it from her shoulders, then she stepped back and admired the view before quickly taking off her own clothes and discarding them to the floor. "You are so undeniably beautiful."

Ilsa blushed and looked away. "No one's ever called me beautiful before."

"Then no one's ever really seen you before."

Ilsa lay down on the bed, and Foster joined her, eager to get as much of her as possible before she had to leave. "I love you, Ilsa Blumstein," she whispered before she lowered her mouth onto Ilsa's swollen clit.

One bliss-filled hour later, Foster took one final look at Ilsa after she'd slipped into a satisfied post-orgasmic sleep. Foster wanted to be sure she'd memorized every contour and every freckle. She had a black-and-white photo of the two of them together, but Foster wanted to remember Ilsa in bright, vibrant colors.

Foster kissed her soft lips one last time before grabbing the clothes she'd tossed aside. She quietly made her way downstairs to dress and retrieve Chernick's journals, then she grabbed the bag of clothes she'd left at the foot of the basement steps and set off to place the body before meeting up with Griffin and the doc at the agreed rendezvous point. She jogged to the place she'd left the woman covered with forest debris and was relieved to find it still there. It wasn't the first time Foster had strangled someone. It wouldn't be the last. But it was the first time she'd killed for her own purposes. Not for a mission, or to maintain her cover, but so she could protect Ilsa. Foster pushed away the unwanted guilt and hefted the body over her shoulder to begin the half-mile trek through the trees to the roadside.

Five minutes later, Foster dropped the body onto the ground. She sliced through the tape and plastic, before pulling off her shirt and putting it on the body. Foster grabbed a new shirt from her backpack and put it on. Her boots and the rest of her clothes followed, and she was glad she'd taken the time to tie the limbs down and together. She didn't want the body's cadaveric spasms to shoot an arm in the air before rigor mortis began to set in.

By the time she'd finished dressing the corpse, which was enough like her to make the situation even more surreal, Foster was sweating hard. She stuffed the plastic and tape into her backpack and shoved her papers and ID into the shirt pocket. She made the short trip to the roadside for one of the rocks that lined the crude walkway and picked one up without putting too much thought into it.

This'll be the hard part. Strangling someone was relatively easy. It was like putting someone to sleep, permanently. But picking up a twenty-pound rock and dropping it onto someone's face was a different prospect. Foster straddled the body, took a deep breath, and raised the rock over her head. She was about to drop it when she considered splatter. The impact from this height would explode the skull, and flesh and blood would fly everywhere, including all over Foster's clean trousers. She knelt down, one knee on each side of the corpse, and pulled the plastic from her backpack to cover her clothes. Then she held the rock at chest height, closed her eyes and saw Ilsa. *Protecting her is why I've got to do this.* The thought gave her fortitude, and she slammed the rock down. The crunching and cracking of bone sounded desperately loud in the still of the night, and Foster paused to look around. The only sound was the gentle deep two-tone hooting of an eagle owl.

Foster didn't look beneath the rock as she lifted it and brought it down on the corpse's head three more times. Sticky moisture covered her fingers, and she was glad it wasn't warm, so it didn't feel quite as real. She remembered the woman bragging about her work with Hitler in Berghof. She wasn't an innocent; she fully supported the genocide of people different from her. *Think of Ilsa.* She hauled up the rock and peered at the face, pulverized beyond recognition. Smashed teeth were embedded in parts of the face they shouldn't be, and Foster couldn't even see where the eyes were. She wiped her bloodied hands on the body's shirt and stood. Everything got a little woozy, and her vision blurred. She stumbled backward, grateful for the solidity of a tree behind her. *Take a breath. I had to do it.*

Foster steadied herself and did one last check of the scene to make sure the setup was perfect. Satisfied the body she'd left would serve its purpose and protect Ilsa from any undue SS attention, Foster continued through the woods to the rendezvous point. She allowed herself one last thought of Ilsa and how soft and peaceful she looked asleep. Ilsa would be safe until Foster could return. And her love had fueled Foster's motivation to take control of Pulsus.

CHAPTER TWENTY-EIGHT

LANDRY LAY FULLY CLOTHED in the bunk she shared with three other prisoners and waited. She gripped the pocket watch Foster had hidden in her tool belt earlier that day. She'd had an unexpected moment of melancholy when she realized it belonged to the British spy she'd come into the camp with. The inscription on the rear of the black copper casing read "Yeshuat Hashem k'heref ayin." Landry had no time for faith or religion, and this quote likened the salvation of God to the blink of an eye, but she liked the sentiment that no matter how dire the situation, redemption or rescue could be in the next moment; it encouraged her to always have hope.

Landry had always loved pocket watches. Her father had a small collection from his travels, which she treasured but never used. *You have no idea who, or what, your father really was.* Her mom's words nestled in her mind like an infected splinter in her finger, and she resolved to challenge her when she got home. She couldn't just say something like that and expect Landry to accept it without question. There'd been a depth of anger and bitterness Landry had never seen in her mother before, and Landry had to know where that was coming from.

She stared at the second hand on its never-ending circular journey around the intricate clock face and decided she'd keep the watch. Usually, she worked hard to ensure missions didn't stay with her, but this one was different. It wasn't the end result that was making her feel this way, though being part of a team that purged the world of cancer was going to feel damn good. It was about having been part of a history that should never be forgotten, and she wanted it to live and breathe inside her. She wanted it to remind her not only of how appallingly the human race could behave when given half a chance, but also of how resilient the human spirit could be.

Ten fifteen p.m. Time to roll. Landry slipped out of her bunk and headed to the toilets at the end of the block, muttering something about a pain in her stomach. She was confident her bunkmates wouldn't raise the alarm when she didn't return, and all she could do was hope they wouldn't be punished when her absence was discovered. The notion that the mission was just the doctor and not the rest of these women made her think again of Foster's idea about making bigger incisions in the past. Maybe she was right, and Pulsus *should* be working toward more impactful outcomes.

Landry propped the two-foot square window open with a torn off piece of her dress and climbed out to drop silently onto the ground six feet below. She stayed close to the block wall, quietly making her way along the grim "shooting alley" to the medical block where she'd have five minutes to explain the plan to Chernick before Griffin arrived with Simson. There were no watchtowers or gun emplacements, because the Nazis figured the women were no threat.

Once she was safely at the medical block, Landry removed the glazing panel of the window she'd deliberately not fixed in properly and climbed through the wooden opening. As she slid down the wall, her dress snagged on the window fastening and tore all the way to her ass. *I fucking hate dresses.*

"Truda, what are you doing here? You'll get us both shot." Chernick's eyes glowed in the dim lamplight, fear flashing through the darkness.

Landry took Chernick by the shoulders, guided her to the nearest chair, and gently pressed her into it. "You need to listen to me." She pulled out her pocket watch and checked the time. "In approximately eight minutes, the man you know as SS Officer Christoph Mahler will come in here, propping up the guard you think of as Johanna Thalberg. He'll leave her here and go to get a

Kübelwagen, which he'll tell the gate guards he needs so he can take Thalberg to the hospital."

"What are you—"

Landry pressed her finger firmly to Chernick's lips. "Quiet and listen. When they get here, you and Thalberg will exchange clothes, and you'll be the one Mahler takes in the Kübel out of the camp. Are with me so far?"

Chernick shook her head vigorously. "You're talking about an escape. Are you out of your mind? It'll never work."

"It'll work. We've done this plenty of times before."

"Done what? Broken out of Nazi concentration camps?"

"All sorts of prisons," Landry whispered. "That's not important right now. What's important is that you understand the plan and are ready to go."

"Who are you...really?"

Landry glanced at the watch again. "We're US Special Forces."

Chernick would only discover Landry's lie in about a decade, when the Green Berets were really introduced in the States. Right now, it was the easiest explanation.

"We're going to get you out of here. Mahler and Thalberg are actually Griffin and Simson, and my name's Donovan. Okay?" Landry allowed Chernick a moment to absorb the information.

Chernick gasped and grabbed a handful of Landry's dress. "My research—Ilsa and the other Thalberg have my journals. Are they in on this?"

Landry tilted her head slightly. "Sieglinde is, but Ilsa has no idea. They're not sisters, and Sieglinde is really called Foster. She'll meet you at the rendezvous point, and she'll have your journals with her."

Chernick suddenly looked distracted and turned away. Landry followed the direction of her gaze to see the five women still strapped in place on the metal tables. She gently brought Chernick back around to face her. "We can't save them, and neither can you. You're going to save millions, possibly billions of lives. We need to get you out of here."

"The greater good?"

Landry nodded. "Exactly. You're an important woman, Bina—so important, the US government has sent my team to rescue you and take you to New York so you can continue your research there." She could see Chernick was torn between her current duties and the thought of what her research might be able to achieve. "The journal you're working in right now, is it here?"

"Yes, I've just finished making an entry."

Landry smiled. "Good timing then."

The main door swung open, and Griffin walked in with Simson draped around his shoulder. She looked up and grinned. "Get your clothes off, Doc."

Griffin opened a filing cabinet, pulled out a sack from behind the files, and threw it to Simson before waving his radio and walking through to the back room to report Simson's life-threatening illness.

Simson took out a set of clothes before passing the bag to Landry. "I don't expect a kiss for that. Getting you out of a dress and back into trousers will be payment enough. Your calves are way too muscular to pull off that look without six-inch heels and a wig. Even then you might end up looking like a drag queen."

Chernick looked puzzled as they exchanged clothes.

"Fair point, Simson. Do you speak English, Bina?" Landry asked, still in German.

"Not enough to understand when someone speaks that fast." She seemed reluctant to admit it.

"Then we'll stick to German when it's important, but the rest of the time, we'll speak English so you can start improving yours. By the time we get to New York, you'll be talking like a native."

Chernick nodded, and as she pulled on Simson's sweater vest, Landry was once again struck by how skinny she'd become compared to her original photos. It must've come across on her face, because Chernick met her gaze and indicated her own body.

"I'm looking forward to eating a few of your famous hamburgers and hotdogs."

Landry laughed, slightly embarrassed at being so obvious. "Wait until you taste a Philly cheesesteak." She checked the pocket watch again and nodded at Griffin. "Griff will take you to the jeep and cover most of you with a blanket. He's already raised the alarm, so they're expecting you both at the gate. Don't panic if they look in on you, just groan and cough—possible communicable diseases usually deter more thorough inspections of a vehicle."

"I hope so. I don't want to end up like Katharina."

"We've got this. Don't worry." She grasped Chernick by the shoulders. "Go."

Griffin took her arm to lead her away, but she spun around suddenly and pointed to her desk. "My journal."

Griffin picked up the leather book and stuffed it down the back of his trousers.

"See you soon," Landry said and watched as they got into the Type 82 and drove away. The gates opened moments later, and the lights dimmed as they made their escape. She fastened her thick belt around the slightly baggy trousers and tugged her shirt out of the waistband a little. "Let's get the fuck out of this death camp."

"Copy that, Donovan."

Simson grabbed the sack containing some blankets, and Landry led the way to the exit window. They climbed out and made their way toward the back wall and electric perimeter.

"You first, Simson."

Simson frowned. "Are you sure?"

"I don't leave any of my team behind, even when they've been assholes." Landry looked into the darkness. "I want to make sure I'm the last one to leave this place."

Simson inclined her head. "You're the extractor," she said before she quickly turned and scaled the two-meter-high wall with exceptional agility, considering her bulk.

Landry pitched the bag to her, and Simson covered a good section of the electric wire with the blankets.

"See you on the other side," Simson said then dropped out of view.

Landry turned to take one last look at the camp, and her face met with the handle end of a whip. She dropped to the ground, and a boot connected with the pit of her stomach, sending her slamming against the wall. She managed to identify the distinctive features of Erika Vogt in the moonlight before her boot smashed across Landry's face, and her head connected with the concrete wall. Black edges appeared around her vision, closing in and threatening her consciousness. She felt Vogt's boot several more times in her gut as she battled with her own body to stay awake.

Vogt crouched down, put her knee on Landry's chest, and fixed one hand around her throat. "Where do you think you're going, Stark?" She punched Landry hard. "I heard the alarm raise for my friend, Thalberg, so I came to visit the doctor to see what had happened."

Another strike, and Landry tasted her own blood.

"Imagine my surprise when I find there's no sign of the doctor in the medical block, and I see two shadows dashing across the camp."

She tightened her grip, and Landry grabbed at Vogt's hand to loosen it so she could breathe. Vogt lifted her knee slightly before slamming it back down onto Landry's chest, knocking the air from her lungs.

"You don't get to leave here, Stark. Not until I've finished with you."

Landry summoned her strength from the memories of what Vogt had done to the thousands of women before her. She thrust her hips and swung her legs into the air, scissoring Vogt's neck between them. Landry pulled her backward, and Vogt lost her grip on Landry's throat as she fell to the ground. Landry sat up and delivered three solid punches to Vogt's gut, then squeezed her thighs tighter around Vogt's throat. Vogt struggled and thrashed, her hands clawing at Landry as the breath escaped her. It took ten seconds to fall unconscious from being strangled, and only a few extra minutes were required to make that lack of consciousness permanent.

"Please..." Vogt tapped Landry's leg repeatedly.

Landry clenched her teeth. Vogt wasn't the mission. If she killed her, it wouldn't be collateral damage, it'd be murder. But Landry had nothing to tie her up with. Vogt wasn't wearing a belt, and if Landry parted with hers, her trousers would follow.

She looked into Vogt's eyes as she began to lose the fight for her consciousness, and they began to close. *What am I looking for?* The woman had proven time and again that she was void of compassion or humanity. She looked up to the wall Simson had scaled, but she was nowhere to be seen. Landry took a deep breath, emptied the emotion from the situation, and focused on the options. If she left Vogt alive, she would regain consciousness in less time than it took Landry to escape. Vogt would raise the alarm, and the mission would be compromised. There'd be no way she and Simson could get to the rendezvous point. Foster and Griffin could still succeed in getting Chernick to New York, but without the PRU, they'd be stuck in 1942 and unable to jump home.

If she killed Vogt, Landry could conceal the body against the wall, and she wouldn't be found until the morning. Hell, they might even think she was part of the escape until they discovered her.

Vogt's grip on Landry's legs softened, and she stopped resisting.

It's for the good of the mission.

Decision made.

Landry raised her left leg, leaving her foot dug into the ground. She slammed both legs down, twisting her right one across and beyond the left, snapping Vogt's neck. She got up and pushed Vogt away from her.

"What the hell is going on?" Simson whispered loudly.

Landry looked up to see her peering over the electric fence. "Slight complication. I'll be with you in two minutes." Landry pulled

Vogt's body out of sight and laid some loose branches over her before scrambling up the wall. She carefully crawled over the electric fence then pulled the blankets with her as she dropped to the ground on the other side.

"What happened?" Simson grabbed the blankets and quickly concealed them in forest debris.

"Vogt blindsided me. Took me a minute to put her down."

"Couldn't happen soon enough. You've done the world a favor."

Landry nodded, then took another look at her pocket watch. "We've got three clicks to cover, and this terrain is hilly. Let's hit it."

CHAPTER TWENTY-NINE

Rendezvous Point, Neustrelitz

"Good to have the team back together," Foster said.

"And even better to be out of a dress." Landry grabbed Foster's hand and pulled her in for a tight bro hug. "I've missed you. Are you doing okay?"

"Not now, Landry. Let's talk later."

Landry tilted her head and looked at Chernick. "How are you, Doc?"

"Better than your face, it seems. Let me look at that."

She stopped Chernick's hand mid-air and winced slightly. "My face is fine."

"Yeah, Doc, a bit of swelling should improve it," Simson said.

She nudged Griffin, and he laughed briefly before he met Landry's glare.

"She can get away with that because we've been working together for a while," Landry said. "You should keep your mouth shut."

"And what about your ribs?" Chernick pointed to Landry's torso. "You're bleeding."

Landry looked down. When she and Simson were racing through the hilly woods, she'd felt nothing, but now she could see the left side of her shirt was wet with ruby red blood. She lifted her shirt to discover a compound fracture in one of her lower ribs.

Chernick pressed her fingers to the area below, and Landry took a sharp intake of breath. "What's the point of having all that muscle if it doesn't protect what's underneath? There's severe bruising here too. What happened?"

"Vogt delayed my exit from the camp."

Chernick leaned back on the hood of the bucket wagon, and the color drained from her skin in seconds. Landry let her shirt fall back into place.

"That woman...is pure evil," Chernick said, her voice trembling. "She's responsible for the deaths of so many of my friends."

Landry placed her hand on the doc's shoulder. "She won't be hurting anyone else."

Chernick looked up, relief and gratitude apparent in her expression. "She is dead?"

Landry looked at Foster and saw something she couldn't define. "Yes. She's dead."

Chernick turned to Foster. "And what of Ilsa? Won't your disappearance mean trouble for her? Why didn't you bring her out with you? She should not stay at such a place. She's too soft for it."

Foster smiled, and Landry waited for an explanation for her apparent good humor. Ilsa was an angle she had no choice but to leave to chance.

"They won't touch Ilsa," Foster said and smiled. "She's got nothing to worry about."

"Did you get her out?" Chernick asked.

The doc clearly wasn't satisfied with Foster's answer, and neither was Landry, but they had to get on the road and didn't have time for lengthy discussions. "We've got a six-hour head start before the morning head count, and Bremen is nearly three hundred miles away with the detour for our US papers." *And the PRU*. "With any luck, we can be in the air before they even figure out we're missing." She pointed to the bucket wagon. "Load up."

"I need to treat your ribs." Chernick stood directly in front of Landry.

Landry patted Chernick's back and gently guided her to the vehicle. "Then you can do it while we drive. Griffin, take the first hundred miles. Simson, ride shotgun. Foster, you're going to have to squeeze in the luggage rack."

They all climbed onboard, and Griffin fired up the engine. After Chernick had managed to patch Landry up as best she could on the move and in the dark, along bumpy, windy roads, Landry turned to Foster. "Tell me more about Ilsa. How did you manage to protect her?" She wished the moon would cast a better light inside the moving vehicle so she could see Foster's face.

"I took care of it." Foster glanced at her briefly. "I don't have to run my every action by you. I made a judgment call, and I'm happy with it."

"If you don't tell me, you'll end up telling it in debrief when we get home." Landry deliberately didn't use any jump terminology while the doc was so close and could overhear them. As far as Chernick was concerned, the team was of this time. She had no reason to suspect anything else, and it was imperative they kept it that way.

Foster sighed loudly. "I had to do something for her, Landry. We shared a villa, and some people knew we were sharing more than that. She would've been the first person they dragged in to interrogate once they discovered the escape involved me and Simson."

"So what *did* you do?"

"I went to Berlin and found a Nazi woman with a similar build to me. I killed her, brought her back to Fürstenberg, and left the body, dressed in my clothes and with my papers in her shirt, by the roadside a half-mile from the camp."

"Fuck, Foster, what about the possible consequences of that?" She'd need more details when they were on the plane and out of earshot, so she could get a handle on exactly what Foster had done. "Unless she was a dead ringer, they'll figure out it wasn't you, and Ilsa will still be in danger."

"No, they won't, not after the way I left her."

Foster looked out the window, and Landry knew she'd done something she wasn't comfortable with. "Explain," Landry said.

Foster shrugged. "There was no face left to recognize."

Chernick put her hand to her mouth and gasped.

"Jesus, Foster. That was some fucking risk. What if you were arrested in Berlin? What if they found the body before we escaped? Did you think about any of those eventualities?"

Foster smashed her hand against the side of the truck. "Damn it, Landry, I loved her. But you don't know a single fucking thing about love, do you?"

Landry didn't respond. Foster was right. She didn't know anything about it, and she didn't try to. She'd never let anyone in, and she really had no intention to. Would she let Jade in sometime in the future? She shoved that aside for now; this wasn't about her. Landry had tried to convince Foster she needed something other than Pulsus, a normal life outside of the missions, but she'd applied that advice in the wrong place *and* the wrong time. Ilsa was clearly a lovely woman, so normal and caring, so massively different from her soldier buddies. It was little wonder that, as vulnerable as Foster was right now, she'd fallen for Ilsa while she was here. Landry couldn't drop the nagging thoughts that she'd failed Foster. How could she lecture Foster when it was Landry's fault that she hadn't protected her from this mission in the first place?

"None of us have the time for love, Foster," Simson yelled from the front.

Foster lightly scoffed. "I had nothing but time."

Landry stayed silent and focused on the darkness of the road before them, as Foster's words echoed in her head. Time worked with them and against them on missions, just as it did in real life. *Real life.* Was she even letting herself have one of those? Or was she just playing at it with no real commitment? She resolved to spend more time with Jade, and her little adopted family, to figure that out. *If the girls are even there.* Cait's wife would live because of this mission, and it was possible that everything could be different when she returned to her San Francisco haven. And what if there was some history in Jade's family that might mean she wasn't born because of the changes they'd made? Suddenly, this time-travel shit seemed like more of a head fuck than it usually did. As the road lay stretched ahead of them, Landry had one thought about the future from which she couldn't escape—she had to have Jade in hers.

CHAPTER THIRTY

July 8, 1942

AFTER THE DETOUR TO the Tollensesee for Landry to collect the PRU and their US papers, Foster took over the driving duty from Griffin. She needed something to focus on other than the heavy silence between her and Landry. Declaring her love for Ilsa to everyone in the truck hadn't been super high on her agenda, and she regretted the words the moment they left her mouth. Blowing up in front of a rookie like Griffin was unprofessional and weak too. She needed him to keep his mouth shut in the debrief, so she asked him to ride shotgun when she took the truck keys.

"What's your take on the first part of the mission? Did you enjoy it?" Foster whispered so that Chernick didn't hear them over the road and engine noise.

"'Enjoy' definitely isn't the right word. Having to fuck a woman is hard enough, but Vogt was harder than shooting heroin for the first time, *and* it never got any easier. And then all the other horrors..." He shook his head. "No. I didn't enjoy it. I hope it was worth it."

Foster laughed quietly. "Yeah, we have to do some crazy shit."

"How many missions have you completed?"

Foster inclined her head and ticked them off in her mind. "This one's unlucky thirteen, if you believe in that kind of shit." Or maybe, because she'd found Ilsa, this was *lucky* thirteen.

"Jesus—in three years?" Griffin asked. "How many years have you lived in those missions?"

"This makes it ninety-five." She could tell him exactly how many years, months, and days she'd spent in other pasts if anyone cared to ask. And she was tired of reliving every minute of them all.

He grinned. "You're looking good for your age. You don't look a day over fifty."

Foster laughed. Griffin was a good guy and working with him had been smooth and easy; her report on his performance would be glowing. Maybe he'd be interested in her version of Pulsus too. Or maybe he'd be a casualty who fell by the wayside. She needed allies, and if anyone would be prepared to join her coup, it'd be an ex-CIA agent. "Watch it, grunt, or I'll kick you out of this truck right now and leave you here to play with Nazi girls for another three years."

"God, no. I'll need some time with my man when we get home," Griffin practically shouted.

Chernick leaned forward. "You're a homosexual and in the army?"

Foster and Griffin exchanged a knowing look. Chernick was operating in a time where homosexuality was an offense punishable by death. Although Hitler wasn't the only one who had that idea, and even in 2076, there were still countries enforcing that penalty. *Those* would be good missions for Pulsus too.

Griffin half turned to Chernick and smiled. "America is a very different place to Germany, Doc."

"That's wonderful to hear," Chernick said before relaxing back into her own seat.

"I guess she doesn't have to know it'll be another seventy years before that's actually true in our military services," she whispered.

Griffin shrugged. "What's regeneration like?" he asked quietly. "It must be strange to keep getting older and then have it reversed. All the years you've lived must make you feel like a vampire."

Foster chuckled "I've never really thought of it *that* way. At least we don't have to drink blood..." She shook her head. "It's a little painful, even with the anesthetic. You can't be fully dosed up or it interferes with the cell reversal process."

"What's the worst injury you've had fixed? That shit amazes

me."

"I've been lucky and have always come back in one piece. You should talk to Landry if you want gruesome stories." She shuddered at the instant image of Landry's broken body in Cartagena. "She came back from our last mission with a punctured lung, three cracked ribs, and a broken nose. It was a lot worse than this time. But they still can't fix malignant cells. Once the body goes bad," she thumbed over her shoulder toward the doc, "like cancer, they can't save you." *And they can do fuck all for your mind too.*

Griffin turned again to look at Chernick and sighed deeply. "It's really something to know that I kind of helped cure cancer."

"Which should make it easier to reconcile when you have to do things like execute a British spy." Foster wanted to gauge his reaction to doing the more unsavory parts of their work. If he was comfortable with it, her plan would be a harder sell.

But Griffin didn't respond immediately and shifted in his seat, then he flicked off some imaginary dirt from his jacket. "I guess that'll be something for me to discuss with Castillo's team."

"Anything else you'll be mentioning?" It was time to stop pussyfooting around and find out if Griffin was an ally or a snitch.

"If you're worried about me saying anything about the Blumstein situation, don't. I had enough backbiting, with agents trying to crawl over the dead bodies of other agents to advance their career in the CIA. I'm just a grunt here, and I like it that way. I got your back. You need to concentrate on the extractor." He put his hand on her shoulder and squeezed. "But I hear you two go way back, so that shouldn't be a problem, huh?"

"Right." Foster eyed the rearview mirror to glance at Landry and met her gaze. That'd be a conversation for the long flight to New York. And she'd have to play it perfectly or Landry would never agree to her Pulsus plan.

She refocused on the road after checking the time. Ilsa wouldn't wake until mid-morning because of the sleeping pills Foster had laced her wine with. She couldn't risk her raising the alarm when

Foster didn't come back after her regular late-night walk. Ilsa would grieve for her and be angry at whoever she suspected of killing her... No one had ever felt that strongly, that protective of her before—maybe not even Landry—but if everything went according to plan, Foster would return to Ilsa's arms only an hour after she left last night. Ilsa would wake and look at Foster as if it was just another normal morning. Foster, though, would take the time to drink Ilsa in all over again, because she wouldn't have seen or touched her for months.

She'd finally found someone she could imagine spending her life with, someone who wanted to spend their life with her. But to make it happen, Foster had to turn her own life—and everyone else's she knew—upside down.

CHAPTER THIRTY-ONE

GRIFFIN SECURED MALE SS uniforms for Foster and Simson and a Luftwaffe flight uniform for Landry, so the four of them could enter the Focke-Wulf aircraft plant and "borrow" an FW 200 Condor. Chernick remained in her slightly oversized guard uniform, ready to act as their accompanying physician. They were counting on taking advantage of the chaos of the recent RAF thousand-bomber raid that had taken place just over a week prior to their arrival. Under the guise that the constant targeting was causing Hitler to consider shifting aircraft production to East Germany and Poland, Griffin would provide the order to fly the plane to Warsaw to see if the evacuation of the plant was feasible.

"You all make very handsome men," Chernick said as they got ready a few miles from the base.

"And convincing, yes?" Landry asked.

"Oh, yes, Donovan." Chernick nodded with enthusiasm. "You all look the part."

They climbed back into the bucket wagon and drove to the base entrance. The sight of the trio in their SS uniforms elicited the prescribed response of terror and fear in the regular soldiers guarding the base entry, and they were all quick to display their Heil Hitler salutes.

Griffin introduced them all before ordering the cadet to take them to the officer in charge. His clipped tones were disturbingly menacing, and Landry almost expected the soldier to pee a little when faced by the three SS officers in the truck with her and Chernick.

"Yes, sir, follow me."

He told the other guard where he was going, before mounting a BMW R75 motorbike and heading into the camp. Foster drove close behind.

Chernick groaned loudly. "This is terrifying."

"I know, Doc," Landry said. "Just try to stay calm. Stay in the wagon and don't speak unless one of them asks you a direct question. That shouldn't happen unless they suspect something— it'd be a blunt challenge to their authority." Landry motioned to their SS triumvirate. "We've done our homework, so you can relax. This plan will work, and we'll soon be on that plane and on our way to New York to your new life."

Foster followed the bike through to the main hangar. The cadet got off and came back to the truck to open the doors for them all to climb out. He waited while they straightened their uniforms and carefully placed their hats, then motioned for them to follow him again. Chernick remained in the truck.

"Oberleutnant Barth, this is Oberführer Eichman, Sturmbahnführers Seiler and Faber, and Major Adler."

Their intel was correct, and each one of them outranked Barth, which should make this easier.

He dutifully saluted each of them. "What can I do for you, officers? I was not expecting such esteemed visitors."

Griffin handed him the folded papers lovingly crafted by the reproduction team at Pulsus. "These are orders from Major General Conrad Hamfeld of Luftkreis III, Berlin. We're here to take possession of a FW-200, fully fueled and battle-ready."

Barth opened the papers, which were an exact replica of orders he would receive in ten months' time. He quickly scanned the details before folding them to hand back to Griffin. "I will have one ready to go in three hours. Perhaps you might like to travel back into town for lunch, or would you prefer to wait here in the officers' mess?"

"Major Adler will stay here and oversee preparations," Griffin said, "but a local lunch for us would be good. Do you have a recommendation?"

"Absolutely. The Bremer Ratskeller by the market has a five-hundred-year history and boasts the oldest wine cellar in Germany. I can send a cadet ahead to book you a prioelken for a little more privacy."

Griffin nodded. "That would be perfect, Oberleutnant."

"Of course, anything for our fine SS officers." He saluted again and ordered the cadet on the motorbike to do as he'd promised. "Enjoy your meals. I will see you in a few hours." He waited until they'd left before he turned to Landry. "Would you like to follow me, Major Adler?"

She nodded and followed Barth. Toward the far end of the hangar stood a pristine FW-200 Condor, an all metal, four-engine monoplane. Once the war had started, the plane was prepared for military service, with front, aft, and dorsal gun positions added. Landry had been briefed about the history of this plane and had neglected to share with the rest of her team that the Condor tended to break up on landing because of the hurried amendments. It was a problem they never really solved. Pulsus was taking a calculated risk, but Landry and her co-pilot, Foster, were excellent in the air. They'd landed planes in several extreme situations, so Landry wasn't worried. Foster had expressed concern that Pulsus was too quick to risk their lives, but as long as they dumped all but their necessary fuel prior to landing, Landry was sure they'd be fine. She tried to ignore the niggling fact that Foster was right about Pulsus' cavalier attitude with the lives of their operatives and extractors.

She grabbed a nearby flight ladder and pushed it up to the cockpit, while Barth instructed several of his staff to prepare the aircraft. She pulled out her pocket watch and flipped it over to read the inscription again. They needed hope and a shit-ton of luck to pull off this part of the mission.

Landry pulled out the Luger PO8 pistol from her hip holster and quickly checked it over. She was used to operating solo on missions, but with so many of the enemy around her, a sense of unease had crept in that she couldn't quite dismiss. She moved through the aircraft to check that everything was where it should be and then climbed the ladders to the front and aft gun positions, where Griffin and Simson would spend the majority of the twenty-five-hour journey to US soil, just in case. Their flight plan took them along the path of least resistance, given the capabilities of the aircraft, and avoided all dangerous airspace, aside from during their approach to New York. The papers they had would hold up to inspection though, and Nelson and Williams, the operatives who had been sent back to 1935 to infiltrate the FBI, would smooth their way through the military hoopla to place Chernick in a university for five years before relocating her to the Brookhaven Research facility on Long Island in 1947. A different extractor would come back to retrieve them once Chernick had a research team of her own in place, and it was clear her work had been successful.

Landry yawned, the jaw-breaking kind that only comes from extreme exhaustion. She checked her pocket watch again; she had another two and a half hours to wait, so she headed back to the cockpit and quickly changed into a flight suit before settling into her chair. She took her Luger from its holster and placed it in the well to her left, keeping her hand on it for easy access. Then she closed her eyes and drifted into a much-needed sleep.

CHAPTER THIRTY-TWO

FOSTER SHOOK LANDRY'S SHOULDER gently. Her holster was empty, and her left hand was out of sight. Foster knew she'd have a tight grip on her pistol, even when sound asleep, and she didn't want her face blown off this close to the end of the mission. She didn't want her face blown off at all. "Major Adler." She reached across Landry and pushed down on her left bicep to keep her gun in place. "Everyone's on the plane and ready to fly to Warsaw."

Landry jumped, and her eyes flicked open. "Seiler. It's time? All on board and accounted for?"

"Yes, Major Adler, everyone's here." Foster grabbed their leather flight helmets and comms and tossed one to Landry before pulling hers on. "We're ready to complete the mission. Time for you to take us home."

Foster peered out the cockpit window and signaled to Barth to take away the chocks, before dropping into her co-pilot seat and fixing her harness. Landry hit the brake and locked the tail, then selected and started the engines in order. Foster put the flaps into position and opened the cowlings.

"Prop pitch to full," Landry said.

Foster nodded, and Landry hit the brake again before easing the throttle up to full takeoff speed. The nose inclined until all they could see was sky. Landry confirmed all was well with the ground crew, and Foster raised the wheels.

They were at cruising altitude before Landry pulled off her headset. "So you love her?"

Foster grimaced. She was hoping they'd put a few hundred miles behind them before this conversation. "Honestly, I don't know. I lived with Ilsa for nearly two years, and I slept with her for eighteen months. When you spend so long on missions, sometimes you have to allow yourself to feel things to get through them in one piece, and she made me feel something different. You don't know what it's like to spend so much time being someone else, acting in ways we swore allegiance to the flag not to." Foster unclipped her harness and turned to Landry. "You're always talking about having a normal life outside of Pulsus, and my time with Ilsa, away from the camp, felt like that. And I liked it. I think I finally get what you've been yammering on about for the past three years. I know you haven't been talking about love, but I couldn't stop it. That relationship developed for the good of the mission, and now the mission's almost over." She didn't want to lie to Landry, but she couldn't reveal everything here when it could be overheard by the others.

"You risked everything, Foster. Your life, the mission, *and* the doc. Hell, you put Ilsa's life above the lives of billions of people the world over for centuries to come."

Foster slammed her hand against the cockpit window. "Don't you think I know that? We all make mistakes on a mission, Landry... Your last one nearly cost you your life."

"That's a low blow."

"Is it?" Foster glared at her. "Seems to me like it's exactly the same thing. You felt compassion for someone, and that same person nearly killed you. I felt love for Ilsa and had to kill *for* her."

There was a small cough before Chernick appeared in the cockpit. "I brought you some cheese and biscuits, Donovan. I thought you'd be hungry." She placed a folded-up napkin of food on the floor between the two pilot seats. "And I need to check your rib dressing to make sure the wound hasn't become infected."

Landry sighed deeply and picked up the food. "Thanks, Doc." She unzipped her flight suit and pulled up her tank top.

Chernick leaned over and slowly removed the wet bandage. "It looks fine from this angle, but I need to put a clean dressing on it. I found a first aid kit back here." She brandished the box in the air. "It will only take a few moments."

Landry unclipped her harness and climbed out of her seat. "You take your doctoring very seriously. It's just a broken rib."

Landry was all charm, even for Chernick. Did she ever turn it off to have a normal conversation with anyone other than Foster?

"It's the least I can do since you saved my life…and having come this far, I'm sure I don't want to die in a plane crash because one of the pilots passed out from septicemia."

Foster laughed. "The doc has a point, Landry."

"Landry. That's unusual." Chernick smiled softly. "Is that your first name?"

Foster groaned quietly. The doc should just get down on the floor and kiss Landry's feet.

"Yeah, it is. You like it?"

Being grilled by Landry was better than listening to Chernick hit on her. What did she think? That they'd be able to hook up once they hit New York? "Fix her up quick, Doc. I need her back in the chair."

Chernick did as instructed and retreated from the cockpit area.

A few minutes later, Landry retook her seat, grunting in obvious pain, but her injuries were far less intense than the ones she'd sustained in the last mission. That was something, at least. She munched on the food Chernick had delivered.

"Nothing like being served tasteless shit for six weeks to make you appreciate real food," Landry said.

Foster nudged her arm. "I need to know you're going to cover for me in the debrief. I can't be suspended from action; I'll go crazy."

"Isn't that the problem?" Landry glanced at her. "I feel like I should've done something before we even came on this mission. I'm not sure you were fit for duty."

Foster smashed her fist onto the yoke. "Fuck that, and fuck you. You can't believe that."

"You told me you were struggling, and I let you come to one of the most heinous times in the history of the world. You might have made the bad decision with Ilsa, but you shouldn't have even been here to make that decision. I failed you." She shifted like she couldn't get comfortable and ate the last of the cheese.

"Jesus, Landry, I think you've been spending too much time with the head shrinks. Or maybe the mainland is making you soft. I didn't tell you I was having issues so you could cut me from the team. I told you so you could help me with them when we get back." *And then help change the way Pulsus works.* This wasn't the way this conversation was supposed to be going.

Simson was the next interloper in the cockpit. "You might want to keep it down. The doc is getting jumpy. She's a clever woman, but I'm not sure how she'll react if she finds out we're time travelers. You don't want to be responsible for sending the woman who could've cured cancer crazy, do you?"

Landry waved her back. "Take her to the far end of the plane where it's noisiest, and make sure she doesn't hear anything. Play cards, go to sleep—do whatever you need to do to calm her down."

Simson shrugged. "You quarrel worse than any lovers I've ever known. Both of you need to get over it," she mumbled as she left the cockpit.

"What the fuck does that mean?" Landry turned to Simson as she disappeared into the back of the plane. She didn't answer. "What the fuck does that mean?" she asked again, this time directing her question to Foster.

It means she knows I'm in love with you. "I don't know. When does she ever make sense?" She felt Landry's stare boring into the side of her head.

Landry sighed. "I'll cover for you, just like you did for me after our last mission. But we need to look at what's going on with you, with or without the head doctors." She shoved Foster's shoulder. "We'll fix it."

Foster nodded and smiled, content with how that'd played out. *We're going to fix all of it, together. And just maybe I'll get the other girl, because I can't have you.*

CHAPTER THIRTY-THREE

July 10, 1942: New York

"IDENTIFY YOURSELF, OR WE'LL blast you out of the sky."

Given the aircraft they were in, the controller at La Guardia Field airport had every right to sound agitated as they entered American airspace.

"This is Special Agent Donovan with the FBI. I've got Special Agents Foster, Simson, and Griffin. We're carrying a high-value rescue, Dr. Bina Chernick. Please confirm Special Agents Nelson or Williams are present."

"Please confirm the landing code, Agent Donovan," the controller said, her mistrust crystal clear.

At least one of them should've made it through their part of the mission. Williams was Nelson's understudy, just in case anything untoward happened to him, but she expected it would turn out to be an unnecessary precaution. There was no real danger to their placement. Only sheer bad luck would have had any impact on their time in the past, and they'd been immunized against all the possible diseases they might have picked up. All they'd had to do was infiltrate and wait. "Papa uniform Lima, Sierra uniform Sierra, two zero, seven-six," Landry said.

Foster smiled widely as Landry relayed the code. The tech guys at Pulsus had an interesting sense of humor.

"Affirmative, Special Agent Donovan, you're cleared to land. Special Agent Williams is waiting in the hangar you'll be directed to."

"Thank you, ground control. Reducing speed on approach.

These German built planes may be built to cross the Atlantic, but they're not built to land so well. Do you have a ground crew standing by?"

"Confirm. Ground crew is standing by."

Landry closed off her mic and called to the rear of the plane. "Simson, make sure everyone's strapped in for landing. This is going to be rough. And be ready for immediate evac once we hit the ground. Put your masks on too."

"You got it," Simson called from the back.

"Would it be ironic if the doc ended up dying in a plane crash after a daring rescue rather than in a concentration camp?" Foster grinned.

Landry chuckled. "That wouldn't be irony; that would be shit luck. Buckle up, buddy. This is going to be the kind of rough you don't get off on."

Foster extended her middle finger. "Fuck you, vanilla girl."

Landry centered the plane on the runway approach and slowed to landing speed, then engaged the landing gear.

"That didn't sound healthy," Chernick shouted over the din of the engine noise.

"Relax, Doc. We didn't rescue you only to let you die on a United States runway. We've never lost anyone before." Landry inclined her head when Foster shot her a sideways glance.

"What about Franco on our second mission?" Foster asked quietly.

"Okay, but we've never lost a mission target before," Landry said quietly then shrugged. "And someone at Pulsus made a mistake recruiting him. Franco was a hotshot sniper with an unwarranted sense of overconfidence and invincibility."

Foster raised her eyebrow. "So he deserved the bullet to the back of his head?"

Landry frowned. "I didn't say that. But he compromised the whole mission, and it could've been avoided if the recruitment process had been tighter...if it had been different."

Foster nodded. "There are a lot of things Pulsus does that could be done differently. And better."

Landry looked at Foster briefly but didn't comment. She was right, and she knew it. But who were they to change any of it? She slowed the plane to just above stalling speed in an effort to combat the compromised weight distribution caused by the plane's militarization. When they hit the runway and bounced, Chernick screamed. There was a loud crack as the plane began to break in half, just behind the wings.

"What's happening?" Chernick shouted, her voice panicked and high-pitched.

"The plane's going to break in two," Foster shouted back. "You'll be fine. That's why you're at the back of it."

Landry couldn't help but laugh. "That's so comforting. I'm sure she'll be really calm now. There's nothing to worry about, Doc," she yelled. "We're almost there." She pulled back on the yoke, keeping the plane as balanced as she could considering it was about to break in two.

They slid past the ground crew as the plane slowed, but as it stopped, it snapped completely and the rear part of the plane fell the remaining few feet to the ground. Landry and Foster scrambled out of the cockpit, while Simson and Griffin carried out an unconscious Chernick.

"What happened?" Landry asked.

"The excitement was too much, and she passed out." Simson shook her head. "It stopped her screaming, which was better than me stopping her."

Griffin opened the side door, and they placed Chernick on a stretcher. She and Foster headed back to the top exit, climbed down onto the wings and dropped onto the ground.

"Nice flying, Special Agent Donovan." Williams greeted her with a firm handshake.

"Thanks, Williams. It's good to see you." She pulled him away from the ground crew and the rest of her team. "Where's Nelson?"

Williams shook his head and sighed. "He was coming out of his hotel on West Fifty-Sixth Street, and a checker cab plowed straight into him. He's at the New York Presbyterian Hospital all busted up with a broken leg. But he's going to be okay."

"Jesus." Landry shuddered to think of what might have happened if Pulsus had sent just one of them. That was one good protocol they had in place. Otherwise, she would've been forced to nominate two of the operatives to stay a lot longer than anticipated to build Chernick's life for her while Landry returned to Pulsus. She wouldn't have wanted to leave Simson with Chernick, but she was desperate to get Foster back to 2076. She didn't want to see her suffer any more than she already had. "Is everything in place for Dr. Chernick?"

"Yes. She's got a teaching position at Columbia, as planned. Everyone's prepared to support a new line of research into cancer. Nelson and I have been assigned to the New York office to make sure Chernick is kept safe. I guess you'll know before we do when the mission is complete."

Landry gripped his shoulder. "Just remember why you're doing this. You'll actually be home before us." Though they knew Chernick had the knowledge and was going the right way to discover the cure for cancer, they had no idea how long it might take her, so Williams and Nelson wouldn't be jumping home with the rest of the team. They had to stay in New York to keep Chernick on the right track, but there was no telling whether that would be in 1947 or 1967. It was another aspect of the operatives' job that made Landry glad she was an extractor. She hated uncertainty, and besides, she really wanted to see Jade. *If she's still around.* She thought about the girls and Priscilla. Letting them into her life, and the way they'd pulled her into theirs, had been so easy and so natural. How would she cope if she got home to new tenants in her building? Was this the cost of doing her job and trying to let people in?

"What's the doc like?" Williams asked.

"She's a good woman." Landry thought about what Chernick

had been through and the difference she'd tried to make to the poor women chosen for the experiments. "Make sure you look after her."

"Landry?" Foster beckoned her over. "The doc wants to speak to you."

"Sure thing." Landry jogged over to Chernick. She was conscious and sitting up on the gurney. "What's up, Doc?" Landry smiled, realizing Chernick wouldn't have seen the iconic animated cartoon character.

"Will you tell these people I'm all right, and I don't need to go to the hospital?"

"Are you sure you don't need to be checked out?"

Chernick shook her head. "I'm certain I'm fine, Landry, though I appreciate your concern. I'd rather just get on with...my new life." Tears slowly formed in her eyes.

"Is the magnitude of what's happening starting to hit home, Doc?" That was something they hadn't talked about or considered. Chernick had been plucked from three years of captivity and cruelty and was suddenly a free woman in a new country. The only expectation placed on her was that she continue her research, which was a scientist's dream scenario, but maybe she wanted more.

"I believe it might well be." Chernick nodded slowly. "Could we go for a meal somewhere, perhaps for one of those famous American burgers you told me about?"

Foster shook her head and glared at her. She obviously wanted to jump home as soon as possible, and so did Landry. The anticipation of knowing if Jade and the girls would still be around was eating at her, but Chernick clearly needed to talk. She shrugged apologetically to Foster. "Sure, I've got some time."

***

The look on Chernick's face when she took a bite of the jumbo burger at Ken's Restaurant made Landry smile. "It's a good thing we didn't get home earlier this week. I hear this place is participating in the rations by doing victory meatless Tuesdays."

Chernick put her burger down, and a look of melancholy passed over her expression. "Home," she repeated slowly. "I suppose I'll be making this my home... I'll never be able to go back to Germany."

"You don't know that for sure, Bina. This war won't last much longer." Landry took a big bite of her own burger and savored it almost as much as the full bottle of beer she'd knocked back as soon as the waitress set it on their table. "Maybe when you've cured the world of cancer, you'll go back there."

"I do like your confidence, Landry. I'm not sure anyone has ever believed in me like you do." Chernick placed her hand over Landry's. "Will you be staying in New York?"

Landry lowered her food and gently put her other hand over Chernick's. "Lots of people believe in you, Bina. That's why they sent us to rescue you." She slowly pulled her hands away and took a quick swallow of her second beer. "But I won't be staying here. I have to go home...to my family." *To the girls. To Jade. And with Foster.*

"Of course." Chernick smiled, and her face flushed pink. "Of course you'd have someone waiting for you at home."

Her statement smarted a little. There was no one actually *waiting* for her at home, and that's the way it had always been. That's the way Landry liked it. But things were changing. "In other circumstances, I would've liked to have stayed," she said with as much sincerity as she could muster. There was no way she would've entertained Chernick sexually. Landry mostly liked her women traditionally feminine, and Chernick was anything but.

Chernick smiled tightly at the platitude, and they ate for a while in silence.

"I'm scared." Chernick popped a gherkin in her mouth and let the statement hang in the air.

Landry washed the last bite of her burger down with a mouthful of beer. "I can't even begin to imagine how you must feel. Being taken away from what you know and brought to an unfamiliar country thousands of miles from home. Do you have any family we could try to bring over?" Sadly, Landry already knew the answer, or she couldn't have asked the question.

"No. I'm the only Chernick left, I'm afraid. My hometown was 'cleansed' of Jews a month before I was imprisoned. The whole village was shot or burned to death."

"I'm so sorry."

"Are any of your team staying here, or do you all live in other parts of the country?"

"Griffin, Foster and I are all from the West Coast," Landry said. "Year-round sunshine. But Williams will be here with you. If you need anything, just ask him, and he'll make it happen. He's a good guy."

"And...will any of you be back this way any time?"

Chernick's enveloping loneliness permeated the space between them. She'd escaped a death camp and avoided unimaginable pain at the hands of Mengele, but it seemed that her main concern was her impending solitude.

Landry sighed and shook her head. "I don't think so. You're the first non-American rescue mission, and I'm pretty sure you're going to be the last. We're usually only concerned with domestic issues."

"Landry, I was alone for the majority of the time I was in Cologne." Chernick pushed her empty plate away and looked around the restaurant. "I had one-night stands every now and then, but until the nurse, I'd been desperately lonely. I'm done with that. I want something...someone, else."

"New York is great place to be a lesbian. If you manage to tear yourself away from your microscope every now and then, you never know who you'll find." Landry decided she'd look Chernick up when she got back to the island. She found herself rooting for the doc to find a long-term true love.

"And until that time, I'll have my research," Chernick said and gave a tight smile.

"Exactly. You're going to change the world, Bina. That's an elite club."

Chernick raised her glass. "To changing the world."

Landry clinked her bottle to the toast and thought about her own words. She was part of changing the world too. She knew she was fighting the good fight and making a difference. But she'd gotten so carried away with that, she hadn't realized that she might be lonely too.

CHAPTER THIRTY-FOUR

LANDRY WOKE IN UNFAMILIAR surroundings to an insistent knock on her door. She stirred in the hard, uncomfortable bed and vaguely recognized the background noise of New York City. It was a far more pleasant environment than the one she'd spent the past six weeks in, where she'd fallen asleep to the sounds of six hundred other women crying or coughing or waking, screaming, from their nightmares. She wondered how Chernick had found her first night out of the camp but figured she'd be pretty okay with it since she'd hooked up with a cute little brunette at Ginger's Bar.

Landry had deflected the attentions of several stunning femmes to keep up the charade of her family on the West Coast, but there was a niggling feeling in Landry's subconscious that it wasn't just the pretense that stopped her from having a little fun. Landry was trying hard to convince herself that she and Jade could simply be friends; she was quite possibly the most beautiful and interesting woman Landry had ever come across. Even at Ravensbrück, she'd been unable to stop thoughts of Jade from invading her mind as she fell asleep each night. Now that she was so close to seeing her again, she could barely concentrate on anything else. Jade and the girls had to be exactly where she'd left them, one hundred and thirty-four years in the future... She just didn't want to contemplate the alternative.

"Landry, are you in there?"

The knocking was even louder this time, reminding her she'd had a few too many drinks trying to numb her feelings for Jade. "Give me a minute." She climbed out of bed and half-stumbled into the bathroom, her eyes struggling to adjust to the bright light through the threadbare curtains. Williams didn't have a big budget for their last-minute hotel booking, and the place he'd put them all in was a fleapit.

She turned on the faucet, cupped her hands full of dirty brown water, and splashed it on her face. She wiped away the sleepy crud from the corners of her eyes and ran her hands over the half inch of stubble all over her head. Six weeks without her proper nutrition regime and a lack of water had made her somewhat gaunt—nothing like the average Ravensbrück prisoner, but maybe more like a cancer patient in the early stages of chemo. She was glad the regenerative tech could grow her hair as well as fix her aging.

She looked at her pale skin against her white ribbed tank. She needed some sun too. She ran her fingers over her forearm and smiled. Her tattoo would give her some color back. She flexed her arms and rolled her shoulder muscles forward, feeling the need to get back to the gym to bulk up again. Between her home setup and Rogue Gym on Mission Street, she'd soon be back to feeling more like herself. She swallowed hard against the intense pain in her ribs and was again glad for her mom's tech.

"Christ, how long are your fucking minutes?" Foster shouted through the door.

"Sorry, buddy." Landry walked back through and let Foster in. She held a tray of coffee aloft and wafted a brown bag in Landry's face. She noticed the old sailor bag slung over Foster's back and hoped it contained what she'd asked Williams for.

"Hungry, stud? Where are you hiding her?" Foster grinned. "Or them?"

"I'm alone." She snatched the bag from Foster's hand and pulled out a cream cheese bagel. "My favorite. What would I do without you?"

Foster huffed. "So we didn't delay the jump for your booty call? Or did you kick her out before you went to sleep?"

Landry detected a hint of anger in Foster's tone and put it down to the jump being deferred. Coming from anyone else, it would've sounded like jealousy, but they were buddies and nothing more. "Sorry to disappoint you, but I have nothing to report in that department. You'd have to talk to the doc if you're after that."

Foster frowned. "You spent all night in a New York nightclub full of lesbians after six weeks without sex, and you came back to the hotel alone?"

"Yep." She took a mouthful of bagel and moaned. "God, this is good."

Foster gave her a shove. "And?"

"And the doc came on to me, so I had to spin her a tale about having a family back home. I couldn't very well go sucking on someone's face after telling her that, could I?"

"I saw that coming a mile off. But if the doc left with someone, how come you didn't stay and find some action for yourself? Or are you saving yourself for your superstar baller?"

Landry shook her head and washed a mouthful of bagel down with a swallow of sweet coffee. "I told you; we're just friends."

Foster walked over to the window, opened the curtains, and dropped her bag onto the table. The woman smoking on her fire escape across the alley waved and smiled. Foster waved back and chuckled. "When it comes to gay women, there's no such thing as 'just friends' if there's even a sniff of chemistry or sexual attraction."

"You and I are just friends who've fucked a couple of times, and it works for us."

Foster snorted. "Sure, but we're soldiers. Your baller girl lives in the regular world with regular people having regular relationships. If she thinks there's a spark, she'll act on it. Trust me."

Landry sighed. Maybe Foster knew what she was talking about. Resisting Jade had been a sweet kind of self-denial, and she didn't know how much longer she could hold out. "You make it sound like women can't control themselves."

"So what if I am? So what if we can't?" Foster threw her arms in the air. "You only live once, right? Even if it does happen to be for two or three hundred years in my case."

"I don't know, buddy." Landry scrubbed her hand over the top of her head. "Isn't that the problem? I can't give her what she needs because of our job."

"Sounds like an easy excuse." Foster balled up the food bag and threw it at Landry. "You're the one always telling me to have a life outside Pulsus, but you've got rules and regulations that mean you're not really fully committing to it. What kind of bullshit is that?"

"Jesus, that Ilsa girl has done a number on you."

Foster had always been so disconnected from love and emotion, just like her. They'd had a couple of rounds of intense sex, but it had just been physical. It was sport fucking. Foster had never been sentimental about anything. Maybe Ilsa was the antidote Foster needed to recover from the poison of the missions.

"It almost makes me wish we could've brought her home with us," Landry said.

"That makes two of us," Foster said softly.

Landry put her hand on Foster's shoulder. "What was it like?" If she could ask anyone what love was supposed to feel like, it was her best bud.

Foster looked slightly bemused. "Love?"

Landry nodded. "Yeah. Love. What's love like?" It felt like a stupid question, but maybe it'd help her figure out what was going on with Jade. She'd never met anyone like her before, and maybe it was just a silly infatuation because they *hadn't* had sex.

Foster dropped into a nearby chair, her expression serious. "It felt like I couldn't breathe around her, but at the same time, she was my oxygen."

"Fuck, man. That's poetic." Landry wanted to know more, but Foster seemed more vulnerable now than ever before. Then again, Castillo was constantly telling them about the importance of sharing their feelings. She had no idea that in order to kill someone, they had to repress their ability to really feel *anything*. Landry decided to risk it. "What does it feel like now?"

Foster hesitated, and Landry wasn't sure if she'd pushed her too far. She scratched at her nose, making Landry think that whatever was going to come out of her mouth, it wouldn't necessarily be the truth. But why would she lie when she'd been so open?

"I'm not sure I've got a handle on it yet." She stood abruptly. "Griffin and Simson are waiting downstairs with Williams. He's going to take us to a quiet place in Central Park to jump back." She picked up the bag and tossed it to Landry. "There's everything you need in there plus the jacket you wanted. Williams said you owe him big for that. He had to steal it from one of the players."

Landry caught it and smiled. "Thanks, buddy."

"I'll go wait with them," Foster said and quickly left the room.

She was hiding something, but Landry wasn't sure whether it was about Ilsa or something else. She'd get it out of her eventually. Foster didn't keep secrets from her, and whatever it was, they'd work it out when they got back to Pulsus and went house-hunting on the mainland. She could stay at a hotel close by while they looked, giving them plenty of time to work on Foster's nightmares and her state of mind. A better friend might invite Foster to stay at her place, but Landry still needed that separation between work and the mainland; Foster was her friend, sure, but she was also her colleague. Selfishly, she didn't want that crossover in her space.

Landry turned the bag upside down and smiled when the navy letterman jacket with its red leather sleeves fell onto the bed. She couldn't resist pulling it on and checking herself out in the bathroom mirror. *Perfect.* Landry felt like an excited high school jock getting ready to go out on a date with the prom queen. *The very sexy, athletic, Latin prom queen.* "Time to go home."

She tossed the jacket aside to take a quick shower and was down in the hotel lobby within ten minutes.

"Did you show the doc a good time?" Griffin asked and gave her a filthy grin.

Landry nodded. "She went back to her hotel with a pretty brunette, so yeah, I think she was content with her new start in life."

"And New York was treated to the great Landry Donovan,"

Simson said. "Can we go home now?"

After their trek through the woods, Landry thought Simson's animosity had mellowed, but apparently she was wrong. Simson was clearly jealous of her friendship with Foster, so how hard had it been to handle Foster's relationship with Ilsa for the past two years? Now that Landry took the time to really look at Simson, she could all but see her skin crawling with repressed aggression. Whatever was happening, she didn't have time to deal with it right now. "Foster says you know a good place for the jump," she said to Williams.

"I do. My car's out front, so it won't take us long."

Landry patted his back and headed toward the lobby entrance. "Let's go."

On the short drive to Central Park, Landry double-checked the details of Williams and Nelson's assignment now that Chernick was their responsibility. They were both great handlers, and she was confident that their part of the mission would run smoothly, particularly given that Chernick had quickly settled into New York's lesbian scene too. They'd know soon enough if the mission was fully successful when they got back to Pulsus and endured the high-speed reality catch-up. Once that was done with, Landry could check on Jade and the girls in the Pulsus database. She tried not to focus on how motivated she was to investigate non-mission elements. She needed some time to herself to really consider how to balance the work-life thing now that she'd added Jade into the mix with the family who'd adopted her. Landry was used to being in control of everything, but the more she let herself have a regular life outside of Pulsus, the more that tightly held control slipped away.

But maybe that wasn't such a bad thing.

CHAPTER THIRTY-FIVE

Foster said goodbye to Williams, then he disappeared to maintain the perimeter. He'd taken them to a densely wooded area toward the back of Central Park, off the regular pathways and away from the crowds. It wasn't like there'd be a blinding flash of light that would have New Yorkers running to report aliens landing, but discretion was still the best bet when four people were simply *disappearing*.

Landry pressed her finger to the recognition plate on the PRU. She created their time circle, and Foster saw her smile like she always did when the luminescent time thread materialized from its center. It was as if she half-expected it not to be there. Foster quelled the irritation barbing at her gut, reminding her that time strings for operatives were always one-way only. She'd attended the training course when the science nerds had tried to explain the physics of it, but she tuned out soon after someone mentioned energy costs and cosmic strings. As long as Landry did her job, Foster didn't really give a fuck about the science. She had more important things to worry about.

Landry pressed buttons on the PRU, and four neon strings extended from the single thread like a giant pull 'n peel blue raspberry Twizzler. Each of the team took hold of one, wrapped it around their wrist, and gripped it tightly.

"Ready?" Landry asked.

Griffin nodded, but he didn't seem sure of himself.

"I won't say the return journey's easier, Griff," Landry said, "but at least your guy's waiting at the other end of this wormhole."

Foster smiled. It seemed ironic that she could say that when she had no idea how to grasp love when it presented itself. Foster stopped herself. If she was going back to 1942 for Ilsa, she had to get over Landry. It wouldn't be fair to disrupt Ilsa's life, only for her to discover that Foster's heart was split in two, and even someone as sweet as Ilsa couldn't draw it back together.

"As long as he never finds out where my dick had to go on this mission, I'll be happy. Let's do it."

Simson simply nodded at Landry. Foster would have to talk with her about curbing that attitude. Foster needed them both for her plan to succeed, and they'd all have to work together. Foster didn't want to contemplate Landry not working with her, but if she did end up doing it the hard way, Simson would delight in using her particular skill set to—to what? How far was Foster prepared to go if Landry wasn't on board with her? *Fuck.* That's something she didn't want to face. "I'm ever-ready, Landry," she said, pushing that thought away. "Let's go home."

The team steadied themselves as Landry pressed retrieve, and they began their journey back to 2076...and all the possibilities of a new future.

CHAPTER THIRTY-SIX

February 14, 2076: Pulsus Island

"WELCOME HOME, LANDRY," HER mom said as she emerged from the jump.

Her mom was always the first one she saw post-mission. Sometimes it comforted her. Sometimes she felt smothered. On this occasion, it did nothing but remind her they'd have to talk about her mom's cryptic parting shot about her dad. Her mom offered a blanket, but Landry waved it away and passed the PRU to Micky, who was waiting eagerly to reclaim their equipment. "I'm nauseous, not cold."

"All that time with the Nazis did nothing to lighten your mood then."

Landry didn't laugh. What they'd witnessed and what that period of history meant for millions of people held no humor for Landry whatsoever.

"Any damage I need to know about that I can't see?" She reached out to touch Landry's black eye.

"I've got a cracked rib that punctured the skin, but fine otherwise."

"And the rest of the team?"

Foster emerged from the shredded time curtain.

"Everyone's fine. Just in need of an age rewind."

"And a mind wipe," Foster added.

Landry agreed, though whether Foster was referring to the memories of the camp or the memories of Ilsa, she couldn't know.

"The pods are ready for you." Her mom began to move away,

expecting Landry to follow behind instead of waiting for the others to exit onto the jump platform. "How was the mission?"

"It was fine. And it worked?" Landry asked, not wanting to discuss the details further with her mom.

She smiled broadly. "Perfectly. It went better than we could ever have envisioned. Chernick completed her first tranche of research and released her findings in 1946, complete with the lead compound required to treat all the major cancers. It only took BodyPose four years to develop the drug, with full FDA approval, and cancer became nonfatal in 1950."

Her mom opened the door to the regenerative pod, and Landry removed her jacket before stepping inside. "Don't let anyone take that," Landry said. "I'm keeping it as a souvenir."

Her mom frowned. "You never want reminders of your missions."

"I want this one," she said, firmly enough that it would deter further comment. "So what else did our good doctor achieve?"

Elena grinned. "Chernick didn't stop there as we thought she would. She went on to assist a gifted geneticist to identify the mutation that caused cancer in all organs and cells. She didn't just find a cure to cancer, she helped eliminate it completely."

Landry smiled as she removed the rest of her clothes and relaxed into the soft cotton of the pod's chair. *Way to go, Doc.* "From what year are you retrieving Nelson and Williams?"

"Now that your team is home, we'll send Harris tomorrow to extract them from 1951." She closed the pod door.

Landry nodded. "So you're leaving her alone now that she's completed the work?"

"Yes, to live out the rest of her life in peace. Chernick left a potentially unmatchable legacy. There's a statue in her honor in Central Park."

Her mom disappeared from view momentarily, and the pod began to warm substantially. Landry felt her body tingle as the sleep gas began to take effect. "Did she spend her life with anyone?"

Her mom popped back to the small window and looked in. "I have no idea. Why do you ask?"

Landry didn't respond. As she drifted into a deep sleep so her mind didn't fight the regenerative process, she thought about Chernick picking up the cute brunette last night—one hundred and thirty-four years ago—and hoped that had stopped the loneliness Chernick was so afraid would consume her. And then she thought of Jade and the girls...

Though the process only took just over an hour, Landry slept hard and felt as fresh as if she'd had twelve hours. After the high-speed catch-up on how the mission had affected history, Landry emerged from the debrief room and walked straight into the brick wall that was Simson.

"You kept Foster safe, right?" Her eyes were flint, her fists clenched.

Landry shoved her away. "Back off, Simson. I always keep Foster safe."

"Bullshit. If you had her best interests at heart, you would've cut her loose months ago."

"Cut her loose from what? What the fuck are you talking about?" Landry squared up to Simson, in no mood for her shit. Simson had the weight advantage by around ten pounds, but Landry was an inch taller. She didn't think Simson would get physical, but Landry was tired of the constant challenge, and maybe standing toe-to-toe with her would calm her the fuck down.

Simson looked at her hard, and then her expression changed. "Jesus, Donovan, you're telling me you don't know? She's in love with you, for fuck's sake. And you let her follow you around like a lost fucking puppy. If you actually cared about her at all, you'd tell her she means fuck-all to you so she could move on and try loving someone else."

The revelation caught Landry off guard. If she'd had a hundred guesses at what Simson was talking about, she'd never have come up with that scenario. "Don't be stupid. Foster's in love with Ilsa."

"Don't play dumb with me." Simson snarled. "You know damn well she loves you."

Landry clenched her jaw and forced herself to stay calm. "I don't know what you're talking about, but it sounds more like *you're* the one in love with Foster, and your jealousy's made you paranoid." She gestured toward the door at the end of the corridor. "Maybe after your debrief, you should head on up to Castillo's department and see if they can fix your head." Landry sidestepped to walk past her, but Simson grabbed her arm.

"Everybody thinks the sun shines out of your ass, Donovan, but you don't fool me; you're a fucking fraud. And if we're ever on opposite teams for real, I'm gonna *really* enjoy fucking you up."

Landry shrugged her arm from Simson's grip. She stretched her neck from one side to the other and smiled tightly. "You couldn't do it in training, Simson, so I guarantee you wouldn't be able to do it 'for real' either."

"Yeah? Maybe one day we'll get to see who's right."

"Sure. I'll look forward to it." Landry walked away in search of Foster. Simson was talking shit. There was no way Foster was in love with her...right?

CHAPTER THIRTY-SEVEN

YOU AND I ARE just friends who've fucked a couple of times, and it works for us. Landry's words bounced around in Foster's head, smashing into her emotions like a wrecking ball around a demolition site. She really didn't get it. And worse yet, Foster had somehow ended up trying to convince Landry she should go for it with Jade, regardless of the restrictions of the job.

But it had to be this way for Foster to have any chance of getting over her, to have her chance at a happily ever after with Ilsa. That didn't mean she had to like it. Or Jade. And honestly, Jade likely didn't stand a chance of getting into Landry's heart. She'd asked the question about love like she was an AI robot, and human emotions were beyond her comprehension. But Foster had felt it. She'd found it with Ilsa, and that meant something.

Foster's comms buzzed, and she saw it was Landry. "Hey, I didn't expect to hear from you today. Are we still house-hunting this weekend?"

"Yeah, sure. Since you probably haven't had the chance to clean your dive up yet, is there any chance you could come over to me tonight?"

"Can't it wait until the weekend?" Foster stretched, realizing she was pretty tired. "I was going to hit the sack and try to get some more sleep." Then it registered that it was the first time she'd ever wanted sleep more than time with Landry.

"I'd really like to chat with you today, buddy."

"Okay. I'll be over in an hour." Foster ended the call and drained the last of the bourbon from her glass. She looked at the bottle, already halfway down after only a few hours home. Foster wasn't quite sure why grabbing the bottle of Widow Jane and a glass was the first thing she'd done when she got back. It didn't feel like a habit. It didn't feel like a need. She'd drunk substantially less over the past four years than she had on previous missions and had nothing but wine in the lodge she'd shared with Ilsa—and wine didn't count as alcohol in her book. And yet, it was the first thing she thought of as she made her way back from the debrief.

Foster blamed it on missing Ilsa already. Ilsa had kept her grounded, safe. When she was around, Foster didn't really feel an itch for liquer. She had to focus on her plan to gain control of Pulsus and to get back to Ilsa, and her weird reliance on bourbon wouldn't help that. She pushed the bottle away, determined to make the change here too.

But something was wrong. Landry sounded serious. She'd promised not to let on about Ilsa, so what was she so desperate to talk about that couldn't wait until Saturday? Surely Simson hadn't let something slip. Foster was certain she could count on her. Whatever it was, Foster had to face it head on. She wanted Landry with her on this journey, so keeping her on her side was paramount.

Refocused, she threw on some fresh clothes, freshened her mouth, and headed across to Landry's place.

"Nice tat," Foster said, seeing Landry's forearm as she welcomed her into her apartment. "Do you think your mom would design me something? I want something I don't have to get rid of every mission though. I'm kinda thinking you like the pain of removal and re-application more than the actual tattoo."

"Ask her next time you see her. Now that she's a lesbian too, she'll probably want to cover herself with them, so your timing could be great."

Foster laughed. "Sounds like you two should go see Castillo for some family therapy."

Landry punched Foster in the chest. "Fuck, no."

She went to the kitchen and came back with a cup of some

hot herbal shit she put in front of Foster. "Aren't you supposed to ask your guest what they want to drink rather than serving them something that smells like an old woman's bathroom?"

"Funny. It's good for you. Cleans out the system, and we could both do with that after this mission." Landry sat in her large reclining armchair and nursed her own cup of whatever the hell it was.

"I think that'll take more than one cup of this shit, but I'll play along." Foster took a small swig and grimaced. "What do you need to talk about anyway?"

"You and Simson. What's going on with that?"

Foster rolled her eyes. "This shit again?"

"Before the mission, it seemed like you'd spent a lot of...time together."

"Yeah, so? My best buddy always fucks off to the mainland, so my choices are limited. We've already talked about this. What's the problem?"

Landry swirled the gunk around in her cup like it was a fine wine. "How well do you really know her?"

"I've known her for decades in missions." Foster shrugged. "What's with all the questions? Why don't you just come straight out with whatever's bugging you? I'm tired, and I want my bed."

Landry took a deep breath. "It's crazy, I know, but Simson says you're in love with me."

"She says what now?" *Shit fuck bastard.*

"Christ, don't make me repeat it."

"You don't actually believe her, do you?" Foster slammed her cup on the coffee table. Something about protesting too much came into mind, and she tried to temper her initial reaction. "I mean, you're a great lay, but you don't have my heart." *You absolutely have my heart...but some of it is Ilsa's too.* Jesus, this was all so fucked.

"No, of course I don't believe her. I'm just wondering what's going on in her head. Seems to me like she's the one in love with *you.*"

"We have fun fucking, that's all. Like you and me did once. She doesn't *love* me. She more or less hates you, but I think that's just jealousy. Or maybe she just wants to be you." Foster fumbled for solid ground. There was no way on earth Landry could find out how she felt. She'd pull away like a freight train into the night, and Foster would be left standing alone in the dark.

"Whatever it is, she needs to calm it the fuck down."

"What do you care anyway?" Foster jutted her chin. "You're heading off to the mainland to spend time with your baller...until you get bored with her."

"Wow, that's pretty harsh. We're just—"

"Friends. Yeah, so you keep saying. I say stop fighting it and fuck her. Maybe it's just because you think you can't have her that she's so tempting. Maybe after you've fucked her, the appeal will wear off, and you can go back to being the illustrious player you really are." *Jesus, shut up.* Why couldn't she stop running her mouth? She was damn sure going to stop Simson running hers.

"Go to hell, Foster. That's not how it is." Landry got up, went to the kitchen, and came back with a glass of something stronger than the tea they'd been drinking.

"No glass for me?" Foster asked.

Landry glared at Foster, her jaw clenching and releasing. Foster had obviously hit a nerve.

"No glass for you."

"Look, I'm sorry." She held up her hands and shrugged. "I'm still sore from Ilsa. You've got a woman waiting for you to act on your attraction, and I can't follow through on mine, because she's nearly a hundred and fifty years in the past. I'm angry, I guess. And maybe envious of what you've got right in front of you and are too chickenshit to do anything about it... I shouldn't have said anything."

Landry took a long drink of the bourbon. Foster could smell it, and she was desperate to head to the kitchen and help herself.

"There was something else she said that didn't sit right," Landry said after a long period of awkward silence.

"Yeah, what?" Foster's heart pounded against her ribs. If Simson had said something about her plans for Pulsus, she was going to end her.

"She said something about us being on opposite sides, like she thought one day we'd be facing off for real, instead of just for the purposes of a mission."

I'm gonna sew her fucking lips together. "That's not going to happen, is it? Simson shoots her mouth off without engaging her brain. I don't know, maybe she just wants to fuck you and doesn't know how to ask, like a school kid picks on the girl she's actually hot for."

Landry shook her head, clearly unconvinced. "No, she specifically said she wanted to fuck me up, not fuck me."

Foster grinned. "Same difference to her. She likes playing rough."

"I'm not convinced. Something's going on with her, and I need to find out what. I got a heads-up for our next mission, and she's on our team again. I need to trust her with my life, and right now, I don't trust her at all." She looked at Foster over her glass. "And I don't know if you should either. There's clearly something about you that's under her skin."

"She's just trying to get in your head, and it looks like it's working. You don't ever need to worry about your life on a mission or any other time. I've always got your back," Foster said. "She's a team player, always has been and always will be, so you don't need to be concerned about missions."

Landry had the power to have Simson removed from their next mission, but Foster needed her there. This was a fuckup that never should've happened; she'd have to bring Simson into line. Whatever her obsession with Landry was, she had to drop it and get with the program. Both she and Landry were essential to her plan, and Foster could do without the playground theatrics. It was a tough enough ask to convince Landry to go against her mom, even with the added issue of her relationship with Jenkin, so Simson complicating things was as welcome as fart in an elevator.

Landry cracked her knuckles. "I can't go on a mission with someone I don't trust one hundred percent."

Fuck, no. "Let me talk to her. I think she's just messing with you. I'll tell her you're thinking of kicking her off the team, and I bet that'll do the trick. She had your back in Ravensbrück. She didn't let you down, did she?"

Landry tilted her head in acknowledgement, swirling the last of the amber liquid in her glass. "Okay. Assess the situation and let me know what you think. But be sure." Landry looked at Foster, her eyes hard and serious. "Be *absolutely* sure."

Foster stood to leave. She had a craving for the rest of the bourbon bottle she'd left on her kitchen counter, and she also wanted to knock Simson's head against a wall before that. "Leave it with me, Landry. I'll deal with Simson." She let herself out of the apartment, jogged a few meters, and dialed Simson. "Get your ass over to my place right now."

Simson laughed lightly. "Craving something specific, soldier?"

Foster took a deep breath and clenched her hand into a fist so tight her knuckles cracked. She wanted to pound on Simson until her arm ached, but not the way Simson would be hoping for. "No. You've fucked up."

"What have I done?" Simson asked. "I didn't say anything at the debrief."

"Just get over here now. I'm not doing this over comms." Foster ended the call and nearly pitched the handset into the lake. There was so much more at stake than before. She needed to go back to Germany. Ilsa was the only cure for Landry, she was sure of that now. If Landry was capable of love, and she actually *had* fallen for Jade, she'd understand why Foster had to go back to Ravensbrück for Ilsa. It'd be hard seeing Landry with someone else, but if Foster was ever going to clean her blood of that obsession, she'd have to swallow her disdain and wish them the best of luck. It wasn't like she wouldn't be able to pull off her plan without Landry but having her on board would make everything so much easier.

The Condor breaking up on landing was just more proof that the Pulsus board couldn't be trusted. They said they weren't prepared to take risks, but they were; they were just taking the wrong ones. Everyone on that plane could've crashed and burned on impact, including the precious doctor. When she was in charge, things would be different. *Everyone* would be important. She could only hope Landry would join her. Locking horns with her best friend and never-would-be lover wasn't something she wanted to contemplate.

CHAPTER THIRTY-EIGHT

February 15, 2076

LANDRY RUBBED HER EYES and forehead as she waited for her chai latte. She'd hardly slept, with thoughts of Jade, the girls, Foster, and Simson driving around her mind in a NASCAR race, each one competing for her attention and bumping the others out of the way. Jade won and the girls came in a close second. That wasn't unexpected. After Foster left last night, Landry searched the Pulsus database for Jade to make sure their cancer success hadn't meant she never existed. She wanted to be sure her memories were still real. Words didn't do justice to the relief that flooded through her body when images of Jade splashed across the wall screen, along with tales of the amazing run of sixty-point-plus games she was having for the Warriors.

Her next search for Beth and Cait's restaurant, La Azucarera, quickly yielded positive results. Knowing that she was going to see them all the next day made her as excited as a five-year-old on Christmas Eve, a totally unfamiliar yet weirdly comforting experience. A couple of missions ago, she'd started to look forward to seeing the girls, but the added draw of Jade this time was something else entirely.

"Landry. Full fat chai." The cardboard cutout barista put Landry's drink on the counter and smiled wanly.

She thanked her and turned, bumping straight into another customer entering the coffee shop. "Oh, shit, sorry," she said, before looking down into the stunning azure blue eyes of Dr. Stowe, Priscilla's ER doctor.

"Ms. Donovan, how nice to see you," Stowe said. "Your friends tell me you've been out of town. Have you been back long?"

"Just hit the shore this morning." Landry pulled at the strap of her duffel bag and felt guilty for not calling her. The fact that she hadn't entered Landry's mind since she'd left the hospital that night, however, was telling.

"What kind of work takes you away for nearly two months?" she asked.

"The kind that makes it hard to make good on promises to a beautiful doctor."

Stowe raised her eyebrow. "How long will you be in the city?"

"A month this time. Sometimes it's just two weeks," Landry said.

"And were you thinking of calling me?"

Landry was about to reply when her phone rang. By strange coincidence, it was Jade. *Just like last time.* She'd sent a text to her as soon as she got off the Pulsus cargo train. "Do you mind? I have to take this."

Stowe shrugged and joined the end of the line to place her order.

"You really weren't kidding about disappearing for big chunks of time," Jade said. "I kinda thought you were exaggerating."

"You missed me then?" Landry grinned and turned away from Stowe's rapacious gaze.

"Only if you missed me."

Landry's grin grew bigger. She'd missed Jade's smart mouth. *I want that mouth on my neck. I want it everywhere.* "I bought you a present to make up for being away so long."

"And why would you do that? We're just friends..."

There was a pause like she was about to say something else but didn't. Landry imagined her quietly laughing. "Where are you? I'll bring it over."

"I'm at the restaurant. Beth is fueling me up ready for the Conference Finals tomorrow."

"For breakfast? That's a happy coincidence since I'm on my

way home right now." Landry looked back at Dr. Stowe. She was beautiful, intelligent, and had an incredible body, but she wasn't Jade. She didn't make Landry's heart race when she spoke, and it wasn't dreams of the doc that got her through the dark, lonely nights in Ravensbrück.

"You better hurry if you want to see me," Jade said. "I have to be at the training facility in two hours."

Landry pulled out the pocket watch from the back of her jeans. *Nine a.m.* If she dropped her drink and ran, she could be at the restaurant in less than fifteen minutes. She'd be a mess when she got there, but she had to see Jade as soon as she could. "Enjoy your breakfast. I'll be with you soon enough." Landry ended the call just as Stowe came to stand beside her. Real close.

"Walk me back to the hospital?"

Her eyes sparkled with the promise of easy sex, but Landry shook her head. "Sorry, Doc, I have to get home."

Stowe inclined her head and smiled faintly. "Someone's waiting for you?"

Landry laughed lightly as she realized that, for the first time ever, someone actually *was* waiting for her. Someone who made her immune to the charms of this gorgeous doctor. "Yeah, they are." And not just Jade, but her little adopted family wanted to see her too. "I'm sorry."

"Mm, me too." Stowe took a step back. "You know where I'll be if things change," she said and walked away.

Things *were* changing; *Landry* was changing. She was going to throw the dice and gamble with Jade's friendship, just like Foster had encouraged her to. Time to make it happen. She threw her cup in the trash and jogged up the street.

The combination of the unusually high temperature, a fifty-pound duffel bag, and the San Francisco terrain conspired to drench Landry in sweat by the time she'd completed the two-mile run home. She was about to slip past the restaurant window and pop upstairs for a quick shower, when Cait spotted her from a window seat and knocked on the glass. Jade sat opposite her, looking amazing in a simple loose sweater with her hair falling softly over her shoulders.

"Get in here," Cait shouted and waved frantically.

Landry pulled at her T-shirt to indicate the state she was in, but Cait had already come through the door to pull her into a bear hug.

"You've been gone for an age. We've missed you." Cait released her and wrinkled her nose. "Why are you so wet?"

Running here now seemed too over eager, and heat crept up the back of her neck. What if Jade was happy with the friend situation? Landry had been gone almost two months. That was too long to wait for anyone, especially with no promises. "Don't you know you sweat more when you're fit?"

Cait frowned. "I thought that was when you were fat. Anyway, come in. Let Beth fix you some breakfast."

They went inside, and Cait hurried off to the kitchen. Landry approached Jade's table slowly, strangely uncertain and unsure of the reception she might get after being away for so long. "Hey."

"Hey, stranger," Jade said. "You look hot."

"Hot sexy or hot sweaty?" Landry wiggled her eyebrows.

Jade flashed the sexy smile Landry had been missing so much, and her eyes sparkled with a hint of lust. "Both."

Landry throbbed when Jade looked her up and down. "I was headed for a quick shower, but you saw Cait drag me in. Sorry."

"No need to apologize. You look even sexier with a sheen of sweat all over your perfect body." Jade put her hand to her mouth and widened her eyes. "Now *I'm* sorry. That's not the way friends talk to each other, is it?" She pushed away her plate and stood. "I'm all done with breakfast. How about you take me upstairs, and I'll snoop around your place while you shower?"

Landry swallowed. Hard. Like a clap of thunder in her head. What was she supposed to say to that?

"You can give me your 'sorry I've been a bad friend by being away for nearly seven weeks slash late Valentine buddy' gift."

Landry grinned. *She's been counting.* "Sure." She cursed her lame response. Usually she was so smooth, but Jade knocked her off her game easier than... That wasn't it. She just didn't need game when it came to Jade. And maybe that wasn't such a bad thing. Slick lines were for one-night stands and not for whatever this was.

"Where are you two going?" Beth moved to envelop Landry in an embrace but stopped just shy when she saw her glistening with perspiration. "You know I want to hug you, Landry, but this is pure silk. Why are you so sweaty?"

"It's hot outside, and this bag," Landry pulled at the strap, "weighs fifty pounds, and I...walked all the way here."

Beth pursed her lips and arched her eyebrow. "I think you ran."

Jade nodded. "I think she did."

Beth motioned to herself and Jade. "I think you couldn't wait to see us all."

"I think you're right," Jade said and bit her lip.

Beth pressed her hand to her heart. "I think you missed us."

"I think—"

"Are you two a double act now?" Landry let out an exasperated sigh.

Beth pulled Jade into an embrace. "Us girls have to stick together when the bois go out of town."

Landry huffed. Truth was, women like Beth and Jade could do pretty much anything and get away with it. When a woman was that beautiful, they had certain privileges.

Jade winked. "Landry was taking me upstairs to check out her inner sanctum while she cleaned herself up."

"Lucky you," Beth said. "It took us ten months to be invited into her apartment even though we only live one floor below."

Jade tapped her watch. "It's kind of taken me two."

"Good point." Beth linked arms with Jade, and the two of them stared directly at Landry.

Landry rolled her eyes, but she had to admit that she liked

the way they were toying with her. "I'm going upstairs. You're *all* welcome to join me."

"Tempting as that is, Cait and I have a restaurant full of people hungry for my spectacular breakfasts. We'll leave you to entertain Jade alone and do come down for something to eat when you've... worked up an appetite." Beth smirked, then walked away without waiting for a response.

"Shall we?" Landry motioned to the door, and they exited the restaurant to take the exterior elevator up to Landry's apartment. She pressed her hand to the fingerprint plate at her front door, and they went inside. Landry dumped her bag on one of the sofas in front of the floor-to-ceiling windows and went to grab a bottle of water from the fridge. "Can I get you something to wash down your power pro breakfast?" Landry glanced over her shoulder when she didn't answer.

Jade ran her hand along the black felt of the full-size pool table. "I have fond memories of the last time I played pool."

Landry recalled the hot kisses they'd shared at Jade's team campus. "You haven't played pool for seven weeks?"

Jade laughed gently. "Presumptuous much?"

"Hopeful." Landry emptied half the bottle, but it did little to cool the sensation of her burning skin, desperate for Jade's touch.

"Friends," Jade said thoughtfully. "What are you doing, Landry?"

"Taking on some water before I go clean up." Landry had never felt so unsure of herself around a woman.

"Do you really want to play games with me?"

No, she didn't want to play games, but she didn't know quite how to move beyond them either. "How about I give you your present?" She went over to her bag and pulled the Jewels letterman jacket from it.

"Oh my God, where did you get that?" Jade pushed away from the pool table and skipped over to Landry. "That must be a hundred and fifty years old! It looks brand new!"

That's because it is. "I figured you already had a Knicks jacket."

Jade snatched it from Landry's hands and put it on. It was just a little too big for her, but that made her look even more adorable in it. The perfect boifriend jacket. Landry imagined her in just that and her underwear, and she had to clench her thighs together in a futile attempt to stop the steady pulsating response to the intoxicating image.

"This is *definitely* a Valentine's Day gift. Does that mean you want to go steady?" Jade grasped a handful of Landry's T-shirt and pulled her a little closer.

Landry had never given anyone a card to celebrate love day, let alone a gift. "Can you call it steady when there's been nearly two months between dates?" Landry inhaled Jade's sweet fig perfume. Mixed with Jade's own scent, it instantly connected with Landry's brain, and testosterone surged through her veins.

"How is it your sweat smells so good?" Jade pressed her leg between Landry's and tilted her head back, so their lips were only a few inches apart.

Landry sighed deeply and pulled Jade closer. "Research suggests that when you smell *the one*, you can't keep your hands off her."

Jade laid both hands on Landry's pecs and pressed firmly. "Is that what you are? *The one?*"

Landry dipped her head so that their mouths almost met. "Do you want to find out?"

"Is this your usual shtick? Because it's very impressive." She ran her tongue over Landry's bottom lip before she sucked it into her mouth and nibbled gently. "If I wasn't just your friend, I'd be in the shower naked with you by now."

The thought of Jade's firm and oh so feminine form stripped bare and pressing against her own made Landry's head spin. "What if I don't want to be *just* your friend?" This attraction was impossible to deny. She'd tried starving the fire of oxygen, and all that had made it do was burn brighter. She hadn't been away from Jade that long, but it felt like years since she'd seen Jade's exquisite perfection, since the velvety tones of Jade's voice had resounded in her ears. She'd never longed for anyone or anything, but Jade held her attention from the moment she saw her. This was different. This was...something else.

Jade slipped her hands under Landry's T-shirt and ran them over the rips of her abs toward her breasts. Her fingertips stopped at Landry's nipples, and she lightly twisted them. "What do you want to be, Landry?" she whispered.

Jade's pure electric touch tingled over Landry's skin, making her want that same touch over every inch of her body. "I want to be the one..." *Jesus, don't stop there,* "who makes you come like you've never come before." She wrapped her hand around Jade's neck and pulled her into a deep, passionate kiss. She broke away. "I want to be the one who makes you pass out from too many orgasms." She walked Jade backward until she was pressed against the pool table. "I want to be the one who makes your fantasies come true." Landry picked her up and sat her on the edge of the table. She parted Jade's legs and pressed herself between them. "I want to be the one you think of as you fall asleep. The one you dream about." She ran her fingers through Jade's hair and caressed her cheek. "I want to be the first person you think about when you wake."

Jade took the hem of Landry's T-shirt and pulled it over her head. She let out a breathy sigh. "That's a lot of want." She trailed her fingers over Landry's hands, along her tattoo, and up to the hard curve of her bicep. She squeezed it and smiled appreciatively. "Do you have what it takes to deliver on those words?"

Landry leaned in and kissed her hard. "That'll be for you to judge."

Jade smiled and placed her fingertips on Landry's lips. "I have very high standards."

"For a woman of your caliber, I wouldn't expect any less." She sucked Jade's finger into her mouth and circled it with her tongue.

Jade unbuckled Landry's belt and jeans and slipped her hand inside her shorts. "Are you wet from sweat or something else?"

Jade's husky voice traveled straight to Landry's core. She wanted to hear that voice whispering sexy promises to her forever. *Forever?* "What do you think?"

Jade withdrew her hand and circled Landry's hardened nipple with the tip of her finger. "I don't want to think. I want to feel. And I want to hear you say it." She pulled away and laughed when Landry tried to kiss her. "Say it."

Landry clenched her jaw. She was so fucking turned on, she wanted to throw Jade on the table and fuck her until the felt was soaked with her sweet juices. "You've made me wet. It's a perpetual state whenever I'm around you. Kiss me...please."

Jade's blue-gray irises were barely visible, edging her dilated pupils, the darkness of which beckoned Landry to crawl into them. She was sure she'd never find her way out if she did, but she really didn't care. She wanted to possess and be possessed. She wanted to be enveloped in Jade's darkness and revel in her light.

Jade grasped the back of Landry's head and pulled her in hard, her craving obvious. "You can start with my pool table fantasy."

Landry nodded and slowly started to remove Jade's letterman jacket.

"No, baby," Jade said, catching Landry's wrists. "Take me like you want to rip me apart. I feel like I've waited years for you, and I don't want to be alone in this. Make me feel your desperation."

Desperate. Wanton. An all-prevailing, unstoppable desire. Whatever it was, Landry *did* feel it too, and it was more powerful than any desire that had gone before it. "I want you so fucking bad, it's painful." She yanked the jacket from Jade's body and tossed it aside. She pushed her back onto the pool table, shoved her sweater up, and unclipped the front fastening on her bra with ease. Pool balls crashed across the surface, making room for Jade's lithe body. She squeezed Jade's breast, while she worked her jeans open with her other hand and then pulled them down, along with her panties. The smell and sight of Jade's pussy filled Landry's senses. She slipped two fingers inside her and pressed her mouth to Jade's clit while she cupped her breasts and pinched her nipples with her other hand.

Jade writhed and moaned beneath Landry's touch, and her blatant yearning intoxicated Landry, driving her to push harder, deeper.

"Fuck me, baby. Fuck me like it's the first and last time."

Landry looked up over the firm, lightly muscled body and olive skin of Jade's flawless physique. It was the view she'd be happy to see multiple times a day for the rest of her life. "It can never be the last time." Without losing her rhythm, she climbed up on the table, knelt beside Jade, and kissed her. Jade slipped her tongue into Landry's mouth, like she was trying to connect their bodies. She lifted her hips up and pushed herself harder onto Landry's fingers. Landry could feel Jade tightening around her as her thrusting became more vigorous and insistent.

"God, baby. Perfect. That's so fucking perfect. Please don't stop."

As if Landry would ever stop. *I need your orgasm more than I need...* Landry remembered Foster's words. *It feels like you can't breathe around her, but at the same time, she's your oxygen.* She slowed her pace, and Jade broke away from the kiss.

"No, Landry."

No, don't be scared? Easier said than done. "No what?"

"Stay with me, baby."

Landry smiled and kissed Jade softly, picking up the rhythm that was taking Jade to the edge. "I'm not going anywhere." She meant it. She really meant it.

She wrapped her hand in Jade's hair and kissed her hard, felt herself dissipate in and around her, only to reform, infused with an unusual and unfamiliar sensation. *I don't want to let go.* Jade called out her name, enfolded Landry in her arms, and begged her to make her come.

"I can't get close enough." Landry pressed her body into Jade's as she brought her closer to orgasm until she came. She yelled

Landry's name and dug her nails into Landry's back, breaking the skin and drawing blood. Landry murmured her pain into Jade's mouth as their kiss rode out Jade's bucking hips before she slowly settled.

Landry lay back on the pool table, and Jade nestled her head on Landry's chest, while she dragged her fingers over the undulations of Landry's abs. "You've got the most beautiful body I've ever seen. So much hard muscle, yet your skin is so soft."

Landry stroked Jade's back gently and said nothing. She was trying to make sense of what had just happened. She'd had sex with so many women, of all shapes, sizes, and presentations, and she'd enjoyed every single one of them. But this...this lifted her up off the pool table, like she was weightless, and the tranquility that swathed her soul was a subtle, yet powerful sedative.

"I can see why you're in such demand," Jade said. "You sure know how to make a girl come." She sat up, pulled on her sweater, and edged off the pool table. "Now all you've got to do is decide whether or not this goes beyond a damn good fuck."

Landry opened her mouth to speak, but something stopped her from vocalizing her disordered thoughts. Words seemed inadequate. And if she revealed her feelings out loud, that would make them concrete and tangible. That would make them real, and she couldn't retract them.

Jade sighed deeply and pulled her panties and jeans back up. When she looked at Landry, there was a sadness in her eyes that took hold of Landry's heart with steel-tipped gloves and crushed it without mercy.

"That's what I thought." Jade shook her head. "I have to get to training. Big game this weekend."

What was she supposed to say? This was more dangerous territory than the mission in Iraq. "Jade..." Couldn't she see it in Landry's eyes? "I don't know what you want me to say." But she did know. But surely it was way too early to be thinking of love.

"I'm keeping this as a souvenir." Jade pulled the Letterman jacket on. "But if you realize what this is," she whispered, then pressed her finger to Landry's heart and then her own, "call me. Don't be frightened by it just because you can't control it."

She walked away and took one last backward glance before she left. Landry lay back on the pool table and looked up at the beams of the ceiling and the light fittings hanging by reinforced steel cable between them. What if the cables failed, and the lights crashed down and set fire to her apartment? She'd lose it all. What if her heart was like one of those spotlights? What if Jade took a bolt cutter to the wires wrapped around it, supporting it, protecting it? Would she lose it all? Or was there everything to gain?

CHAPTER THIRTY-NINE

 Simson to show the recruits how both fighters could take a beating and still stay upright, but she'd been a little overzealous, choosing to continue Simson's punishment for mouthing off to Landry with physical recriminations. It ended with Simson in the regen lab to fix some broken bones before they walked to Rik's Place for a perfect end to the day.

Simson swiped her card and bought them a bottle of Elijah Craig to enjoy while Foster filled her in on the sketchy details of their next mission.

"Are we good now that you've given me a code red?" Simson dropped onto the chair opposite Foster.

Code red was a good descriptor, since there'd been plenty of blood. "Sure. We're square if you've learned your lesson, and you back off Landry."

Simson nodded. "I'll leave her be until you say otherwise."

"Good." Foster dropped two ice cubes into her glass and poured a generous measure of the spicy sweet bourbon. She sniffed it appreciatively before she took a smallish sip. She was making a conscious effort to drink less. She wanted to stay the woman she'd been with Ilsa, but it was proving difficult. The nightmares hadn't abated, and they wouldn't until her plan had been put into action. But now, Foster saw the vivid dreams as motivation to get back to Ilsa. Until then, she needed a little of this stuff to take the edge off and help her catch little slices of sleep.

"So, how many guys did our serial killer dispatch?"

"I did a quick search after Elena gave me the mission outline," Foster said. "They think she's responsible for over three hundred men who were found tortured and murdered during a thirty-year period all over the States."

Simson raised her eyebrows and looked impressed. "Wow. But we've only got to save one? Are we being authorized to kill the killer if we find her?"

"Yes, and, no, of course not. We've got narrow parameters for our work, don't we?" The mission was another example of the board's short-sightedness and lack of willingness to do what was truly necessary, but Foster didn't say any of that. As usual, there weren't many patrons in the bar, but she still didn't want to discuss her intended coup anywhere other than the inside of her apartment, where she could be sure there was no surveillance.

"What's so special about this guy...Muniz, did you say?"

"Lyman Muniz." Foster nodded. "A biophysicist who would've probably gone on to invent a sustainable and economic alternative to fossil fuels. He was one of Jenkin's buddies."

"Probably? Aren't they supposed to be absolutely certain, given that it costs eight hundred million dollars per mission?"

Each mission *was* that expensive, but no one would expect time travel to be as cheap as buying a Muni card. "Given the potential gains, they're willing to take a chance on this one. Plus, we're bringing him back with us, so Pulsus will own the tech that saves the world from melting. This one's more like an investment, I guess. They'll spend eight hundred million saving him but make billions once he finishes inventing, researching—whatever the hell he's going to do."

Simson sipped at her liquor. "What're your thoughts on that? Seems a little off our sphere of activity."

Foster emptied her glass and got up, taking the bottle with her. "Let's go to my place and talk some more." Now that she'd worked out her strategy to take control of Pulsus, it was time to fill Simson in, and Rik's Place wasn't the right location for that particular conversation.

They walked in silence until they got back to Foster's place, and she closed the door behind them.

"This is exactly what I've been afraid of. The board is out of control." Foster filled two glasses and gave one to Simson before she dropped onto her couch. "We're running missions for their financial gain."

Simson shook her head. "What're we going to do about it?"

Foster liked Simson's terminology; it signaled her complete buy-in and loyalty. "This mission is the perfect chance for us to set our takeover in motion. We're going back to 2035, which is the same time that the Cagle gang were at the height of their success, running their operation from Boystown, Chicago. One of their departments was mercenaries for hire: top quality, ex-military, and highly trained."

Simson grinned. "Our own little army."

"Exactly."

"Where does Donovan and getting the PRU fit in?"

Foster cracked her neck and emptied her glass. "We need the PRU to take our band of mercenaries back to Pulsus to enact our hostile takeover. When Landry jumps to 2035, I'll explain what we're doing and why. I'll ask her nicely for the PRU."

"What about her mom?" Simson asked as she refilled Foster's glass. "She practically runs Pulsus with Jenkin. How will you get Donovan to go against her mom?"

"She hates Jenkin. She thinks she manipulated her mom into a relationship. I'll use that to convince her to join us, and then she'll give me the PRU."

"And if she doesn't?" Simson's mouth curled into a twisted smile.

Foster didn't want to say the words she knew would light Simson's face like a Christmas tree. She didn't want to think of her best friend turning against her when she needed her most. "Then you'll have to persuade her to give it to me."

Simson's smile turned into a full-on grin. "I get to persuade her *my* way?"

Foster could almost smell Simson's excitement at that prospect.

She took a slow drink and nodded slowly. "You'll do what you have to do to get me the PRU."

"And you won't stop me when it gets serious?" Simson asked.

Foster had seen Simson inflict damage on countless recruits. The torture methods she'd used on several of their missions together always yielded results. Foster could only hope that Landry came on board with them or that she broke before Simson did irreparable damage. "I won't stop you. If Donovan won't join us, then she's against us. There is no middle ground." She swallowed hard, realizing what she was saying and what it meant for their friendship. "I need the PRU, and if the only way to get it is to let you loose on Donovan, then so be it."

"It'll take time. She won't break easily." Simson laced her fingers together and looked gleeful. "I hear she was tortured for seventy-five hours on the Iraq mission and still didn't crack."

"That's true. Everything you've *ever* heard about Donovan is true, and there's so much more you haven't heard. You'll have all the time you need to get me the PRU."

Simson held her glass up in a mock toast. "She'll be my Michelangelo. My masterpiece."

"Don't get ahead of yourself. I think she's starting to see that a change is needed too." Foster swallowed the last of the bourbon straight from the bottle, hoping that if she said it out loud enough times, it'd make it true. She didn't want to have to destroy her best friend *for the greater good*, but if it had to be, at least she wouldn't be the one forced to physically do it.

CHAPTER FORTY

February 18, 2076

Landry and Foster had looked at five apartments and houses yesterday, and Foster hadn't liked any of them. The last one they were viewing today belonged to a teammate of Jade's who was moving out of the city into a multi-million-dollar house on Edwards Avenue, Sausalito, and she needed to lose this place in Dolores Heights. Jade had offered to show them around.

Landry smiled and waved at Jade, perched on the hood of the latest Ferrari Spider. She wished Foster wasn't there so she and Jade could have sex with the warmth of the engine under her hand and the spring sunshine on her back. They hadn't seen each other since the amazing sex on Landry's pool table. They'd had plenty of phone and text contact, but Jade had kept the conversations light, flirty, and fun, and it hadn't felt awkward at all, which was quite the feat, considering the situation. If anything, it'd been Landry wanting to talk about what had happened between them, but she didn't really have the first clue how to broach the subject.

Landry introduced Jade to Foster, and when she grunted, her impatience with the house search came over loud and clear. "You were great last night. Some of your three-pointers were unbelievable."

"For your size, you're surprisingly good at them," Foster said.

Jade laughed. "Thanks. I haven't heard that before."

Landry frowned at Foster and punched her arm hard.

Jade opened the door and turned off the alarm system. She gave them the full real estate agent spiel as they toured the three floors of the property, and every statement was met with a pointed remark from Foster.

"*I love how close this place is to Dolores Park.*"

"Maybe you should live here then."

"*There are five garages underneath the house, off to the side, if you've got cars or motorbikes.*"

"How many vehicles does one person need?"

"*It was built in the 1900s but was split into three condos in the fifties. The previous owner purchased all three units and restored it to its former size and glory.*"

"So it could fall down at any minute."

"*The outdoor deck has recently been re-varnished, and all the furniture is for sale with the house.*"

"Being a realtor should be your fallback career when you get too old for basketball."

"That's a great idea." Jade smiled sweetly. "What do you plan to do when you're too old to be a soldier?"

Foster huffed. "I'm going back to the deck for a better view."

Landry caught hold of her arm before she left. "Why are you being such an asshole?" she whispered as Jade wandered away to the kitchen.

"I haven't got stars in my eyes, Landry. Doesn't make me an asshole."

"Apparently, it does. If you don't like the house, let's go, and we can stop wasting Jade's time. I'm sure she's got better things to do than this, and we've got plans tonight, so what's your problem?"

Foster shrugged her arm away from Landry's grasp. "No problem, stud. Go get her."

She walked off, leaving Landry deciding which one of them to go after. It didn't take long to make the choice. She found Jade grabbing a bottle of water from the fridge. "Can I get one of those, please?"

Jade tossed Landry a bottle, and she took a long drink. The city's spring felt more like a Vegas summer, and the ice-cold water was unusually welcome.

Jade leaned against the counter and gestured outside. "How long has Foster been in love with you?"

"Why do people keep saying that?" Landry shook her head. "We've been friends a long time, and we've worked a lot of missions together. We're just close, that's all."

"Have you ever fucked her?"

Landry spluttered on the water she was drinking. "What the—? Why?"

"Answer the question. Have you fucked her?"

"Yeah, but—"

"But nothing. The woman's in love with you." Jade wiped some invisible dust from the marble surface. "I can't blame her, not after *feeling* you in action, but I don't know how you can't see it. Her pores are seeping jealousy."

"First, what I did with you was different from anything I've *ever* done with any woman before you." Landry's breath caught when Jade smiled and looked pleased with herself. She crossed the kitchen and stood as close as she could without touching Jade. "And secondly, we were just friends with benefits. That's all it ever was: soldiers relieving tension with no fear of emotional entanglement."

Jade gently stroked Landry's face. She caressed her throat and traveled down to her chest. "Maybe that was the case for you, hotshot, but she's all entangled in your funk, and she's fallen hard."

"She's in love with someone else. Someone from our last mission." As soon as she heard herself blurt the sentence out, she realized how desperate she sounded, how desperately she didn't want it to be true. Foster couldn't be in love with her. All they'd ever had was hard and fast sex. There'd been no emotional connection. Not like...not like with Jade.

"And you think you can't be in love with two people at the same time?" Jade chuckled. "Or that she's not using someone else to try to get over you?"

Fuck. "I don't know anything about that. I've never been in love before—"

"Before now?" Jade winked and smiled.

That wasn't what she'd been about to say, but that didn't mean she might never say it. "Presumptuous much?" Landry said, echoing Jade's words from earlier that week.

"Hopeful."

Landry took Jade's hand and kissed her fingertips. "Are you still coming over tonight so I can cook you my specialty?"

Jade arched her eyebrow. "I'll know if it's one of Beth's, you know."

"I do know, because your new best friend would straight up *tell* you that's what she'd done." Landry heard the footsteps of Foster's heavy boots on the oak floor. "So you're coming?"

"Oh, I hope so." She flashed a wicked smile before she looked over Landry's shoulder at Foster. "Seen enough?"

Foster nodded. "I've got to get back. Drop me at the station?"

"Sure." She shrugged, and they both followed Foster out of the building.

Foster jogged down the front steps and turned to look at the house. "Tell your friend I'll take it. Send me the deets, and I'll transfer the whole amount to her account today."

"It doesn't quite work like that, but I'll put you both in touch, and you can figure out the escrow and such," Jade said, then she locked the door and raised her eyebrows. "I didn't realize working for Uncle Sam paid so well."

Foster laughed. "Is that who Landry told you we work for?"

What are you playing at? "No. It isn't." She glared at Foster.

"She's kept more or less silent about the who. I suppose I assumed that you work for the government."

"Have you seen Landry's building?" Foster scoffed. "She couldn't afford that on a government salary."

Landry shook her head and put her finger over her mouth to signal Foster to shut the fuck up.

Jade looked puzzled. "I've seen her apartment. What do you mean, building?"

Foster's smile grew broader when she obviously realized she knew something Jade didn't. "The apartment? She owns the whole building, sweetheart."

"Perhaps you'll tell me all about your work tonight over dinner, in *your* building." Jade gave Landry another one of her sweet smiles.

Landry felt the competition heat up, but she really didn't want to believe everybody was right. Was Foster really in love with her?

"In the perfect little family restaurant, right?" Foster said and sneered.

Fuck. Landry closed her eyes and sighed.

"Oh no," Jade said, shaking her head. "I'll be dining in the penthouse restaurant."

She sounded so innocent, but her voice was laced with possessive undertones. It wasn't a quality Landry had ever found attractive before but hearing it from Jade made her twitchy.

"Has Landry cooked for you before?" Jade asked and fluttered her eyelashes.

That was the kicker. Foster knew Landry never took women home, and she'd never even seen the inside of Landry's bedroom in her place on Pulsus. They'd met in the restaurant yesterday, rather than her apartment. And even though Landry's apartment had three bedrooms, Foster was staying in a hotel.

Jade knew all of that. She knew exactly how special she was to be invited into Landry's retreat. Foster had been an ass to her though, so she deserved it.

"Forget the ride. I'll see you back at base, Donovan," Foster said and just walked away.

Landry frowned. The only time Foster had used her last name was when they met three years ago. She looked down the road at the disappearing Foster and back to Jade, whose mischievous eyes and smile sparkled brighter than the LA sun.

"You should go after her. You're breaking her heart."

How come Landry was the only one who hadn't seen Foster was in love with her? "Should I?"

"Of course...if only to explain that she should concentrate on the other woman in her life, because I've already pinned you down."

Landry laughed. "You're too tiny to pin me down." But if she did, metaphorically, could she share *everything* with Jade, including the details of her work? Her mom would go ballistic, and Pulsus would probably kidnap Jade and keep her prisoner on the island for the rest of her life. But what would it be like to have that trust in someone, to have a sounding board, or someone just to come home to and complain about a bad day or an awful mission?

Jade pulled Landry close to her and whispered, "You might be tall and packing an incredible amount of muscle, but I can show you some moves that'll have you on your back and happy to be so." She stepped back. "But maybe we're getting ahead of ourselves. You should go after your temperamental friend, and I'll see you at your place tonight."

"This isn't a test? I won't lose points if I leave?" Landry was half-joking, but honestly, she wasn't sure if this was a pass/fail situation.

Jade smiled widely. "I'll see you tonight. Go."

Landry wrapped her hand around Jade's neck and kissed her. "I'm going to work you out."

"We'll see if you have the patience for that."

Jade jogged down the steps, got into her car, and drove off, leaving Landry to catch up with Foster. All Landry wanted to do was jump into her own car and follow Jade wherever she went. She was already looking forward to finding out exactly how Jade planned to get her on her back.

But first...Foster.

CHAPTER FORTY-ONE

LANDRY WAS FALLING IN love with Jade. There was no getting away from it. Foster wouldn't deny Jade was a nice piece of ass, and she had a quick wit, but she didn't have the chops to hold Landry's attention long-term. How could they have an honest relationship when Landry would never discuss her work and had to be away for months on end without Jade knowing where she'd been or what she'd been doing?

But that wasn't Foster's problem anymore. When she rescued Ilsa, she'd share her work with her, and Ilsa could be a big part of it; she could be part of something bigger like she wanted. All Foster had to do was concentrate on *that* relationship, which would be much easier once the next mission was complete, and she could go back for her. With Ilsa by her side, ignoring her feelings for Landry would be easier. They had to be.

"Has being an asshole made you work up much of an appetite?"

Landry's approach had been silent. Either that, or Foster had been so caught up in her own thoughts, the world had faded into the background. It'd been a long time since she'd been among regular people without being on a mission, and she'd found it a bit overwhelming. She couldn't wait to get back to her hotel room to pack and head to the island. "Ha fucking ha. I'm not hungry, but I could use a drink. Being around all these civilians is unnerving."

"I'll take you for tea but nothing stronger."

Foster stuffed her hands in her pockets. "Christ, doesn't choosing a place to live here earn me a real drink?"

"Nope. There's a great Japanese garden in Golden Gate. I'll get my car."

Foster sighed. Being around Landry wasn't helpful, but she was a hard habit to break. Foster loved her company, but if she was constantly around her, how could she make the transition from obsession to acceptance of just friendship? That had been easier to swallow when friendship was something Landry only offered her. It had always meant more to Landry than love, but it looked like her relationship with Jade was changing her perspective. That said, she had chased after Foster instead of staying with Jade... "Fine. As long as you don't make me drink the same herbal shit you gave me the other night."

Landry smiled and punched Foster on the shoulder. "I won't...I'll make you try some *other* herbal shit instead."

On the drive to the park, they chatted mainly about the house Foster had just committed to buying, but she could feel something wasn't quite right. When she'd accidentally brushed Landry's hand as they both reached to change the music at the same time, Landry had pulled away abruptly.

They walked in awkward silence to the tea garden, and Foster let Landry order her some fancy beverage from the hostess dressed in a traditional kimono, with the obi-jime tied so tightly to create an impossibly minute waist that Foster thought she'd struggle to breathe.

"I've been wanting to say that I'm sorry I was so hard on you about Ilsa," Landry said when the hostess left them. "I'm glad you managed to experience love while you were in that shithole."

Now her weirdness made sense. Landry didn't do apologies. Not that she was often wrong about much, which was both infuriating and inspiring. She struggled to find the appropriate response and settled with, "Thanks."

"How have you been coping, you know, with the nightmares? Were they better in Germany?"

Foster smiled briefly. "How could they be? But it was nice having someone comfort me." She thought about Ilsa wrapped in her arms. How she woke at the sound of Foster's yelling and gently stroked her face until Foster came around. Then she'd curl up into Foster's embrace again, and her soft breathing would soothe Foster back to sleep. She wanted that again, and she was going to make it happen.

"How's sleeping alone?"

"It sucks." Foster wasn't sure where Landry was going with her questions, so she kept her responses short. She didn't want to trip herself up and ruin everything. Their hostess came back with cast iron teacups and pots. She picked hers up and examined it. "This looks like something a kid would drink from."

Landry poured some of the tea into her tiny iron cup. "Imagine it's a shot of bourbon."

Foster detected an edge to Landry's voice. The apology obviously had nothing to do with the recently developed atmosphere. "So you'll come to my housewarming barbeque?" Maybe a change of subject would distract Landry from whatever she was chewing on.

"Sure. You'll invite Jade?"

I'd rather pull down my pants, sit bare-assed on the grill, and offer my rump steak to guests. "Of course. She found it for me. Would be rude if I didn't."

"You didn't seem to mind being rude to her at the house."

Foster laughed lightly. So Landry was being protective over her pretty girl. "Didn't look like it bothered her."

"Why *were* you such an asshat?"

Foster took a sip of the too-hot tea and burned her lips. She took a swig of the cold water their hostess had also placed on the table and looked away. She wasn't doing a great job of keeping Landry's focus off the topic she really wouldn't be able to handle her tackling. With a master's in psychology, Landry was probably reading her like the clichéd book. The question took physical form and hung between them. Landry simply stared at Foster and waited for her response. "I don't know. I guess I don't know how to be around civvies anymore."

"Really? So it's got nothing to do with you having deeper feelings for me?"

Fuck shit. "This again? I told you, Simson was bullshitting you. How big is your fucking ego that you think I'm in love with you?" *Fuck shit fuck.* It was clear from Landry's expression that she wasn't fooled this time.

"It's not just Simson—"

"Who then? Your girlfriend?" Foster scoffed. "Can't she handle you having a best friend? You should tell her that jealousy doesn't look good on her." Foster's raised voice made the family at the adjacent table looked at her disapprovingly. She stopped scratching at her nose and smiled to placate them.

"You're lying to me, Foster." Landry ran her hand through her hair and shook her head. "Did I lead you on? I thought we were both clear what we did was sport fucking?" she asked, making the family's mom glare in their direction again.

So Landry had finally figured it out, with a lot of help from Jade and Simson. There was little use in protesting further. If she admitted it, if it was out in the open, maybe it would help her get over it. If she could tell Landry the things that really revved her engine, she'd stop being so fucking sexy, and Foster could focus on Ilsa. "I don't know what to tell you. I can't help the way I feel, and believe me, I've tried. I never meant to fall in love with you, just like you never meant to fall in love with Jade, I guess."

"Don't bring Jade into this. This is about you and me. How long have you felt this way?"

From the first time I saw you in recruit training. "Not that long."

"You should've told me," Landry said. "I never would've said yes to sex. I don't want to be responsible for messing with your heart."

"You were never messing with my heart. I knew you didn't—and wouldn't—ever feel the same." She laughed, but Landry didn't join her. "Look, now that you know, can't we just forget about it?" She was trying hard to, and it did help to have said all this shit out loud. "I've gotten over Ilsa, and I can get over you. Maybe I'll end up with a really hot neighbor, and she'll fall for me like Jade obviously has for you." She hadn't wanted to outright lie, but she couldn't share her intention to bring Ilsa back home to stay in her fancy new house to live happily ever after. Not yet.

Landry sighed and rubbed at her forehead. "This ruins everything. Why did you have to...fall for me at all?"

Foster laughed. "It's not like I could control it, you asshole! But it doesn't change anything. We haven't fucked for an age, and you knowing doesn't mean I expect you to fall in love with me. Just give me some time to get over you, that's all."

Landry sipped at her tea and narrowed her eyes. When she did that, it was impossible to tell what the hell she was thinking, good or bad.

"Maybe Jade can fix you up with a woman as well as the house," Landry finally said and smiled.

"That might be an idea. I suppose trying a civilian relationship wouldn't be that bad. You could be on to something with this 'life outside Pulsus' thing."

"Seriously though, how do I make this easier for you?"

By helping me bring Ilsa back. "I'll let you know when I figure it out."

Landry nodded. "Okay, buddy. However you want to do this, just talk to me."

"Sure." That was already the plan. Foster just had to hope Landry was open to what she had to say and would join her without hesitation.

And then Simson wouldn't get to bust up her gorgeous face.

CHAPTER FORTY-TWO

Landry took her time getting ready for Jade's arrival. She chose her favorite button-down black shirt and teamed it with a dark blue tie and jeans, then she glanced over her collection of boots and sneakers but decided to stay barefoot, rather than add more height that would dwarf Jade. She always liked to look good for a night out with any woman, but this was a night *in*. Her first. And Jade wasn't just any woman. She was the woman who'd cast a line and snagged Landry's heart. She'd been looking for balance, something to offset the darkness of their missions, and Jade was offering that. All Landry had to decide was whether to choose freedom or embrace the charms of sweet captivity.

The doorbell chimed. Landry took one last look in the mirror and swept her hand through her hair before she answered. She swallowed hard and wiped imaginary drool from her mouth as Jade stepped inside. "Hi."

"Hey," Jade whispered.

She turned to allow Landry to remove her long coat, and Landry sighed deeply at the sight of Jade's simple white sweater dress and knee-high boots. She resisted the desire to slip her hands around Jade's waist and pull her close enough to feel her heartbeat.

Jade sniffed the air. "Is that chili?"

"Yes and no." She hung Jade's coat and headed back to the kitchen, where she'd been simmering her one and only specialty dish while she fretted over which outfit to wear.

"Meaning?" Jade took a seat at the breakfast bar.

Landry poured a glass of pinot noir and pushed it across the counter. "I put a hundred different types of beans in it, so technically, it's not the chili you're used to."

"Beans?" Jade took a sip of her wine and licked her lips. "That's a bold choice for a date."

Landry smiled. "Is that what this is?"

Jade inclined her head and arched her eyebrow. "Isn't it?"

Landry spooned the chili into bowls, just to have something else to focus on other than Jade's piercing gaze. "Is that what you want it to be?" she asked, taking a seat beside Jade.

"I told you after the Pool Table Incident," Jade ran her finger over the lip of her wine glass, "you've got to figure out what you want. This can be whatever you want it to be." She shrugged and spooned some sour cream onto her chili. "But enough about that for now; why don't you tell me how things went with Foster."

Landry rolled her eyes and dunked a chunk of bread into her bowl. It didn't seem appropriate to discuss a woman in love with her with Jade, the woman Landry seemed to be falling in love with. But she recounted the tale anyway.

Jade smiled and nodded her head. "I told you. A woman's intuition is never wrong."

"I'm a woman, but I didn't see it." How had she'd missed Foster's infatuation when everyone else around them had seen it?

Jade gestured toward Landry with her spoon. "Perhaps you don't want to acknowledge that love even exists."

"Studying psychology as a fallback career?"

"Nope, just a hobby. And you're a complicated study, Landry Donovan."

"I am?" It was usually a good thing in her line of work, Jade had torn down her walls, and she was powerless to rebuild them.

"No, not really, but everyone likes to think they're hard to work out." Jade's laugh filled the room. "Just kidding. Yes, you are."

"In what way?"

Jade pushed her bowl of chili away, stood, and wandered over to the leather sofa by the window. The soft wall lights cast shadows on her flawless, beautiful face, and her eyes sparkled enticingly, enchanting Landry further. What the hell was Jade doing to her? And why couldn't she stop it?

"You seem determined to keep people at a distance, even though you've got a wonderful, loving, and open heart."

Now it was Landry's turn to laugh. Having an open heart was something she'd never been accused of. "How the hell do you work that out?" She joined Jade on the couch, sitting close enough for their thighs to touch. She needed the proximity desperately.

"Don't be coy." Jade shook her head and motioned wildly around her. "Let's talk about Foster's bombshell earlier; this building is yours? Cait and Beth think they're renting from someone who's so loaded they don't need to hike the rent, despite the value of the property and surrounding area going through the roof. And they have no idea it's you."

Jade dropped her hand onto Landry's thigh and looked at her pointedly, clearly waiting for an explanation. Why were they talking about everything other than what Landry wanted to talk about... even though she also *didn't* want to talk about it. She was so fucking hot for Jade, spontaneous combustion might be a possibility. She sighed gently. "You can't tell them I own it."

"Why? Because you're an international drug dealer, and you bought it with blood money?"

Landry grinned widely. "You have an overactive imagination."

"And *you* have an unusually high income and a mysterious occupation you can't tell anyone about." Jade twirled a piece of her hair between her fingers. "Your best friend was extremely dismissive about the government job. *Is* there something I need to worry about?"

Landry placed her hand over Jade's and squeezed. "No, of course not. We work for a very rich philanthropist, baby. That's all I can say. I'm sorry if that's not enough, and I'd understand if it wasn't, but..." She hoped to god it *was* enough.

Jade bit her bottom lip. "Promise me it's nothing illegal."

"I promise." Landry had avoided making promises to anyone for years, yet it tripped from her tongue all too naturally.

"Then I guess that'll have to do for now," Jade said. "You were about to explain why the girls shouldn't know who their mysterious benefactor is."

Landry shook her head at the swift ease with which Jade had switched from serious to playful again, though she was glad of that particular talent. "Raising a child is an expensive business. They don't need to be wasting their hard-earned money on unnecessarily high rent. And I don't want them thinking they owe me anything either. Them thinking that they're paying a faceless corporation or random rich person means they can just get on with living their lives and looking after Priscilla."

Jade ran her fingers over Landry's forearm, tracing the fine branches of the tree. Her touch left trails of fire on Landry's skin, and she took a steadying breath.

"Cait already owes you her life," Jade said quietly.

"That's not true. I stopped her from getting a bad beating; I don't think it would've gone any further."

Jade rubbed her other hand along Landry's thigh, making it almost impossible to concentrate on the conversation.

"Actually, you're wrong. Every one of those people are now in prison for murder."

Landry frowned. "How on earth do you know that?"

"After Cait told me about the attack, I did some digging. They did exactly the same thing to another woman six months later, except no tall, handsome stranger stepped in to save her."

"Really?" That new knowledge felt like a punch to the gut. She'd gone on a mission shortly after and never thought to follow up with the police, especially after she'd had sex with the arresting officer. That would've been awkward. But it wasn't like Landry could've done anything about it, other than killed them at the scene, and then she would've been the one in prison. "Still, they don't need to know." She put her hand over Jade's. "Will you promise me you won't say anything? Ever."

"You should just wear glasses, then *no one* would realize you're a superhero."

"Jade..."

"Fine. I won't say anything. What about the medical bills you paid for them?"

"So, not only a spare time shrink, but also a private dick." Landry shrugged. "What about the medical bills? I have the money, and they don't. Priscilla's life was in danger, and the hospital was messing around. It was the right thing to do, but again, I don't want them thinking they owe me anything."

Jade moved her hand slowly along Landry's thigh until it rested lightly on her crotch. "I'm not criticizing, baby; I'm proving my point. You act like you want to keep people at a distance, but the ones you let in... You'd give them the world if they needed it."

She said nothing. What was there to say when everything Jade said was true, even if she was only realizing it now that Jade had said it? And then there was the red-hot heat of Jade's hand through the denim of her jeans making her ache to be inside her again. Jade pulled Landry's pocket watch from her jeans. Her breath whispered on Landry's neck, and she took a deep one of her own, trying hard to control the need threatening to devour her.

Jade turned it over and over in her hand. "What's the story behind this?"

"Foster found this one for me on our last mission, mainly for the quote on the back. I inherited my dad's collection too. He loved them." The memory stirred Landry's need to quiz her mom on that pre-mission cryptic statement.

"*Yeshuat Hashem what?*" Jade asked. "What language is that?"

Jade traced the intricate stenciling on the casing. God, Landry wanted to be the watch under her hand. "It's Yiddish. It means that no matter how grim the situation is, salvation could be just around the corner."

"Salvation?" Jade gave her a serious look. "I didn't peg you as the religious type."

"I'm not. Not at all." She took the watch, touching Jade's fingers for longer than necessary, and slipped it back into her pocket. "But

I like the idea of always having the hope that rescue or recovery can come along in an instant."

Jade smiled. "You wear it, but you haven't looked at it once this evening."

"That's because you're such wonderful company," Landry said. "Time is a huge part of my work, so I don't like to look at a clock or watch when I'm on vacation. I don't want to know that time's running out."

Jade frowned. "How is it running out?"

Landry sighed, not really wanting to think about tomorrow or any other day. What she wanted to do was enjoy and relax into what was happening tonight. "You have a basketball game. I have another mission in a few weeks. I'll be gone maybe two months." She paused, unsure that if she said the words, she'd scare Jade off for good. "And I have to tell you again that it's possible I might not come back at all."

Jade caressed Landry's cheek. "So we shouldn't keep *wasting* time then." She kissed her hard and wanting, her hand pressed firmly on Landry's crotch.

"I was hoping you might say something like that." She wrapped her hand around Jade's neck and gently pulled her into her lap. She drew her fingers up the outside of Jade's thigh and stopped at the hem of her dress.

Jade put her hand over Landry's. "There's just the small thing of where you think this is going, Landry. As much as I thought I could do a friend with benefits gig with you, it turns out that I can't. I want more. But what do you want from me?"

Landry looked deep into Jade's eyes and saw something she'd never looked for or seen in the eyes of another woman. Tomorrow. And the next day. And she also saw no logical reason to hold back anymore. "Everything. I want everything from you."

"And if I give you everything, what do I get in return?"

"All of me...if you want it."

"If you're sure you can give it, I'll take it."

Landry nodded. "I'm sure. And you can handle my job?"

"I'll do my best." Jade pressed her lips to Landry's and traced her tongue over them. "Do we get the bed this time?"

Landry slipped one arm under Jade's knees and stood up. "Your wish is my command." She walked to the end of the corridor and pushed open the bedroom door with her foot.

Jade giggled a little and began to undo Landry's tie. "To say you never have women here, that's an awfully big bed."

"I move around a lot in my sleep. I sleepwalk occasionally." Landry lowered Jade to her feet.

"If you do it in your sleep, how do you know?" She pulled Landry's tie from around her neck and tossed it onto the bed.

"I wake up in strange places. In front of the curtains, in the kitchen, in the shower. It's one of the reasons I never sleep anywhere other than here when I'm not at work." Landry ran her fingers through Jade's soft hair and kissed her neck.

"Any ideas why you do it?" Jade asked.

"Usually when something's on my mind, and I can't resolve it. I woke up putting the comforter over the pool table last night."

Jade laughed and began to unbutton Landry's shirt, her perfectly manicured fingers moving deftly over her body. "What was on your mind last night?"

"You were." Landry swallowed, willing herself to stay the course and be open and honest. "You've been on my mind since we met."

"Smooth." Jade pulled Landry's shirt from her jeans and slipped it from her shoulders. She kissed and nibbled Landry's chest and murmured appreciatively into her skin. "I know I've already told you, but your body is stunning. I don't think I've ever been with a woman with so much muscle. Have you always been this ripped?"

"I had a rough childhood, and I never wanted to be that weak again, so I bulked up. It doesn't bother you?"

"God, no. I've always loved women with big muscles. I've just never had one."

Jade worked open Landry's buckle and then her jeans. Landry

watched, mesmerized, and she almost growled when Jade slipped her hand inside to cup her pussy through her briefs. Landry pulled up the hem of Jade's dress and removed it in one fluid movement. She swallowed hard at the sight of Jade's matching white lace bra and panties and the unbelievably sexy way they contrasted against her olive skin.

"I never realized I was such a cliché," Landry whispered between the steamy kisses that seemed to lift her from the ground, defying the earth's gravitational pull.

"Meaning?"

"Seeing you in that dress, and in that lingerie, makes me think I only *ever* want to see you looking like that."

Jade bit Landry's neck gently. "I admit to a similar sin. Your style makes me twitchy."

She dropped to her knees, pulling down Landry's jeans. She stepped out of them, and Jade pressed her mouth to Landry's briefs. Her hot breath swept straight to Landry's sex, and she wrapped her hand in Jade's hair, keeping her in position. "Now you're making me wish I had something else to offer you."

Jade nibbled at the soft cotton and traced her tongue over Landry's hardened clit. "Maybe next time, handsome." She pulled Landry's shorts down and tongued between Landry's lips.

Landry moaned, and her legs buckled slightly. "There's no way I can stand if you're going to do that."

Jade stood and pushed Landry back onto the bed.

Landry edged farther onto it and smiled. "You're pretty strong for a little one."

"Told you I'd be able to get you on your back." Jade got onto her knees between Landry's legs and started again.

"It's not really a position I'm familiar with."

Jade stopped for a moment and caught Landry's gaze. "You'll get used to it."

Landry relaxed into the cool cotton sheets and concentrated on the growing throb between her legs.

Jade looked up and met Landry's gaze. "Close your eyes and relax, baby."

"I need to see you." Landry twisted her fingers into Jade's hair while Jade circled Landry's clit slowly and firmly. The pressure built, quicker and more intense than Landry was used to, and Jade's rhythm had her approaching her orgasm in no time. She moaned and pushed her hips up. Jade moaned in response, never breaking contact. Just as Landry was about to come, Jade slipped two fingers inside her and began to fuck her, without missing a stroke with her tongue. The throbbing became too intense to hold, and Landry let go, releasing herself, and her love, to Jade.

Jade didn't stop. She continued to lick, suck, and fuck until Landry couldn't take any more and pulled away, the pleasure too much. Jade raised her head, and her chin and mouth were slick with Landry's wetness.

"Wow, you needed that, huh?"

Landry laughed, slightly embarrassed. "You're to blame for that." She reached down and felt how wet she was. "I've never come that much, even for myself."

Jade crawled up Landry's body and lay against her. "I like that. I like doing something no one else has ever done to you."

Landry held Jade in her arms and didn't comment on how right she felt there, how well she fit. *Like the jigsaw piece you can never find that completes the puzzle of your life.* They lay in the kind of silence that comes from being completely, and inexplicably, at ease.

"I like listening to your heartbeat."

It beats for you. Oh, fuck, does it? That's so cheesy. "Yeah? Is it tuneful enough to keep you interested long-term?"

"I don't see why not."

Landry flipped Jade onto her back and straddled her. She unclipped her bra to release Jade's full breasts and took her nipple into her mouth. Jade writhed beneath her and moaned loudly.

"And might this keep you interested long-term?" Landry asked, as she slipped her fingers inside Jade.

Jade let out a breathy gasp and took a handful of Landry's hair. "I don't see...why not."

Landry worked her fingers deeper into Jade and used her other hand to pull the panties off altogether. Jade groaned and pushed her body onto Landry's fingers, daring her to go deeper and harder. Landry looked into Jade's eyes, and the raw honesty she saw in them took her breath away. She picked up the pace in response to Jade's grinding and the tightening grip she had in Landry's hair.

"Baby, I'm gonna come. Fuck me harder."

Landry smiled at Jade's demand, glad that her honesty bled into her sexual need. "Fuck, you're so beautiful."

Their thrust and pull synced perfectly. Jade's breathing quickened, and she begged for Landry to pump faster. She lifted her hips from the bed as she orgasmed, and Landry slipped beneath her. As she came down, she rested on Landry's lap, and powerful tremors shuddered through her. Landry kept her fingers inside Jade and began again just as she'd settled on Landry's stomach.

"Oh, fuck." Jade dug her nails into Landry's shoulders.

She started off slow and hard, building back up to the rhythm that had sent Jade over the edge. She writhed on top of Landry, allowing her to catch nibbles of Jade's body as she rose up and down. She was quick to come again, and shortly after, once more.

Landry slowly withdrew her fingers and began firm movements over Jade's clit. Once again, she responded, and another powerful release flowed through her body. Landry raised her hand to her nose to breathe in Jade's scent and sighed deeply. "You smell amazing." She probably couldn't describe it, if asked. Could pure have a scent signature? She did know it was the sweetest aroma that her brain had ever processed.

Jade giggled. "You're dirty."

"You like me that way."

"I do. And you make me *very* glad I'm multi-orgasmic."

Jade rolled off Landry and lay with her head on Landry's chest, looking up at her.

"I have no idea how this is going to work, baby." Landry ran her hand from Jade's shoulder to her hip. She really didn't know, but she knew she wanted to try.

Jade outlined gentle circles on Landry's chest. The intimacy was alien but welcome, like her heart was exposed and yet simultaneously protected, and Landry had no desire to build another wall around it. Most probably, Jade would run a bulldozer straight through it anyway.

"We don't need all the answers, handsome. If we're meant to be, it'll fall into place."

A wave of calm swept over Landry. Lying there with Jade was quite possibly the most peaceful she'd ever been in her entire life. In the years after her mom had died, her memories echoed a life that had been chaotic, and the only order she found was in the military. Her new memories, of all that time *with* her mom, were disordered in a different way she couldn't figure out. In both of them, her life meant little to her. She went on missions, first for her country, and then for Pulsus, with little regard for the personal consequences. Suddenly, with Jade, there was an existence to share and to cherish. There was meaning to the time between missions, and she wanted to hold Jade in her arms forever.

"Will you stay the night with me?" Landry felt a catch in her throat but still managed the words she'd never spoken.

"I'd love to, baby, but I can't. I have to catch a flight to LA in the morning for the final playoff game, so I need to get home for an early night."

Landry clenched her jaw shut and closed her eyes.

"If you promise to let me sleep," Jade whispered, "you could stay with me..."

The breath Landry caught in her throat released. "That's a mammoth ask, but if it means I get to wake up and you're the first thing I see, it'll be worth it."

"See how good you are at this romance thing already? You've got all the right lines." Jade kissed her and climbed off the bed. "It's a fifty-minute drive, but if we're quick, we could probably get a few more orgasms in before I have to sleep." She winked, and her wicked smile had Landry jumping off the bed to follow her.

They dressed swiftly and headed to the underground parking.

"I should give you my address," Jade said as she climbed into her Spider. "I don't think your old-fashioned muscle car will be able to keep up."

"We'll see." Landry kissed her and closed Jade's door. She jumped into her Mustang, revved the engine unnecessarily, and honked her horn.

As they headed out of the city on the 101 across Golden Gate Bridge, the traffic thinned considerably. Landry called Jade over Bluetooth.

"Are you missing me already?" Jade asked when she picked up.

"Do I get bonus points if I am?" Landry bit her lip and shook her head at herself for acting like a lovestruck teen.

"No, but it'll get you something special when we get to my place."

After Marin City, they hit Highway One, which was more suited to the Ferrari, but Landry was still on Jade's tail. "Did you want to be a race car driver when you were a kid?" Landry asked.

"What's the matter, hotshot, can't you keep up?"

Landry laughed. "You haven't lost me yet."

"Losing you is the last thing I'm trying to do, handsome. I've only just found you."

The highway was dark, and their headlights were the only lights for miles. "Is there a place to pull over anywhere on this road?" Landry asked, not even trying to disguise her lust.

"Why?"

"Fresh air sex is hot," Landry said.

"Mm, another night. What I've got in mind isn't something we can do on the hood of our cars."

Landry grinned and let out a husky breath. "Damn, you're sexy."

"You're going to find out how—fuck!"

The rest happened so fast. Jade shouted and then screamed. She continued to scream as she lost control coming out of the hairpin bend by Lone Tree Creek. Her car skidded off the road and careened down the deep valley.

"Jade!" Landry slammed on her brakes and held it steady as the back end threatened to spin out. "Jade!" She watched helplessly as the Ferrari rolled and smashed into a tree. Jade's screaming stopped abruptly. Landry threw the door open and tried to get out, but her seat belt stopped her. "Fuck." She released the restraint and jumped out. "Jade!" Landry called out, but there was no answer. She listened to the phone for breathing, whimpering, *any* sign of life, but she couldn't hear a sound. "I'm coming." She ran down the steep incline toward Jade's car. With the force of the impact, it was highly likely the car might blow up. "Jade. Talk to me, baby. Tell me you're okay."

Landry's breathing faltered as she reached the Ferrari lying on its roof. The door had burst open with the collision, and Jade was half-hanging from her seat, with just her belt keeping her in place. The thick branches of the tree had forced themselves through the windshield and the driver's side window. One had penetrated Jade's thigh, and her gushing blood had turned her white dress ruby red.

"God, no." Landry leaned in and held her ear to Jade's mouth. Her breathing was shallow and labored, but at least she was alive. She couldn't pull the branch out in case it had severed an arterial vein; the best chance of saving Jade's leg at all would be to saw through the branch, wrap the wound around the broken piece still inside her, and take her to a hospital. "It's going to be okay," she said, trying to convince herself more than Jade, who still hadn't made a sound or movement.

Landry paused. They were almost an hour from the hospital.

It was likely by the time they got there, the badly damaged nerves would be dead from the trauma. Her leg would be lost. Her basketball career over. She was only thirty minutes from the Pulsus train stop though. She could take Jade to Pulsus, and her mom could regenerate the leg tissue. *Then what?* It was strictly forbidden to speak to anyone outside the organization about their work, let alone bring an outsider onto the island.

Landry scrambled back up the bank, opened her trunk, and pulled out her tool kit. "Stay with me. I'm here. We'll get through this." She ran back down to the car and used a laser saw to carefully slice through the branch three inches above Jade's thigh. Then she pulled out a can of skin sealant, another Pulsus invention that shouldn't be off the island, but Landry didn't give a damn. She sprayed around the branch and tossed the can back into the bag before putting it on her back.

"I'm going to take care of you, Jade. Don't worry about a thing." She released the seat belt and supported Jade's weight as she took her down from the seat. Landry carried her up the ridge, placed her gently in the backseat, and took a deep breath as she turned the car around before making the most important call of her life. "Mom, you have to do something for me. I've never asked you for anything, and I never will again. But I need you to do this for me. I need you to say you will before I even ask you."

"What's happened, pumpkin? Are you in some kind of trouble on the mainland?"

"Please, Mom. Just tell me you'll help me."

"I'll do anything you need me to, you know that."

"Meet me at the regen lab in forty minutes." Landry pushed the car to its limits as she took the corner. "Don't tell anyone else."

"Landry, what's this about? You're scaring me."

"Please, Mom, no questions. Just say you'll be there. I need you like I've never needed you before."

There was a short pause on the other end of the line. "I'll be there."

"Thanks, Mom." Landry ended the call and glanced through the rearview mirror at Jade's unconscious body.

The woman she loved.

The woman Landry was about to risk *everything* to save.

~ THE END ~

Of course I'm not going to leave you on that cliffhanger! Here's chapter one of Change in Time so you don't explode with anticipation before its release in a few months! And if you want to keep up with all my author news, why not sign up to my newsletter and bag yourself a free short story? Link: bit.ly/RJNyxNews

Ciao for now,
RJ Nyx

CHANGE IN TIME

CHAPTER ONE

LANDRY PULLED HER CAR into the lot and jumped out. She opened the rear door and tried hard to steel herself against the vision of how damaged Jade looked. She slipped her arms beneath Jade's limp body and took her out of the car before kicking the door shut. "Everything's going to be okay, baby. I promise."

It must've been the hundredth time she'd said it in the thirty minutes since the accident. She didn't make promises unless she was sure she could keep them, and worse yet, this one depended on her mom. She pressed her ear to Jade's chest; her breathing was shallow, but Landry took it as a sign of hope. Her mom was a damn fine surgeon, but she couldn't bring people back from the dead.

"Donovan, is that you?"

Landry nodded, thankful it was Garrett at the cargo platform. "Sure is, hoss. I need to go back to the island." As she walked toward him and into the platform lights, Garrett's expression changed.

"Whoa there, cowboy. Who have you got there?"

"I've called ahead. Elena Donovan is expecting us. I need you to get us home."

Landry could see Garrett processing the information. Everyone knew Elena was Landry's mom and thought she had special treatment. Landry usually tried to make sure that it wasn't actually the case, but in this instance, it was probably best for Garrett to believe it.

"No one called me, Donovan. You know I can't let you take a civilian to the island. I'll lose my job."

Landry stepped as close to him as she could with Jade in her arms and tried to stay as calm as possible, considering the storm of emotions in her head. "Step aside, Garrett, or you'll lose a lot more than that." Nothing and no one was going to stop her from getting Jade on the island to see her mom, and if that meant putting Garrett down, that's what she'd do.

Garrett looked at her for a moment, as if assessing the threat, then he moved out of the way.

Landry nodded. "Take this train as fast as it goes, hoss."

"If you're sure, cowboy." Garrett still looked uncertain but jogged off to the cab to set the train on its return to the island.

Landry got into the first open carriage and settled gingerly onto a seat, careful not to move Jade too much. She rested Jade's feet on a luggage rack to elevate them in an effort to cope with the blood loss. Landry was far too aware that if she didn't get Jade to her mom fast enough, the potential decrease in circulation could result in gangrene and the removal of Jade's leg. With no road to concentrate on, she only had Jade to look at, which didn't fill her with hope. Jade's skin was drained of its usual color, and her lips were tinted blue. Landry lifted Jade's hand and saw the same effect in her fingernails.

As the train began to move, she pressed her lips to Jade's forehead and kissed her gently. "I'm going to take care of you, I promise." *Another promise I don't know if I can keep.* She placed her head on Jade's chest and closed her eyes. There was nothing else she could do right now. She was at the mercy of the high-speed train, and when she got to Pulsus, Jade would be in the hands of her mom. She hoped Jenkin wouldn't be there too. A confrontation with her boss and her mom's lover wasn't what Landry needed. If Jenkin tried to keep her mom from helping Jade, Landry could only hope her mom would make the right choice.

The train pulled into the island station five minutes later. There was no one guarding the platform, but the cameras and body scanners between there and the regen lab would monitor her arrival and track her movements. Security would be alerted to the presence of a non-Pulsus employee, so she had to get there before they tried to stop her.

She thanked Garrett before putting Jade in her car and flooring it to the regen lab, where her mom waited at the door on the ground floor.

"Landry, what on earth are you doing? Is this the girl you were telling me about?"

Landry sidestepped her and headed for the elevator. "Mom, I don't need your judgment right now. I need your help. She can't lose her leg... I can't lose her."

Her mom said nothing as they got in, and she pressed for the surgical level.

"What did you tell Jenkin?"

"I told her you had an emergency, which is all I knew at the time. She'll soon find out what's really going on when security alerts her to this breach."

Landry pulled Jade closer to her. "You can't let her stop you. Promise me."

Elena stepped out of the elevator and looked back at Landry. "You don't have to lecture me, sweetheart. I took an oath to do my utmost to save people, always. I won't let her die."

Landry followed her mom to an operating room and waited as she prepped for surgery.

"Lay her on the table."

Landry did as her mom had instructed and stepped back. Her mom activated the pod, and the body scanner zipped up and down the length of Jade's body in seconds. Her blood pressure and temperature appeared on the glass screen beside the table, along with detailed analysis of Jade's organs.

"She's in hypovolemic shock. I need an IV to extract and replicate her blood to have any hope of replenishing what she's lost before she suffers any kidney or brain damage. You got her to me in time to save her life, but I can't guarantee her leg."

Landry felt her own legs falter and sought support from a

nearby blood station. She heard "heart strength," "dobutamine," and "gangrene" but was already fixated on her mom's previous words, "I can't guarantee her leg." She didn't hear anyone approaching until it was too late, when strong hands grabbed her, and her arms were forced behind her back.

"What the hell have you done, Donovan?" Jenkin stepped in front of Landry.

"You should let me go right now unless you want this to get nasty."

She scoffed and turned away. "Elena, what do you think you're doing?"

Jenkin moved toward her mom, and Landry kicked out, sweeping Jenkin's legs from under her. She crashed to the floor, and the security guards pushed Landry to her knees.

"Don't even think about trying to stop her." Landry still managed to stumble forward despite the best efforts of the people holding her.

Jenkin got up and brushed her clothes down, her eyes flaring with anger and bruised pride. "I won't stop her from saving your girlfriend. But I will wipe her memory and have her put back home none the wiser. And then I'll deal with you."

Jenkin nodded to her security detail, and Landry felt a blunt blow to the back of her head. She fell to the floor, dazed, and was vaguely conscious of her wrists and ankles being fixed into bindings.

"JJ, that wasn't necessary," her mom said.

"Just because she's your daughter doesn't mean the rules don't apply to her, Elena."

"I know that," her mom said, her voice stern and harsh, "but you didn't have to knock her out."

Landry grunted as she was hauled to her feet. "They'll have to hit me harder than that if they want to knock me out."

Jenkin turned to face her again "Maybe this'll work then, tough guy." She pulled something from her pocket and pressed it to Landry's neck.

A sharp pain stung before everything went black. *Jade.*

Other Great Butterworth Books

Dead Pretty by Robyn Nyx
An FBI agent, a TV star, and a serial killer. Love hurts.
Available on Amazon (ASIN B09QRSKBVP)

Secrets of Her Heart by Karen Klyne
Some secrets keep us safe. Others keep us alone.
Available from Amazon (ASIN TBC)

Ship of Dreams by Brey Willows
Two captains, one ancient relic, and a destiny written in the clouds.
Available on Amazon (ASIN B0DRW1X75N)

Encrypted Hearts by E.V. Bancroft
Even amid the chaos of war, love is the hardest code to crack.
Available from Amazon (ASIN B0DKG7BHMJ)

Unwritten by Helena Harte
No strings is fun 'til it unravels.
Available from Amazon (ASIN B0DGQFFHYB)

Chucking Putty at the Queen by Simon Smalley
A heartbreaking, humorous, and courageous exploration of what it takes to be ones authentic self.
Available from Amazon (ASIN B0DGGBV22W)

The Promise by Addison M Conley
When the world keeps pulling you under, who do you reach for?
Available on Amazon (ASIN B0DDY9FH6Z)

Back to Back by Jo Fletcher
."When Fred and Ruby's worlds collide, can love rise from the rubble?"
Available on Amazon (ASIN B0D6M499K2)

Sanctuary by Helena Harte
Passions ignite and possibilities unfold. Welcome to the Windy City Romances.
Available from Amazon (ASIN B0D4B42RRW)

An Art to Love by Helena Harte
Second chances are an art form.
Available on Amazon (ASIN B0B1CD8Y42)

Music City Dreamers by Robyn Nyx
Music brings lovers together. In Music City, it can tear them apart. Available on
Amazon (ASIN B0994XVDGR)

Let Love Be Enough by Robyn Nyx
When a killer sets her sights on her target, is there any stopping her?
Available on Amazon (ASIN B09YMMZ8XC)

Nero by Valden Bush
Banished and abandoned. Will destiny reunite her with the love of her life?
Available from Amazon (ASIN B0BHJKHK6S)

Warm Pearls and Paper Cranes by E.V. Bancroft
A family torn apart by secrets. The only way forward is love.
Available from Amazon (ASIN B09DTBCQ92)

Judge Me, Judge Me Not by James Merrick
*One man's battle against the world and himself to find it's never too late to
find, and use, your voice.*
Available from Amazon (ASIN B09CLK91N5)

Scripted Love by Helena Harte
What good is a romance writer who doesn't believe in happy ever after?
Available on Amazon (ASIN B0993QFLNN)

Call to Me by Helena Harte
Sometimes the call you least expect is the one you need the most.
Available on Amazon (ASIN B08D9SR15H)

What's Your Story?

Global Wordsmiths, CIC, provides an all-encompassing service for all writers, ranging from basic proofreading and cover design to development editing, typesetting, and eBook services. A major part of our work is charity and community focused, delivering writing projects to under-served and under-represented groups across Nottinghamshire, giving voice to the voiceless and visibility to the unseen.

To learn more about what we offer, visit: www.globalwords.co.uk

A selection of books by Global Words Press:
Desire, Love, Identity: with the National Justice Museum
Aventuras en México: Farmilo Primary School
Times Past: with The Workhouse, National Trust
Young at Heart with AGE UK
In Different Shoes: Stories of Trans Lives

Self-published authors working with Global Wordsmiths:
Steve Bailey
Ravenna Castle
Jackie D
CJ DeBarra
Dee Griffiths
Iona Kane
Maggie McIntyre
Emma Nichols
Dani Lovelady Ryan
Erin Zak